SPIDER-MAN

THE BLACK COSTUME

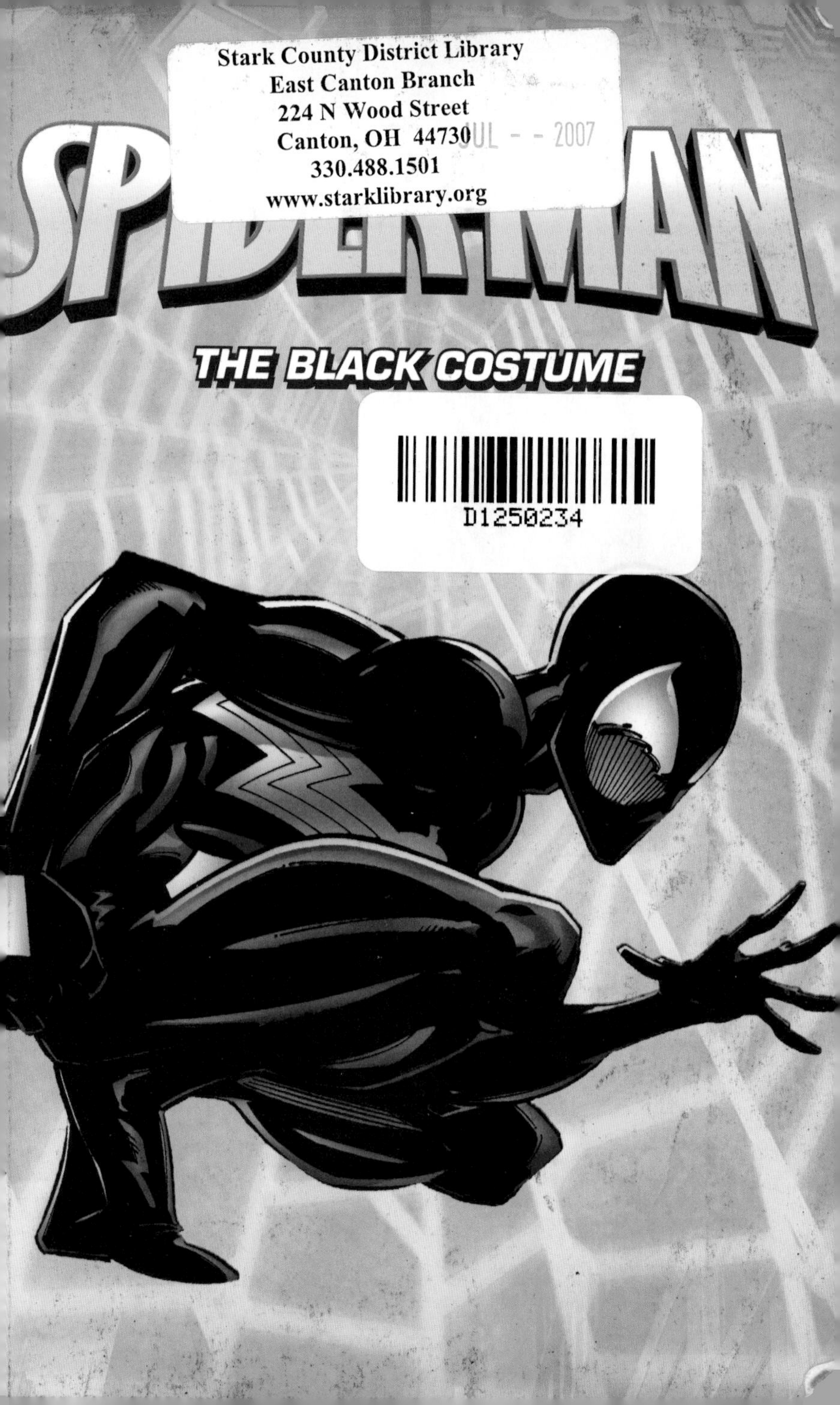

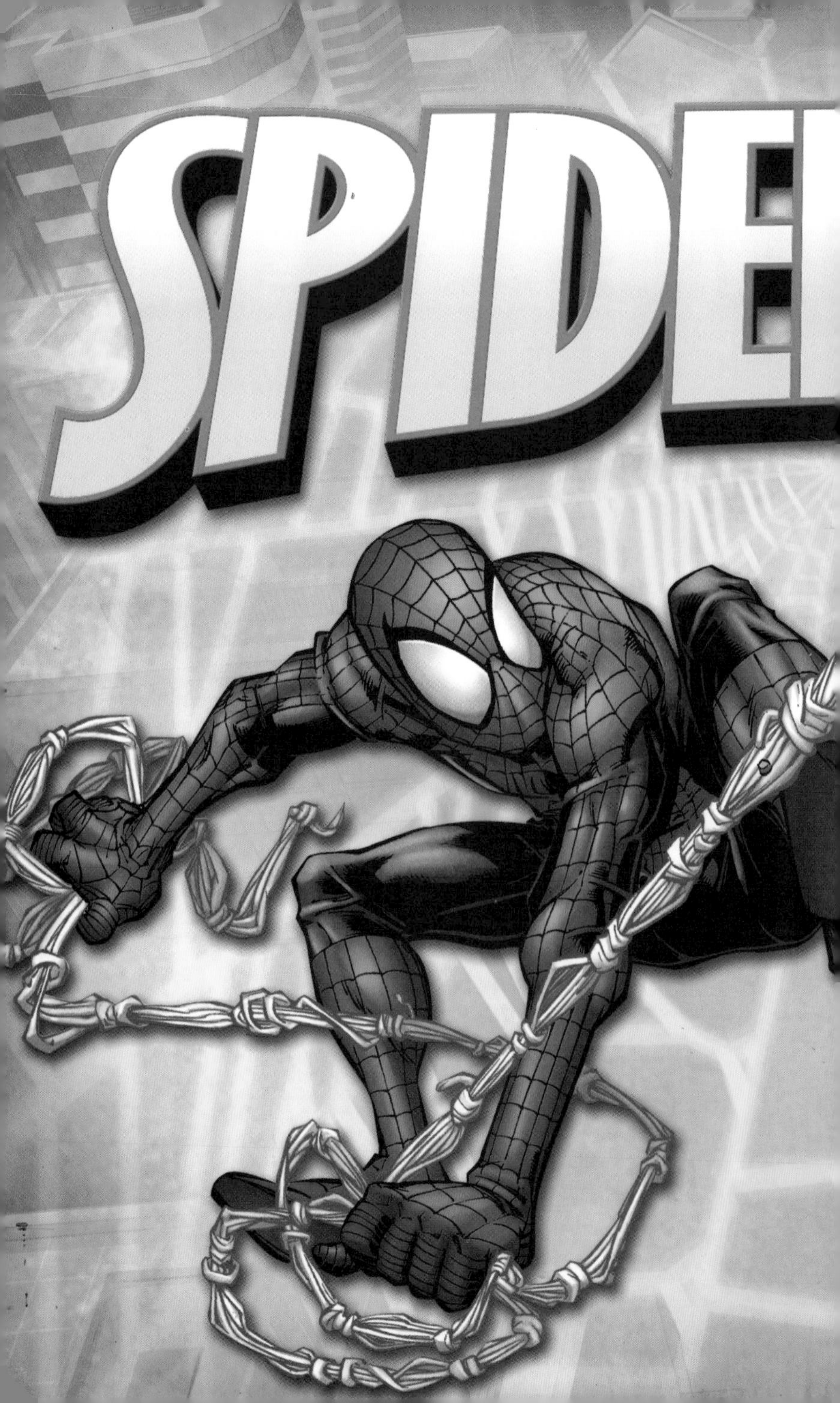
SPIDE

R-MAN

THE BLACK COSTUME

Writer
Fred Van Lente
Artists
Cory Hamscher
with **Michael O'Hare**
Colors
Guru eFX
Letters
Dave Sharpe
Cover Art: **Patrick Scherberger, Roland Paris,
Cory Hamscher & GURU eFX**
Assistant Editor: **Nathan Cosby**
Editor: **Mark Paniccia**

Collection Editor: **Jennifer Grünwald**
Assistant Editors: **Michael Short & Cory Levine**
Associate Editor: **Mark D. Beazley**
Senior Editor, Special Projects: **Jeff Youngquist**
Senior Vice President of Sales: **David Gabriel**
Production: **Jerron Quality Color**
Vice President of Creative: **Tom Marvelli**

Editor in Chief: **Joe Quesada**
Publisher: **Dan Buckley**

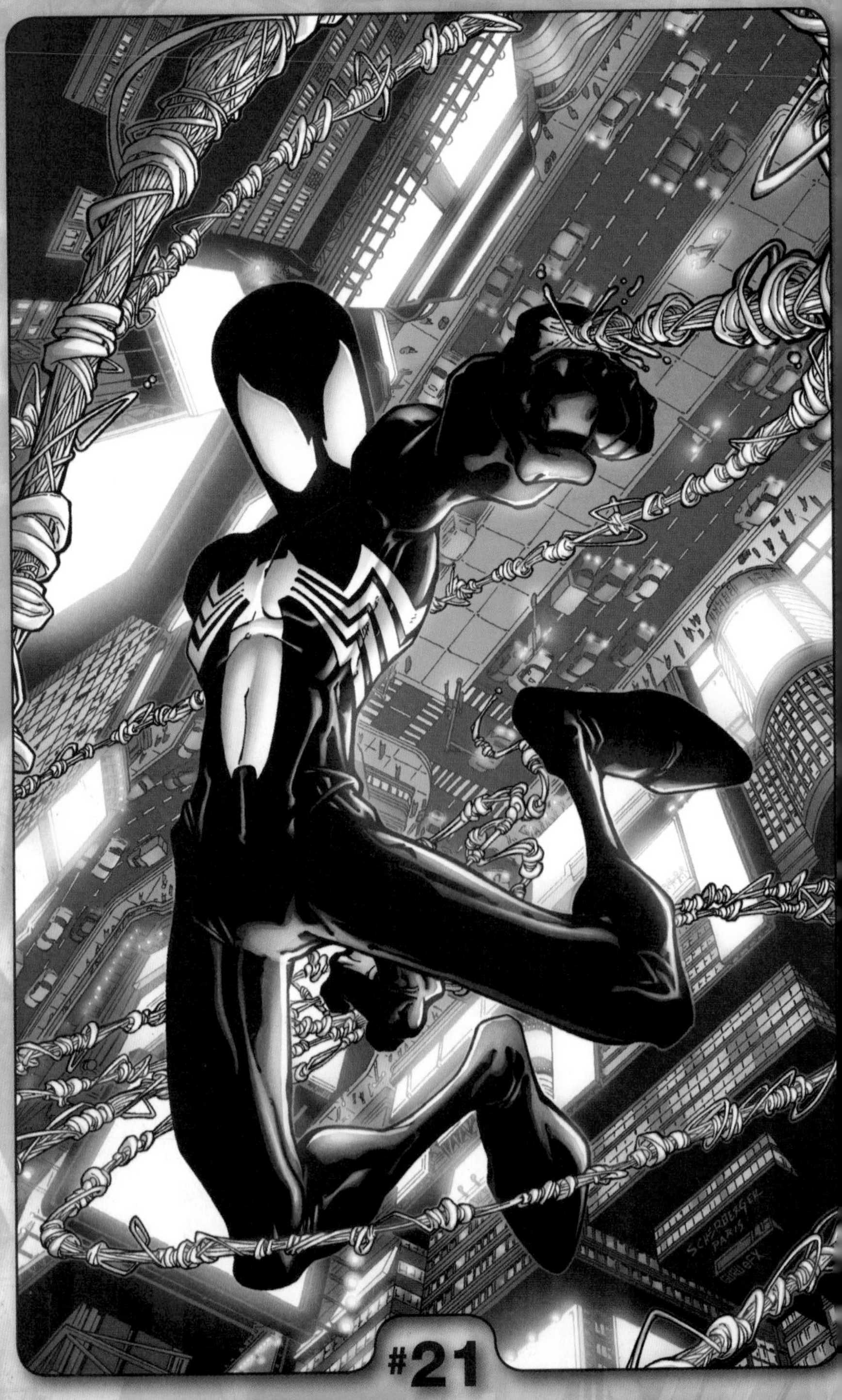
#21

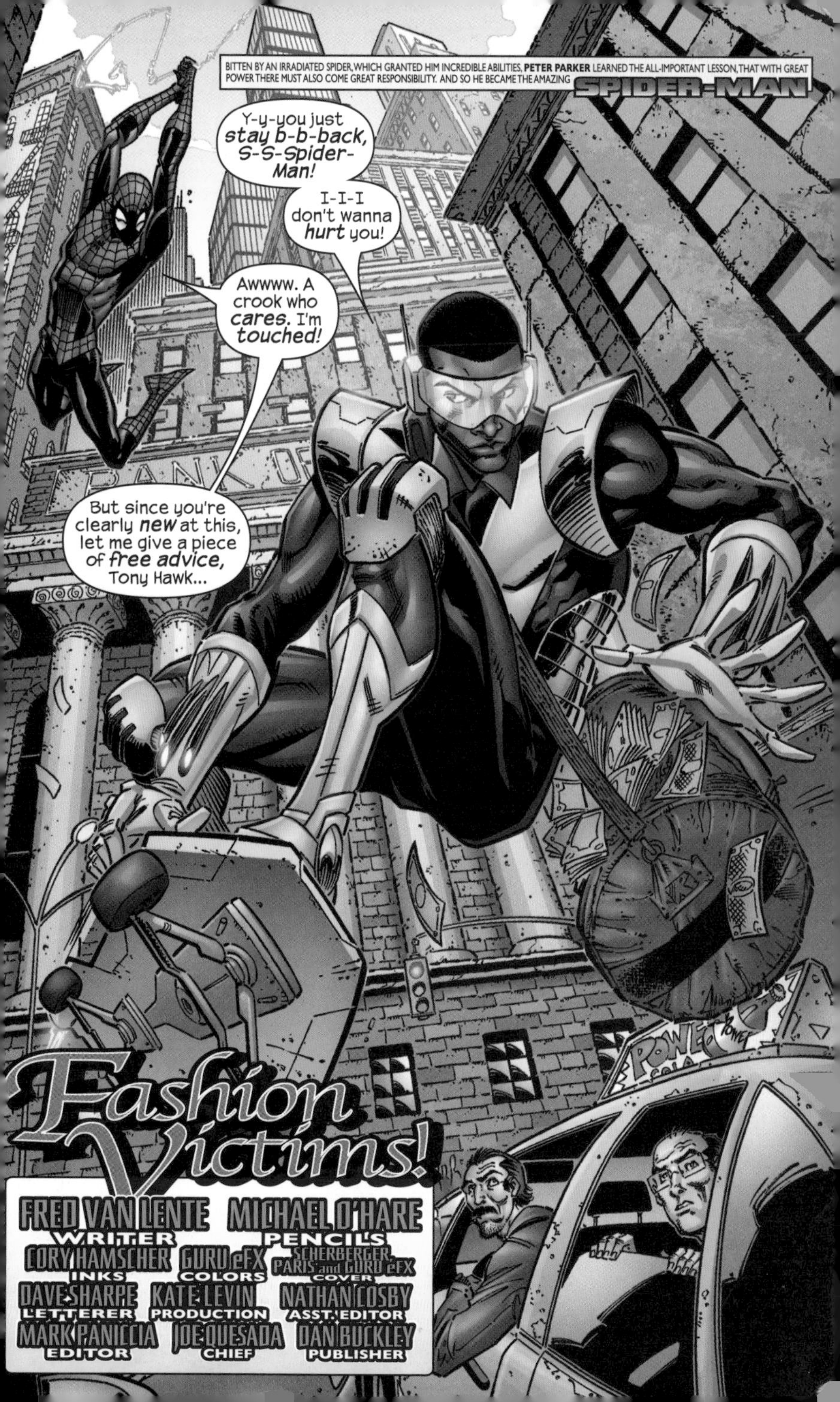

BITTEN BY AN IRRADIATED SPIDER, WHICH GRANTED HIM INCREDIBLE ABILITIES, **PETER PARKER** LEARNED THE ALL-IMPORTANT LESSON, THAT WITH GREAT POWER THERE MUST ALSO COME GREAT RESPONSIBILITY. AND SO HE BECAME THE AMAZING SPIDER-MAN
Y-y-you just *stay b-b-back,* S-S-Spider-Man!
I-I-I don't wanna *hurt* you!
Awwww. A crook who *cares.* I'm *touched!*
But since you're clearly *new* at this, let me give a piece of *free advice,* Tony Hawk...
BANK OF
POWE
Fashion Victims!
FRED VAN LENTE WRITER
MICHAEL O'HARE PENCILS
CORY HAMSCHER INKS
GURU eFX COLORS
SCHERBERGER, PARIS and GURU eFX COVER
DAVE SHARPE LETTERER
KATE LEVIN PRODUCTION
NATHAN COSBY ASST. EDITOR
MARK PANICCIA EDITOR
JOE QUESADA CHIEF
DAN BUCKLEY PUBLISHER

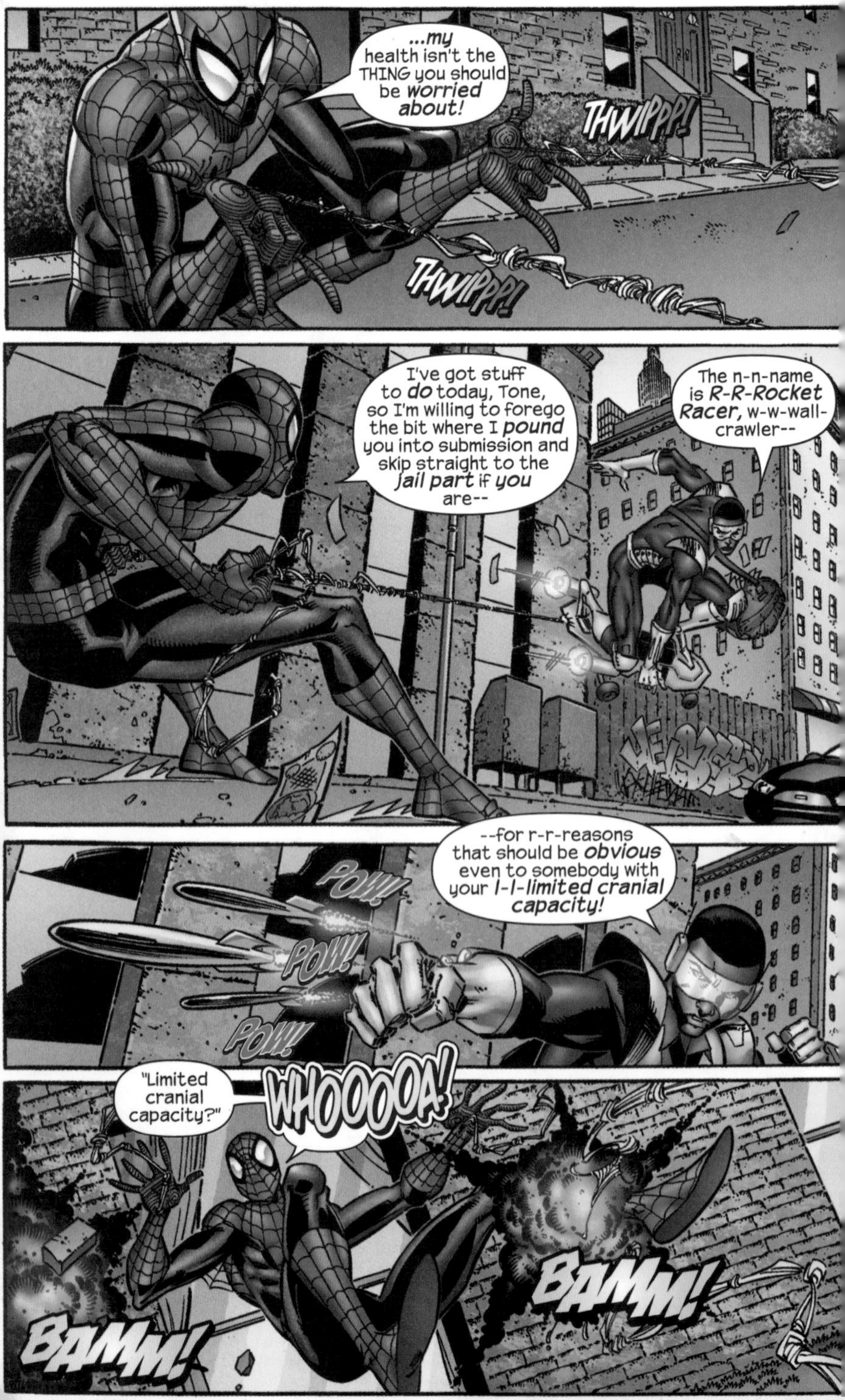
...my health isn't the THING you should be worried about!
THWIPPP!
THWIPPP!
I've got stuff to do today, Tone, so I'm willing to forego the bit where I pound you into submission and skip straight to the jail part if you are--
The n-n-name is R-R-Rocket Racer, w-w-wall-crawler--
--for r-r-reasons that should be obvious even to somebody with your l-l-limited cranial capacity!
POW!
POW!
POW!
"Limited cranial capacity?"
WHOOOOA!
BAMM!
BAMM!

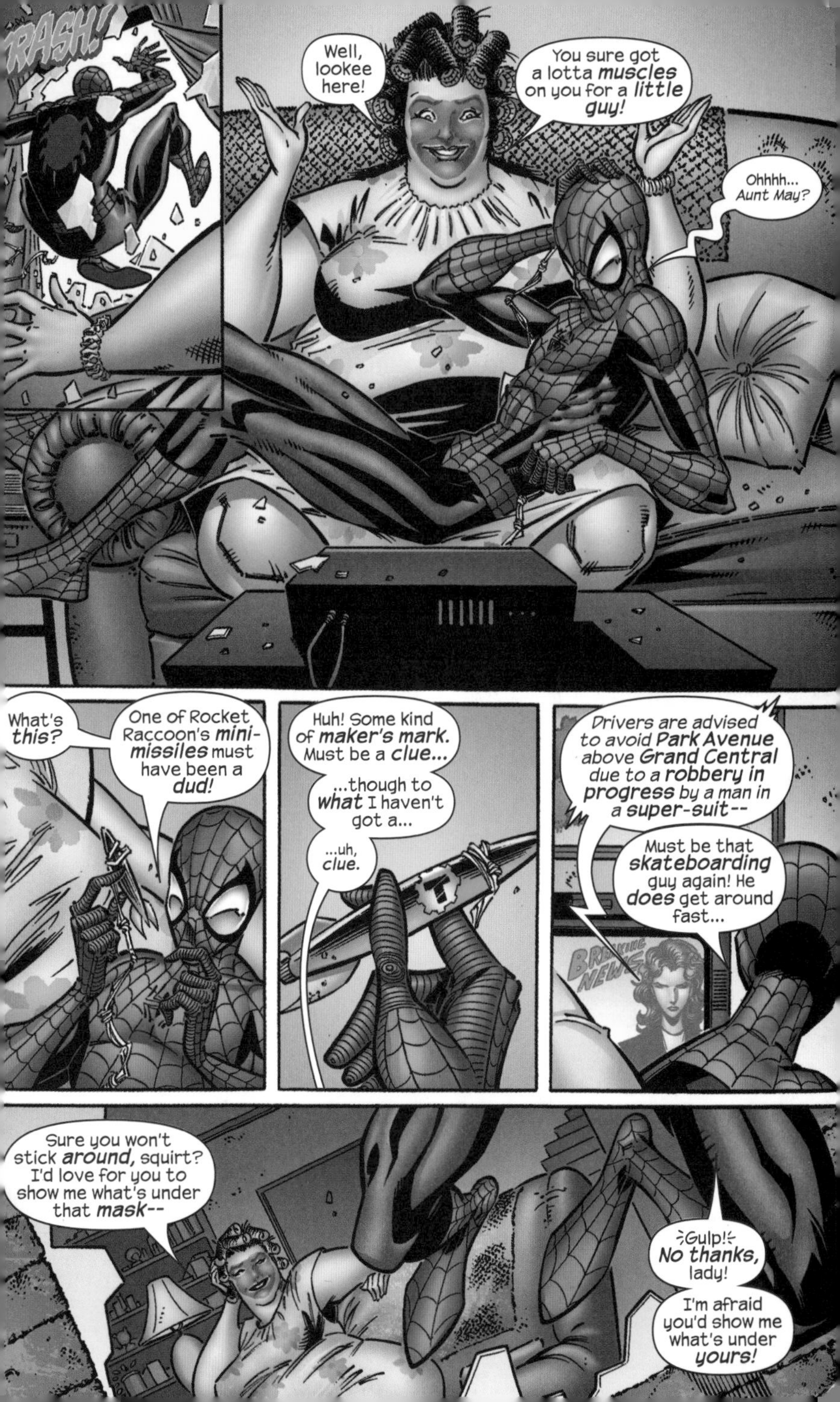

RASH!
Well, lookee here!
You sure got a lotta muscles on you for a little guy!
Ohhhh... Aunt May?
What's this?
One of Rocket Raccoon's mini-missiles must have been a dud!
Huh! Some kind of maker's mark. Must be a clue...
...though to what I haven't got a...
...uh, clue.
Drivers are advised to avoid Park Avenue above Grand Central due to a robbery in progress by a man in a super-suit--
Must be that skateboarding guy again! He does get around fast...
BREAKING NEWS
Sure you won't stick around, squirt? I'd love for you to show me what's under that mask--
Gulp! No thanks, lady!
I'm afraid you'd show me what's under yours!

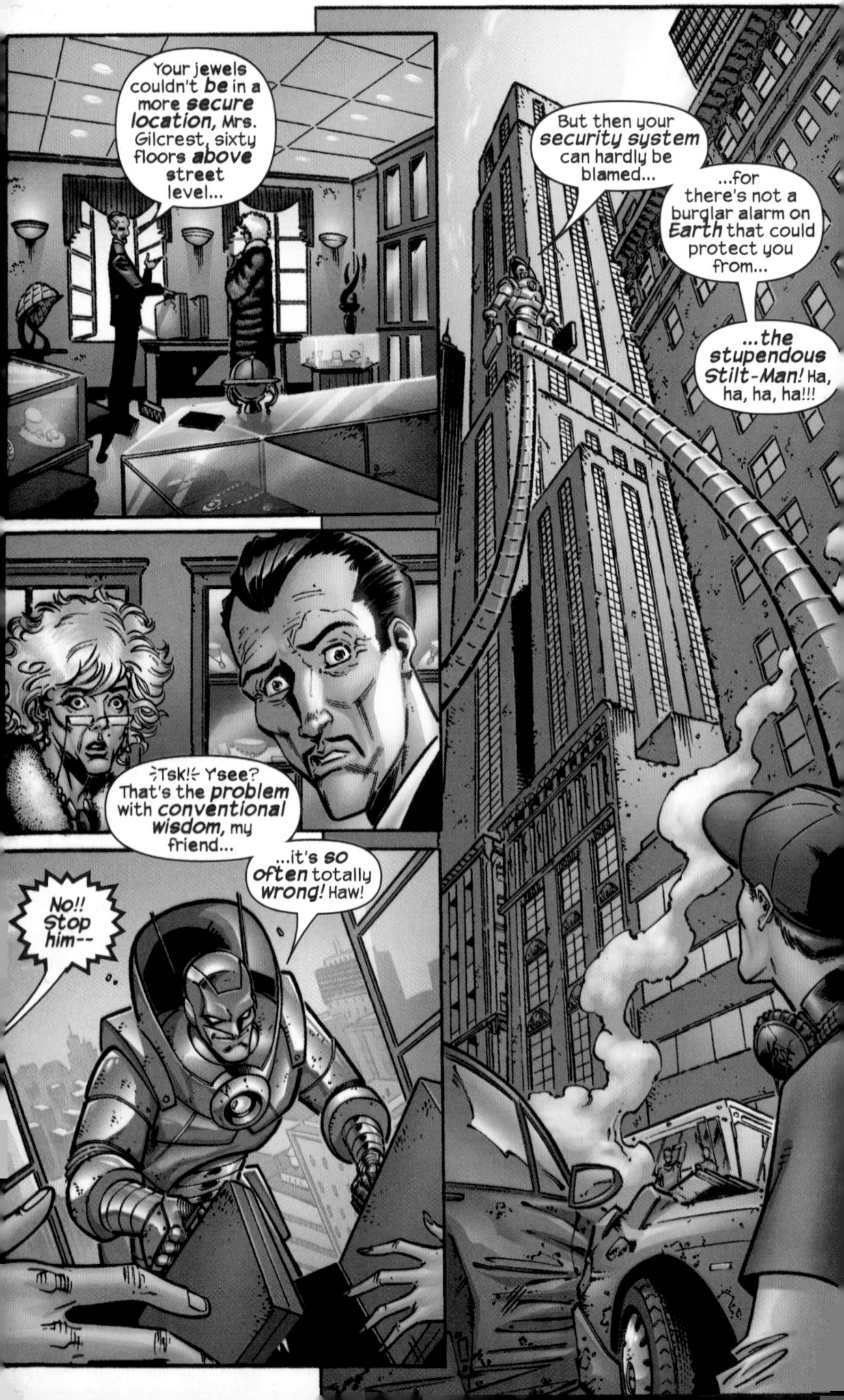
Your jewels couldn't be in a more secure location, Mrs. Gilcrest, sixty floors above street level...
Tsk! Y'see? That's the problem with conventional wisdom, my friend...
...it's so often totally wrong! Haw!
No!! Stop him--
But then your security system can hardly be blamed...
...for there's not a burglar alarm on Earth that could protect you from...
...the stupendous Stilt-Man! Ha, ha, ha, ha!!!

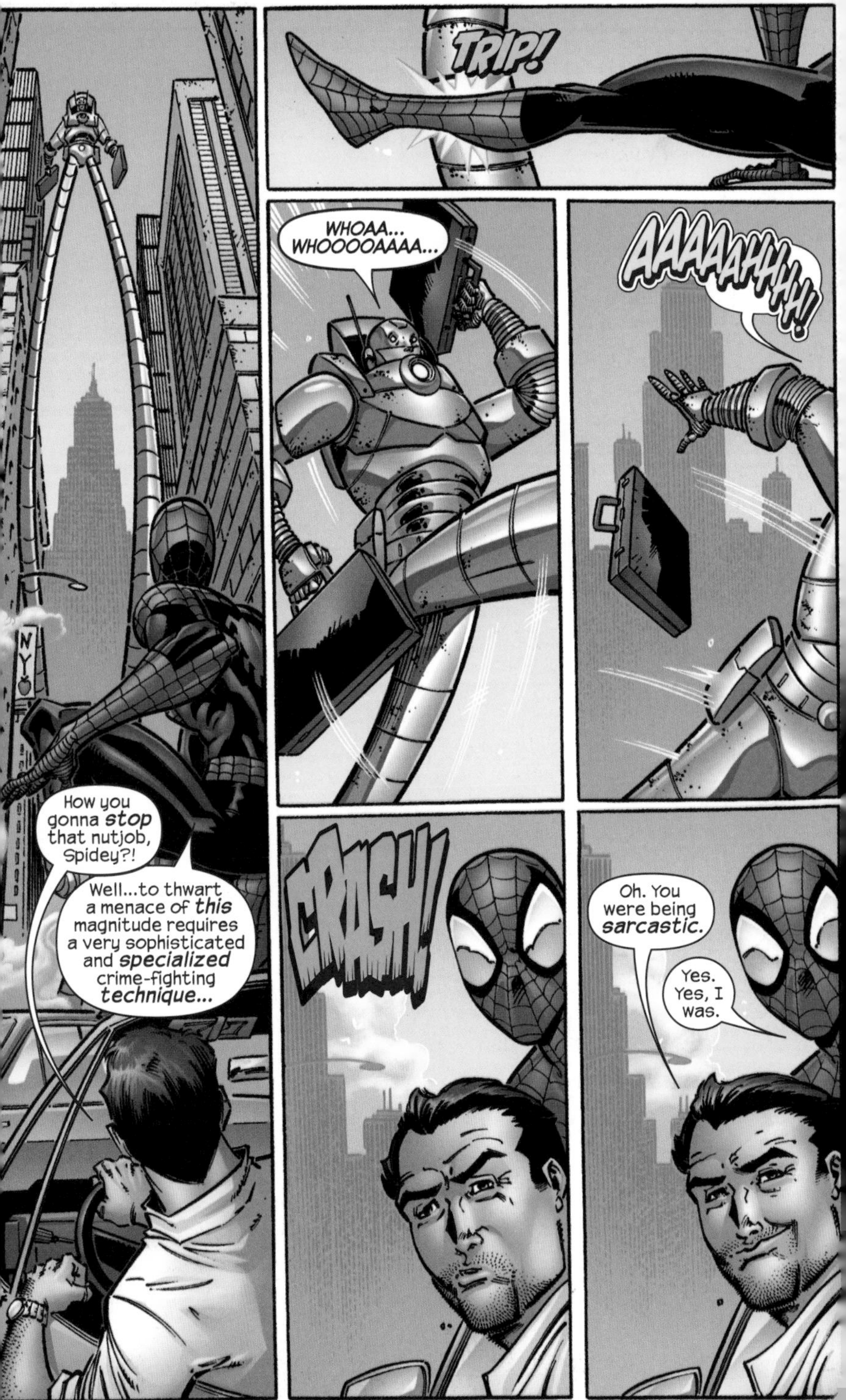

TRIP!
WHOAA... WHOOOOAAAA...
AAAAAHHHH!
NY
How you gonna stop that nutjob, Spidey?!
Well...to thwart a menace of this magnitude requires a very sophisticated and specialized crime-fighting technique...
CRASH!
Oh. You were being sarcastic.
Yes. Yes, I was.

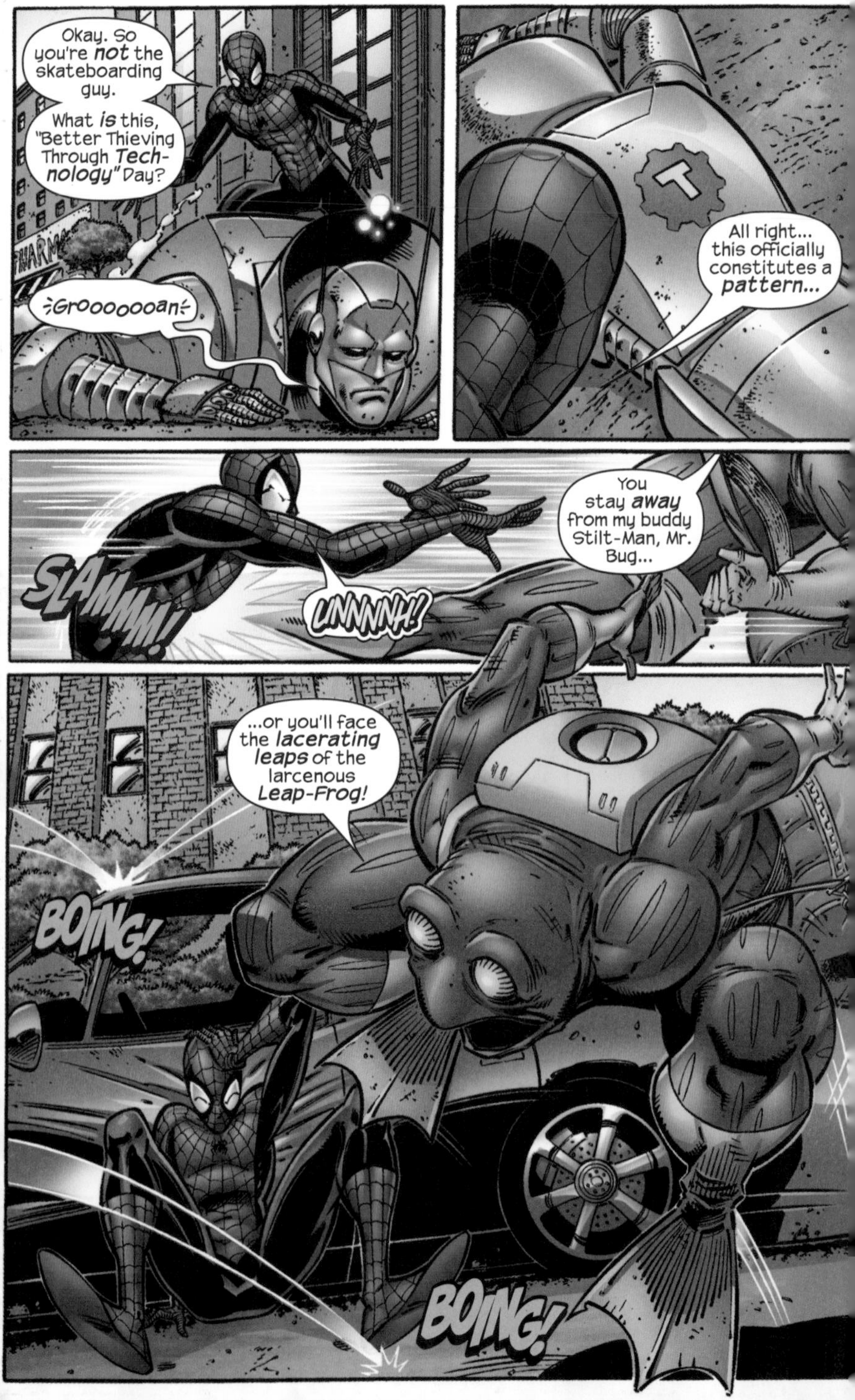
Okay. So you're *not* the skateboarding guy.
What *is* this, "Better Thieving Through *Tech-nology*" Day?
Grooooooan
All right... this officially constitutes a *pattern*...
You stay *away* from my buddy Stilt-Man, Mr. Bug...
SLAMMMM!
UNNNNH!
...or you'll face the *lacerating leaps* of the larcenous *Leap-Frog*!
BOING!
BOING!

That's a risk I'm willing to *take.*

ZWOK!

Now, where *was I?* Oh, yeah. Listen up, *tall guy*--

Stilt-Man!

Whatever!

You gonna tell me where all you technologically-enhanced *freaks* are *coming* from of your own *free will*...

...or am I gonna have to use *harsh language?*

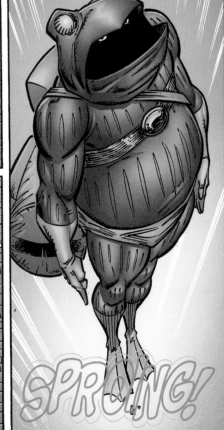

SPROING!

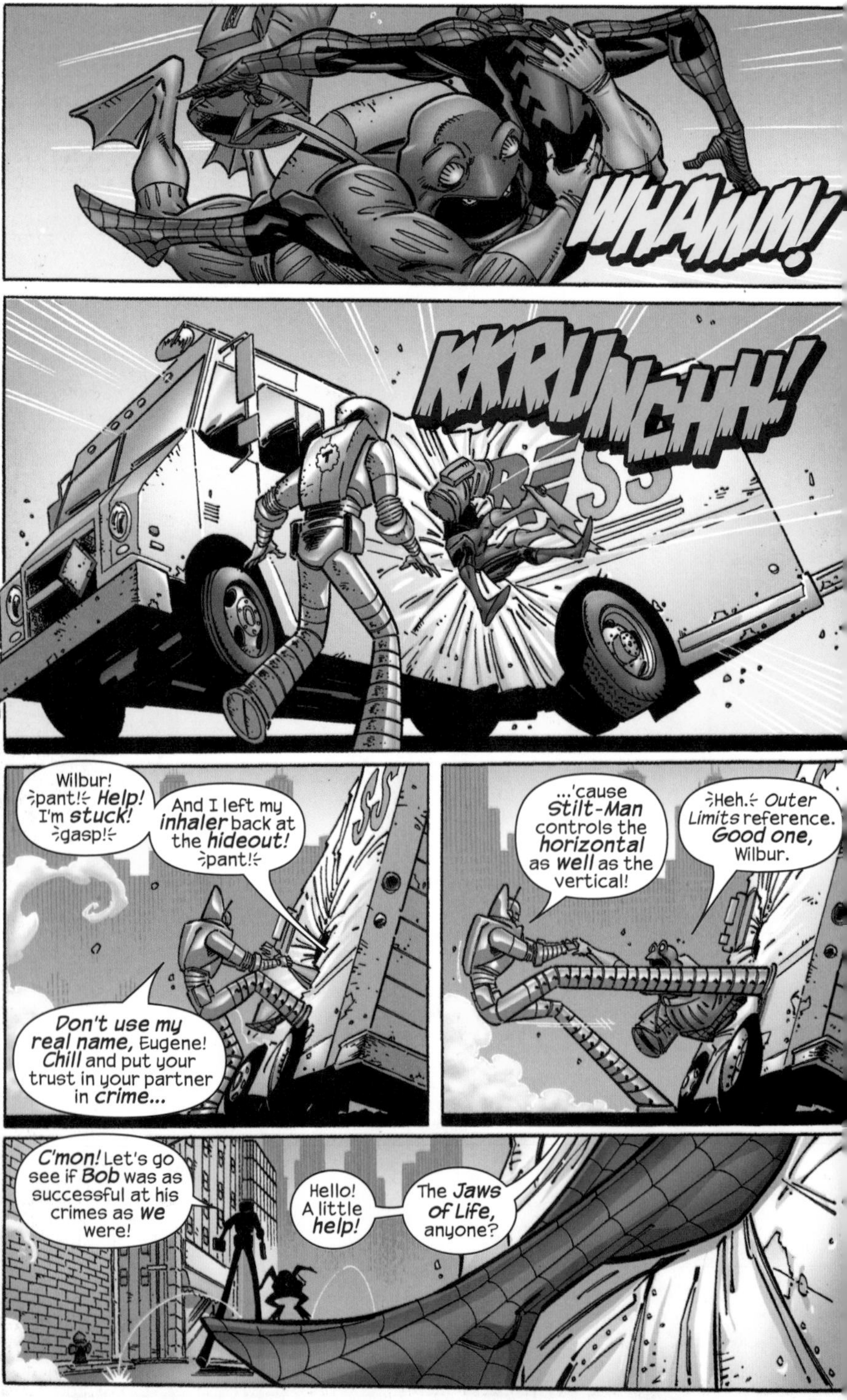

WHAMMM!
KKRUNCHH!
Wilbur! ⁓pant!⁓ Help! I'm stuck! ⁓gasp!⁓
And I left my inhaler back at the hideout! ⁓pant!⁓
Don't use my real name, Eugene! Chill and put your trust in your partner in crime...
...'cause Stilt-Man controls the horizontal as well as the vertical!
⁓Heh.⁓ Outer Limits reference. Good one, Wilbur.
C'mon! Let's go see if Bob was as successful at his crimes as we were!
Hello! A little help!
The Jaws of Life, anyone?

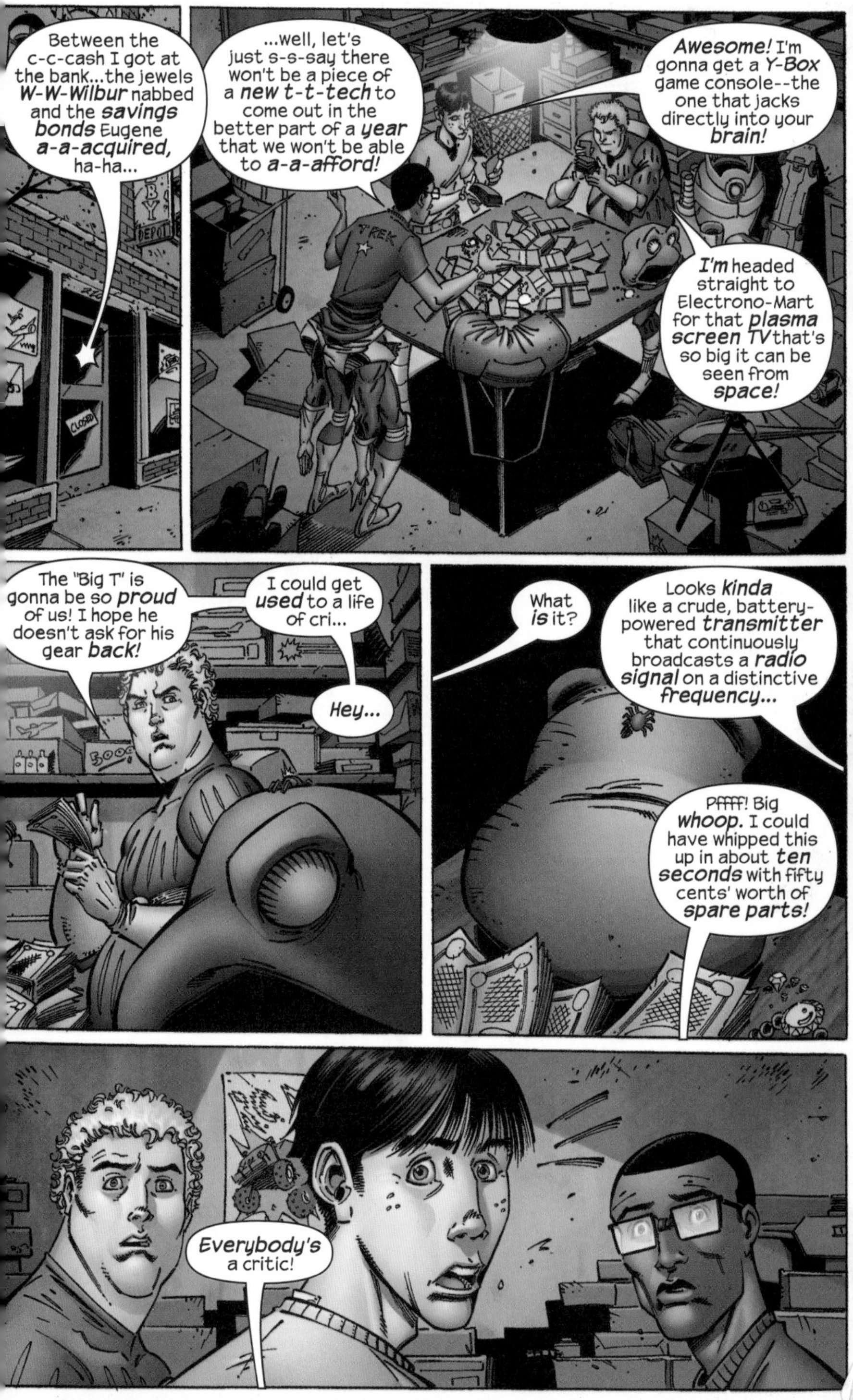

Between the c-c-cash I got at the bank...the jewels W-W-Wilbur nabbed and the savings bonds Eugene a-a-acquired, ha-ha...
...well, let's just s-s-say there won't be a piece of a new t-t-tech to come out in the better part of a year that we won't be able to a-a-afford!
Awesome! I'm gonna get a Y-Box game console--the one that jacks directly into your brain!
I'm headed straight to Electrono-Mart for that plasma screen TV that's so big it can be seen from space!
The "Big T" is gonna be so proud of us! I hope he doesn't ask for his gear back!
I could get used to a life of cri...
Hey...
What is it?
Looks kinda like a crude, battery-powered transmitter that continuously broadcasts a radio signal on a distinctive frequency...
Pffff! Big whoop. I could have whipped this up in about ten seconds with fifty cents' worth of spare parts!
Everybody's a critic!

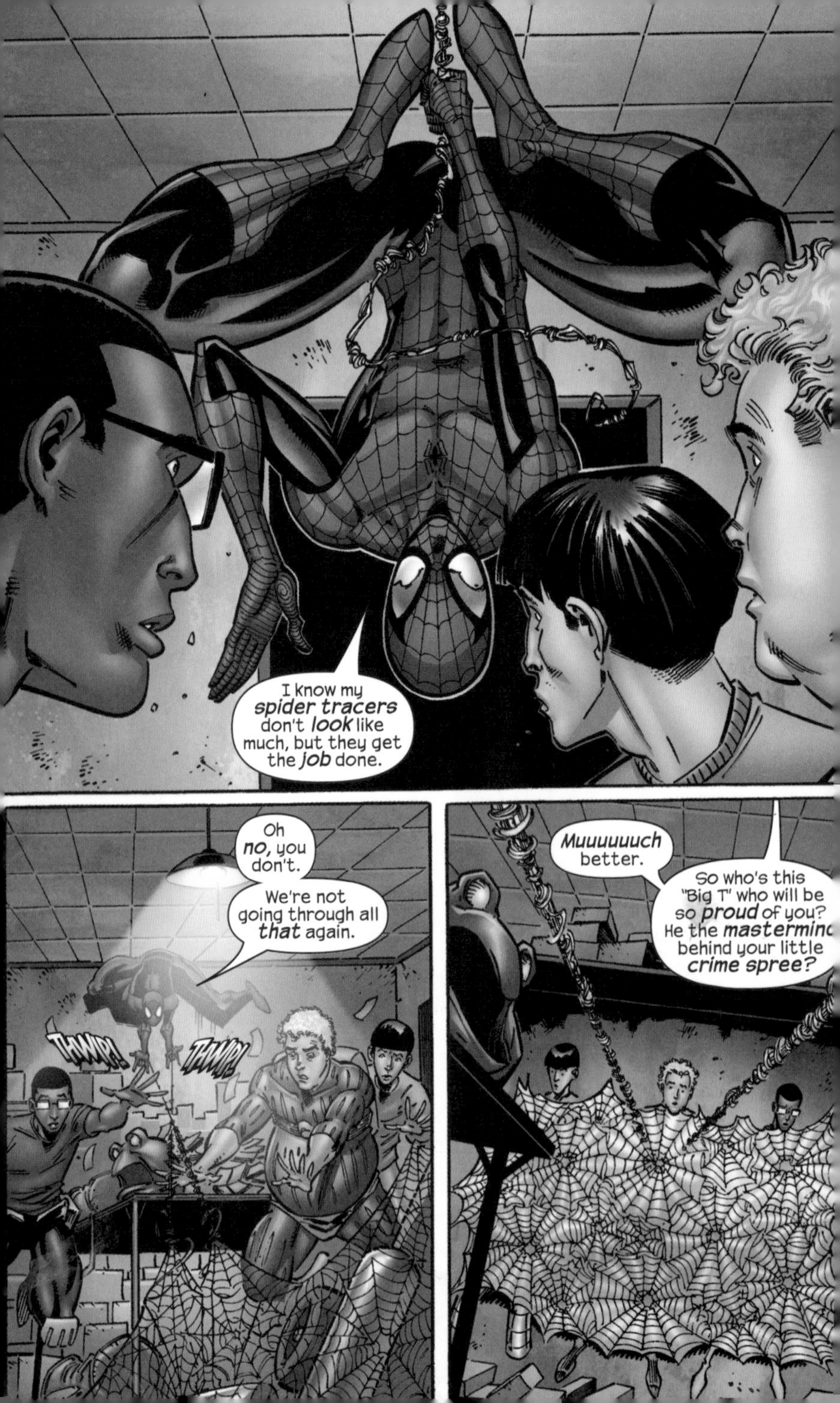
I know my *spider tracers* don't *look* like much, but they get the *job* done.
Oh *no,* you don't.
We're not going through all *that* again.
THWIP!
THWIP!
Muuuuuuch better.
So who's this "Big T" who will be so *proud* of you? He the *mastermind* behind your little *crime spree?*

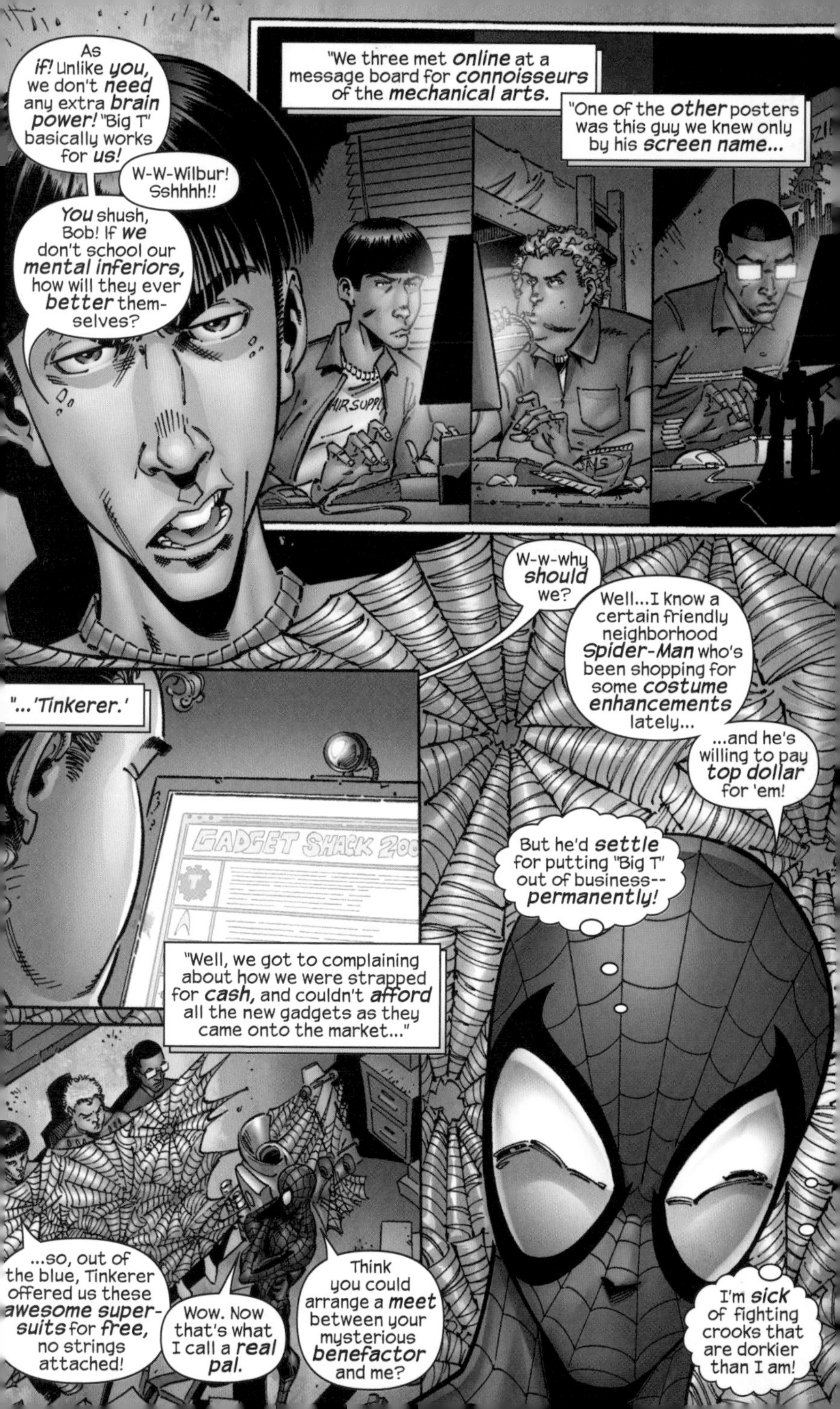

As if! Unlike you, we don't need any extra brain power! "Big T" basically works for us!
W-W-Wilbur! Sshhhh!!
You shush, Bob! If we don't school our mental inferiors, how will they ever better themselves?
"We three met online at a message board for connoisseurs of the mechanical arts.
"One of the other posters was this guy we knew only by his screen name...
"...'Tinkerer.'
GADGET SHACK 200
"Well, we got to complaining about how we were strapped for cash, and couldn't afford all the new gadgets as they came onto the market..."
...so, out of the blue, Tinkerer offered us these awesome super-suits for free, no strings attached!
Wow. Now that's what I call a real pal.
Think you could arrange a meet between your mysterious benefactor and me?
W-w-why should we?
Well...I know a certain friendly neighborhood Spider-Man who's been shopping for some costume enhancements lately...
...and he's willing to pay top dollar for 'em!
But he'd settle for putting "Big T" out of business--permanently!
I'm sick of fighting crooks that are dorkier than I am!

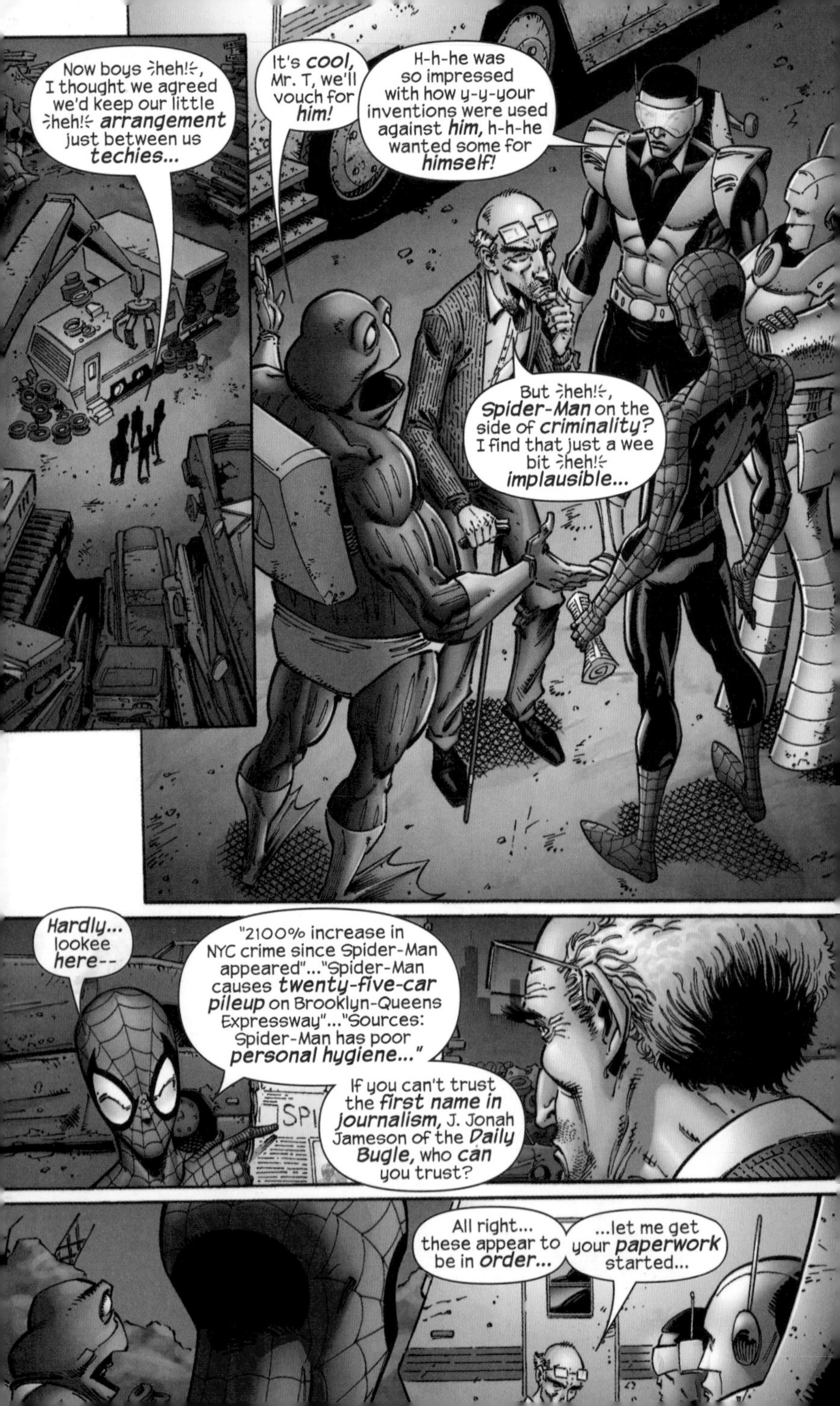

Now boys ⫶heh!⫶, I thought we agreed we'd keep our little ⫶heh!⫶ arrangement just between us techies...
It's cool, Mr. T, we'll vouch for him!
H-h-he was so impressed with how y-y-your inventions were used against him, h-h-he wanted some for himself!
But ⫶heh!⫶, Spider-Man on the side of criminality? I find that just a wee bit ⫶heh!⫶ implausible...
Hardly... lookee here--
"2100% increase in NYC crime since Spider-Man appeared"..."Spider-Man causes twenty-five-car pileup on Brooklyn-Queens Expressway"..."Sources: Spider-Man has poor personal hygiene..."
If you can't trust the first name in journalism, J. Jonah Jameson of the Daily Bugle, who can you trust?
All right... these appear to be in order...
...let me get your paperwork started...

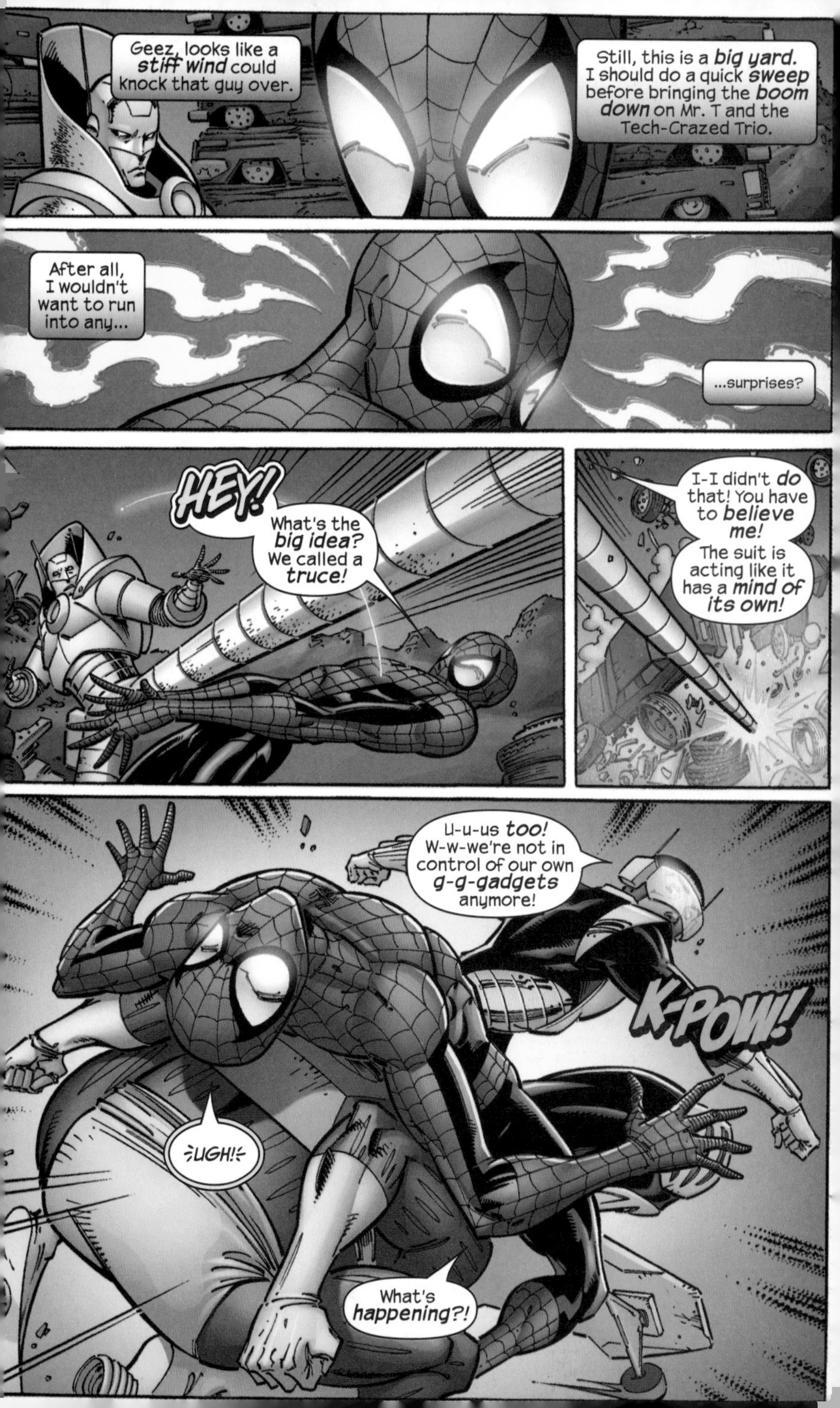

Geez, looks like a stiff wind could knock that guy over.
Still, this is a big yard. I should do a quick sweep before bringing the boom down on Mr. T and the Tech-Crazed Trio.
After all, I wouldn't want to run into any...
...surprises?
HEY!
What's the big idea? We called a truce!
I-I didn't do that! You have to believe me!
The suit is acting like it has a mind of its own!
U-u-us too! W-w-we're not in control of our own g-g-gadgets anymore!
K-POW!
UGH!
What's happening?!

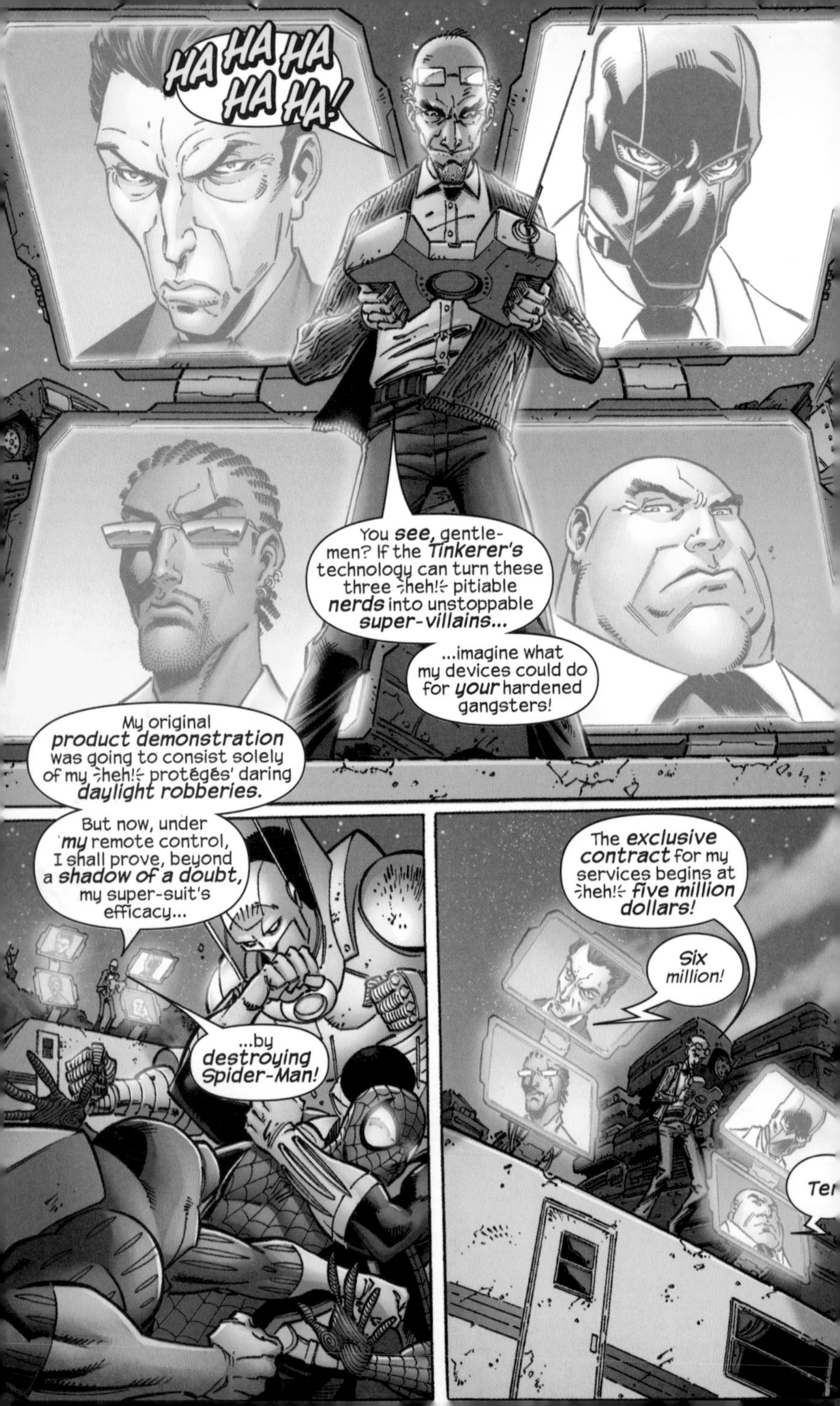
HA HA HA HA HA!
You see, gentlemen? If the Tinkerer's technology can turn these three -heh!- pitiable nerds into unstoppable super-villains...
...imagine what my devices could do for your hardened gangsters!
My original product demonstration was going to consist solely of my -heh!- protégés' daring daylight robberies.
But now, under my remote control, I shall prove, beyond a shadow of a doubt, my super-suit's efficacy...
...by destroying Spider-Man!
The exclusive contract for my services begins at -heh!- five million dollars!
Six million!

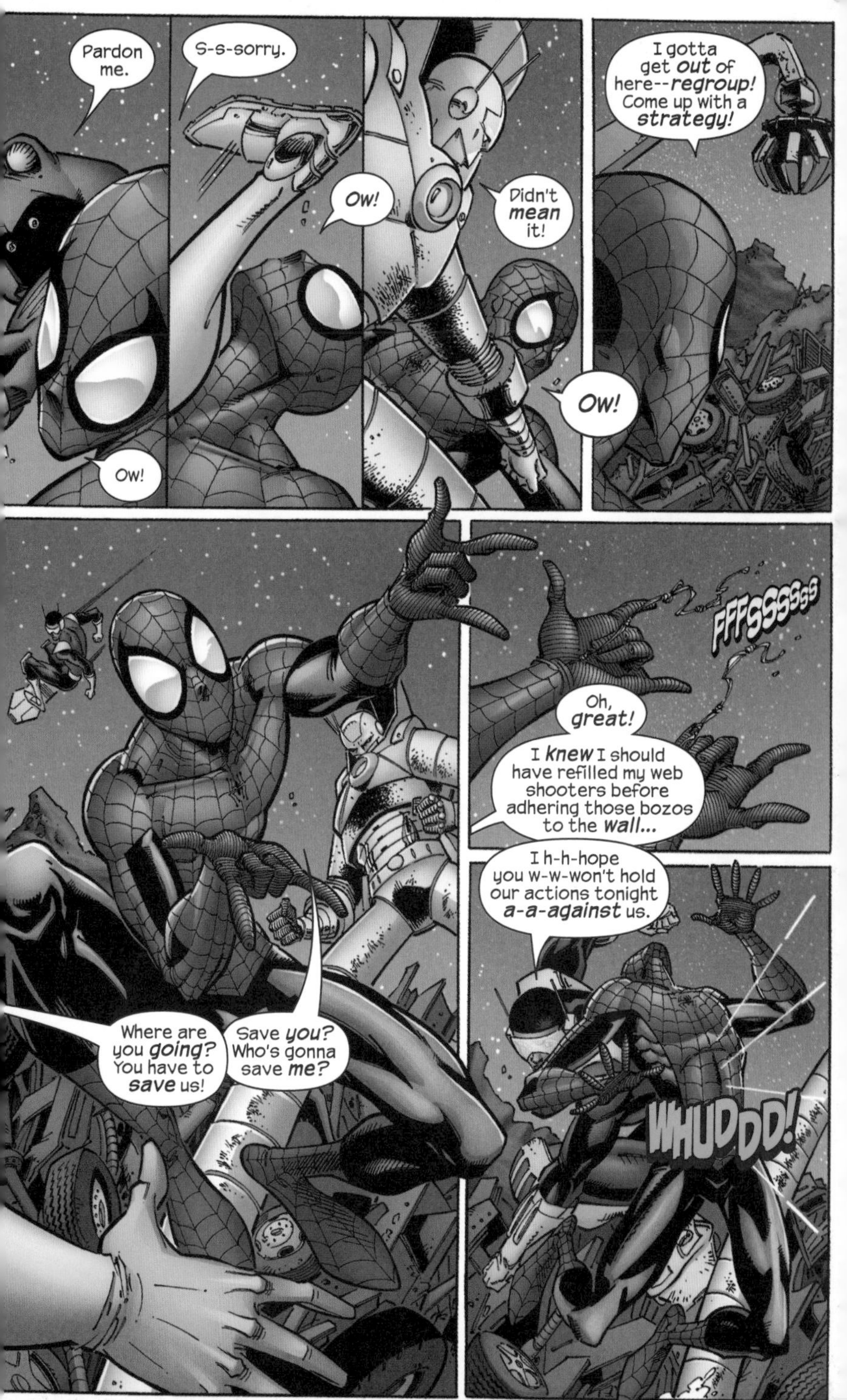

Pardon me.
Ow!
S-s-sorry.
Ow!
Didn't mean it!
Ow!
I gotta get out of here--regroup! Come up with a strategy!
Where are you going? You have to save us!
Save you? Who's gonna save me?
FFFSSSSSS
Oh, great!
I knew I should have refilled my web shooters before adhering those bozos to the wall...
I h-h-hope you w-w-won't hold our actions tonight a-a-against us.
WHUDDD!

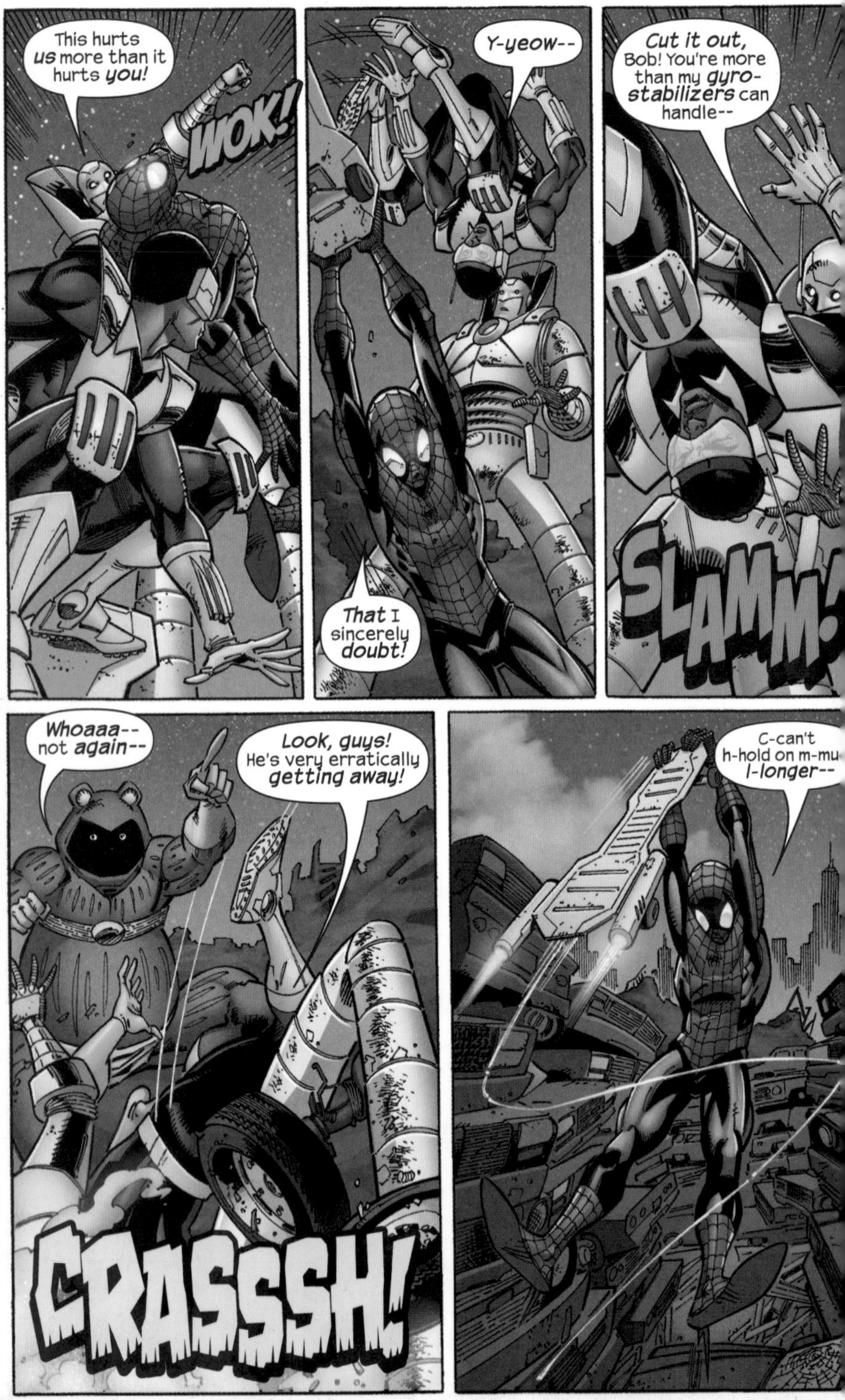

This hurts us more than it hurts you!
WOK!
Y-yeow--
That I sincerely doubt!
Cut it out, Bob! You're more than my gyro-stabilizers can handle--
SLAMM!
Whoaaa-- not again--
Look, guys! He's very erratically getting away!
CRASSSH!
C-can't h-hold on m-mu l-longer--

YAAHHHH!

≈Whoof!≈

That *spider-agility* does come in mighty *handy*.

But I'll need more than *that* to get me out of *this* mess--

--I could use some kind of *edge*, especially since my *web-shooters* are empty!

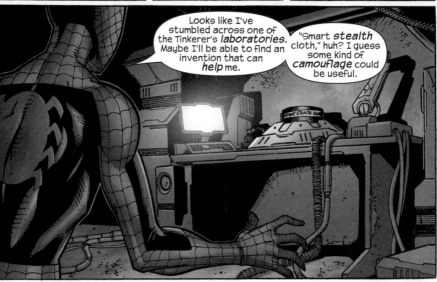

Looks like I've stumbled across one of the Tinkerer's *laboratories*. Maybe I'll be able to find an invention that can *help* me.

"Smart *stealth* cloth," huh? I guess some kind of *camouflage* could be useful.

But this doesn't look like any kind of *fabric* I've ever seen.

Almost more of a *liquid metal*, like *mercury*--

MART STEALTH CLOTH

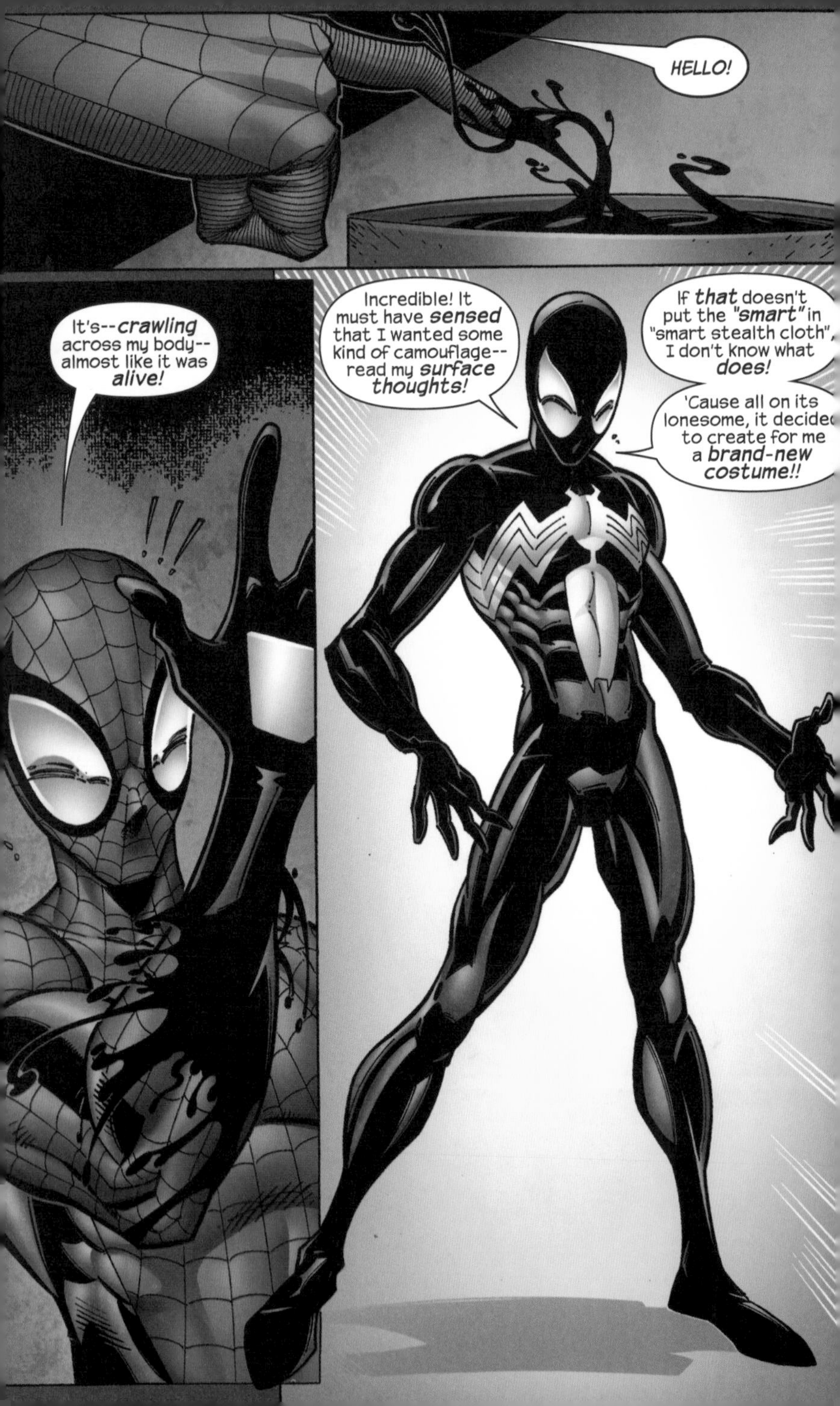
HELLO!
It's--*crawling* across my body--almost like it was *alive!*
Incredible! It must have *sensed* that I wanted some kind of camouflage--read my *surface thoughts!*
If *that* doesn't put the *"smart"* in "smart stealth cloth", I don't know what *does!*
'Cause all on its lonesome, it decided to create for me a *brand-new costume!!*

Gentlemen... our prey is *cornered.* That means we near ⊱heh!⊰ *endgame.*

One hundred million dollars!

One million ten!

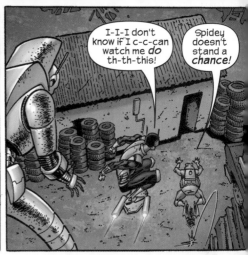

I-I-I don't know if I c-c-can watch me *do* th-th-this!

Spidey doesn't stand a *chance!*

Let's just hope his end is *quick* and relatively *painless!*

KRASH!

B-b-but...I didn't see him l-l-*leave,* did y-y-*you?*

Of *course* not!

I bet you he's hiding under one of those *work-benches* over there!

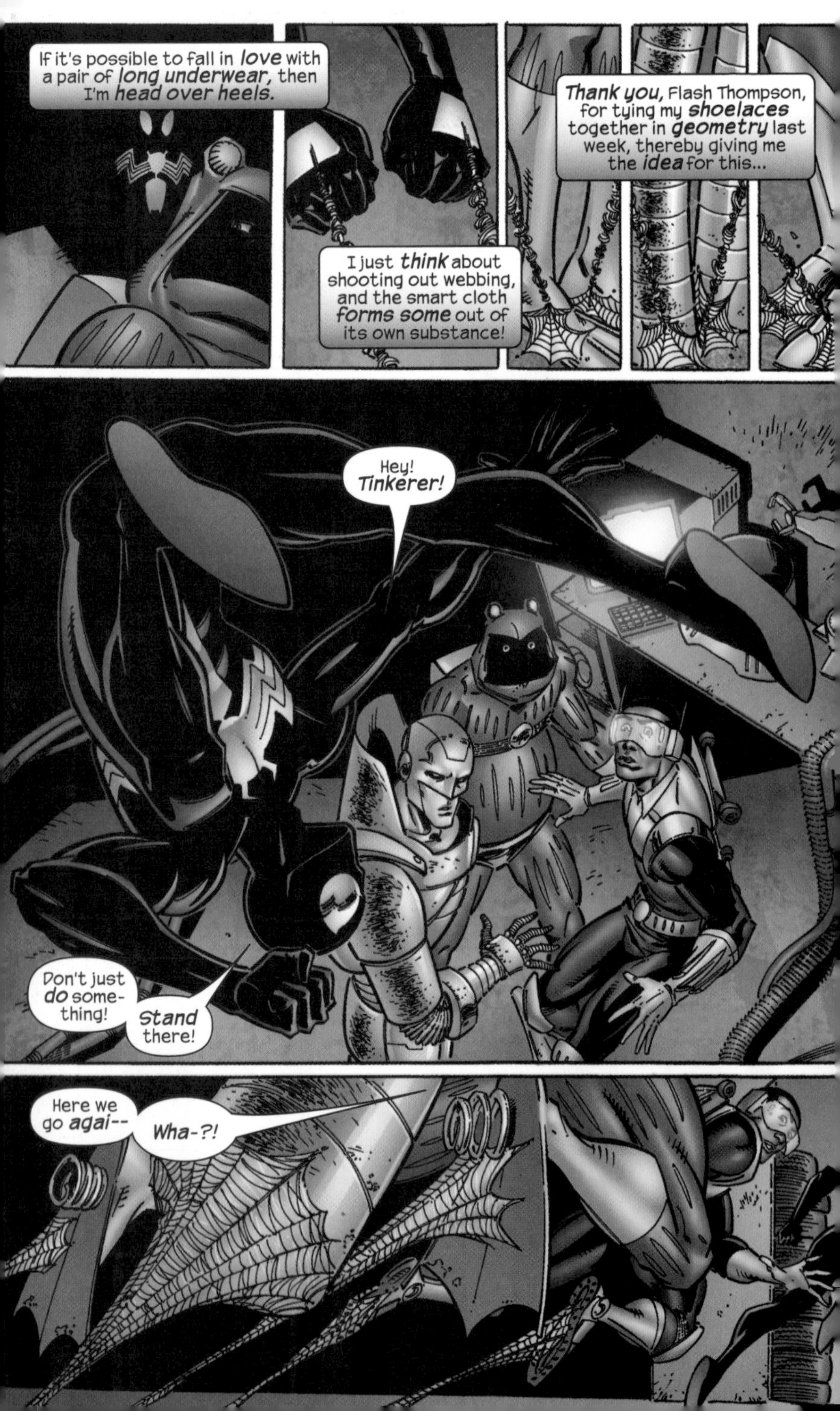
If it's possible to fall in *love* with a pair of *long underwear,* then I'm *head over heels.*
I just *think* about shooting out webbing, and the smart cloth *forms some* out of its own substance!
Thank you, Flash Thompson, for tying my *shoelaces* together in *geometry* last week, thereby giving me the *idea* for this...
Hey! *Tinkerer!*
Don't just *do* some-thing!
Stand there!
Here we go *agai--*
Wha-?!

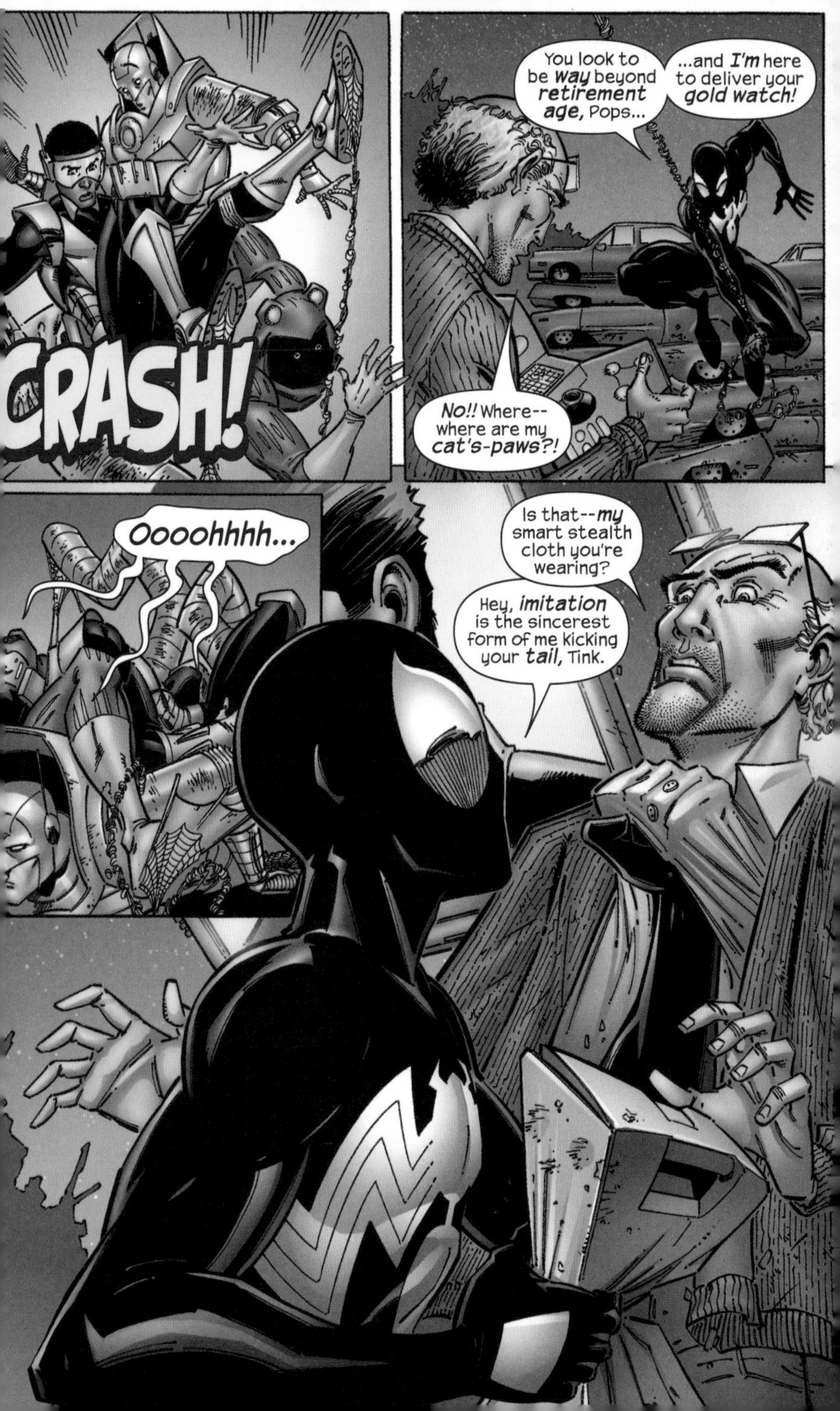

CRASH!
You look to be way beyond retirement age, Pops...
...and I'm here to deliver your gold watch!
No!! Where-- where are my cat's-paws?!
Oooohhhh...
Is that--my smart stealth cloth you're wearing?
Hey, imitation is the sincerest form of me kicking your tail, Tink.

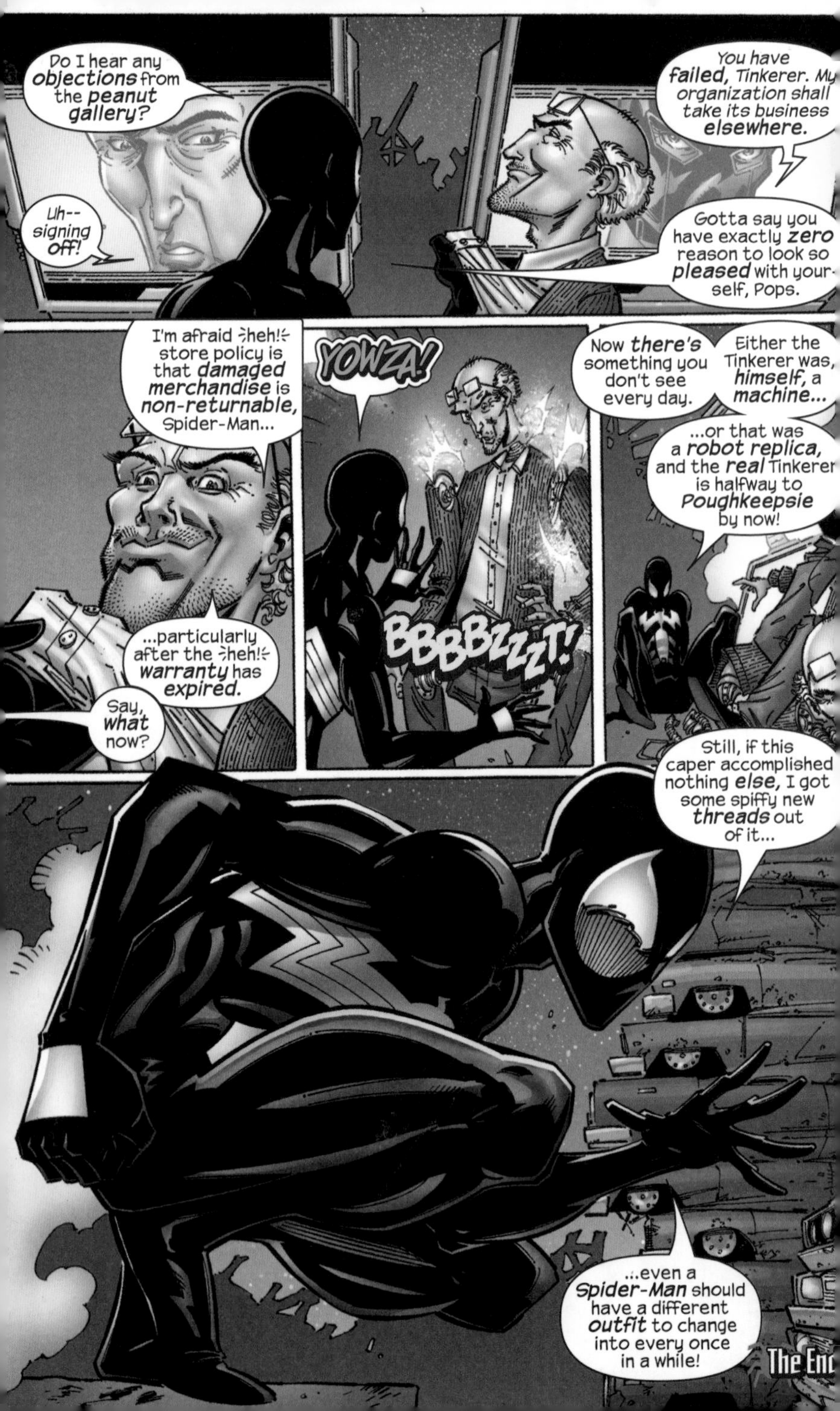
Do I hear any objections from the peanut gallery?
Uh-- signing off!
You have failed, Tinkerer. My organization shall take its business elsewhere.
Gotta say you have exactly zero reason to look so pleased with your-self, Pops.
I'm afraid -heh!- store policy is that damaged merchandise is non-returnable, Spider-Man...
...particularly after the -heh!- warranty has expired.
Say, what now?
YOWZA!
BBBBZZZZT!
Now there's something you don't see every day.
Either the Tinkerer was, himself, a machine...
...or that was a robot replica, and the real Tinkerer is halfway to Poughkeepsie by now!
Still, if this caper accomplished nothing else, I got some spiffy new threads out of it...
...even a Spider-Man should have a different outfit to change into every once in a while!
The End

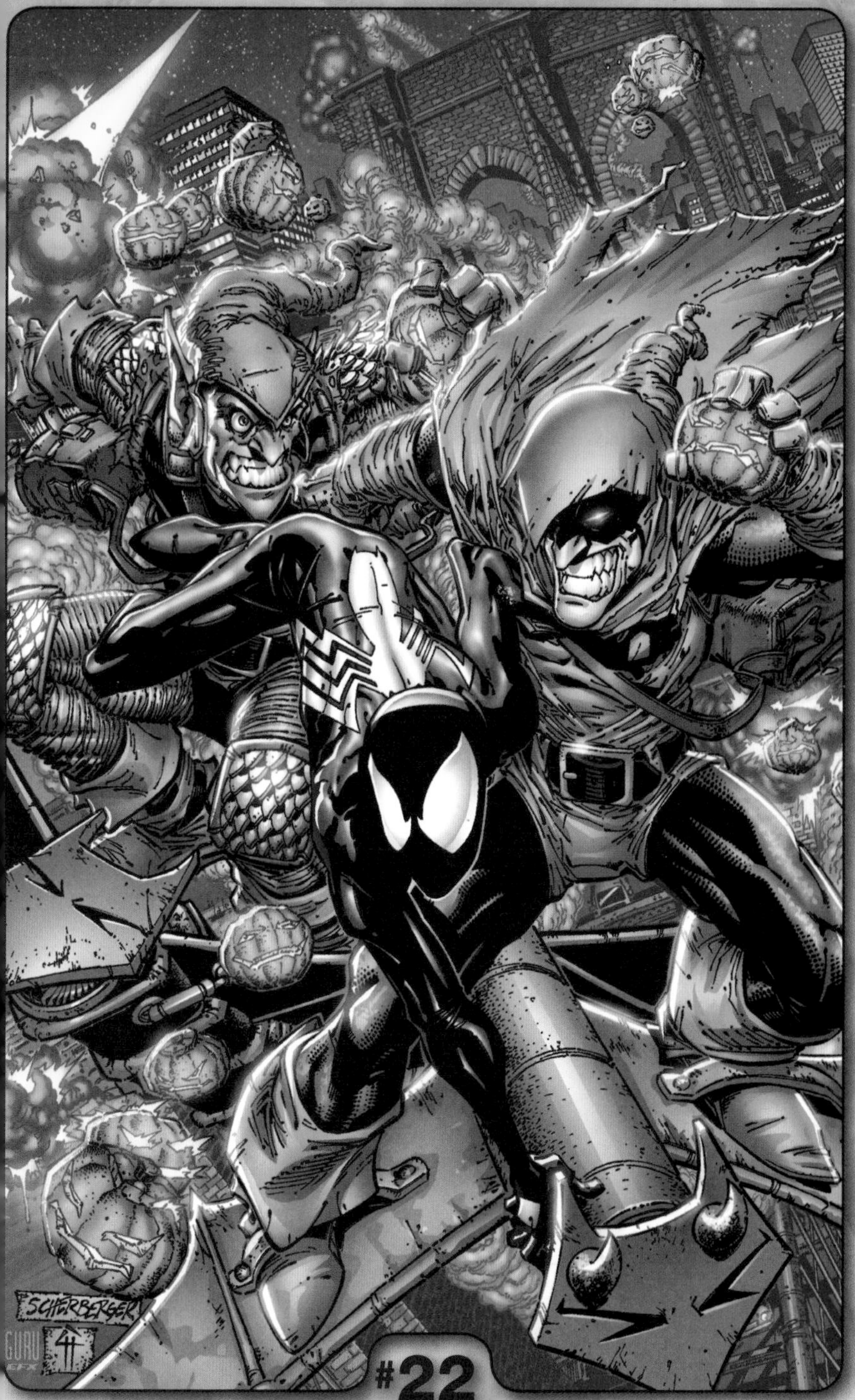
SCHERBERGER
GURU EFX
#22

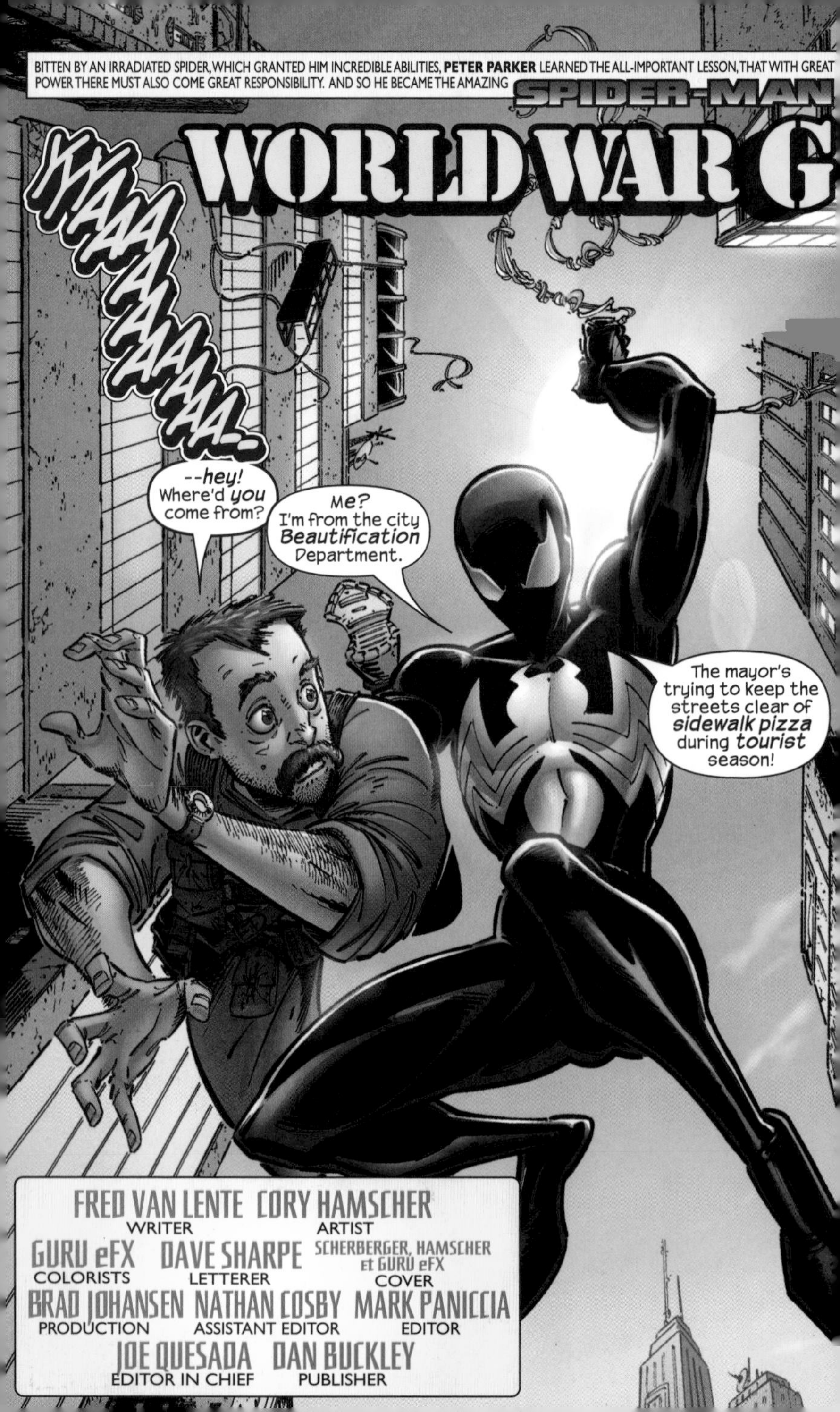
BITTEN BY AN IRRADIATED SPIDER, WHICH GRANTED HIM INCREDIBLE ABILITIES, PETER PARKER LEARNED THE ALL-IMPORTANT LESSON, THAT WITH GREAT POWER THERE MUST ALSO COME GREAT RESPONSIBILITY. AND SO HE BECAME THE AMAZING SPIDER-MAN
WORLD WAR G
YYAAAAAAAAAAA--
--hey! Where'd you come from?
Me? I'm from the city Beautification Department.
The mayor's trying to keep the streets clear of sidewalk pizza during tourist season!
FRED VAN LENTE WRITER
CORY HAMSCHER ARTIST
GURU eFX COLORISTS
DAVE SHARPE LETTERER
SCHERBERGER, HAMSCHER et GURU eFX COVER
BRAD JOHANSEN PRODUCTION
NATHAN COSBY ASSISTANT EDITOR
MARK PANICCIA EDITOR
JOE QUESADA EDITOR IN CHIEF
DAN BUCKLEY PUBLISHER

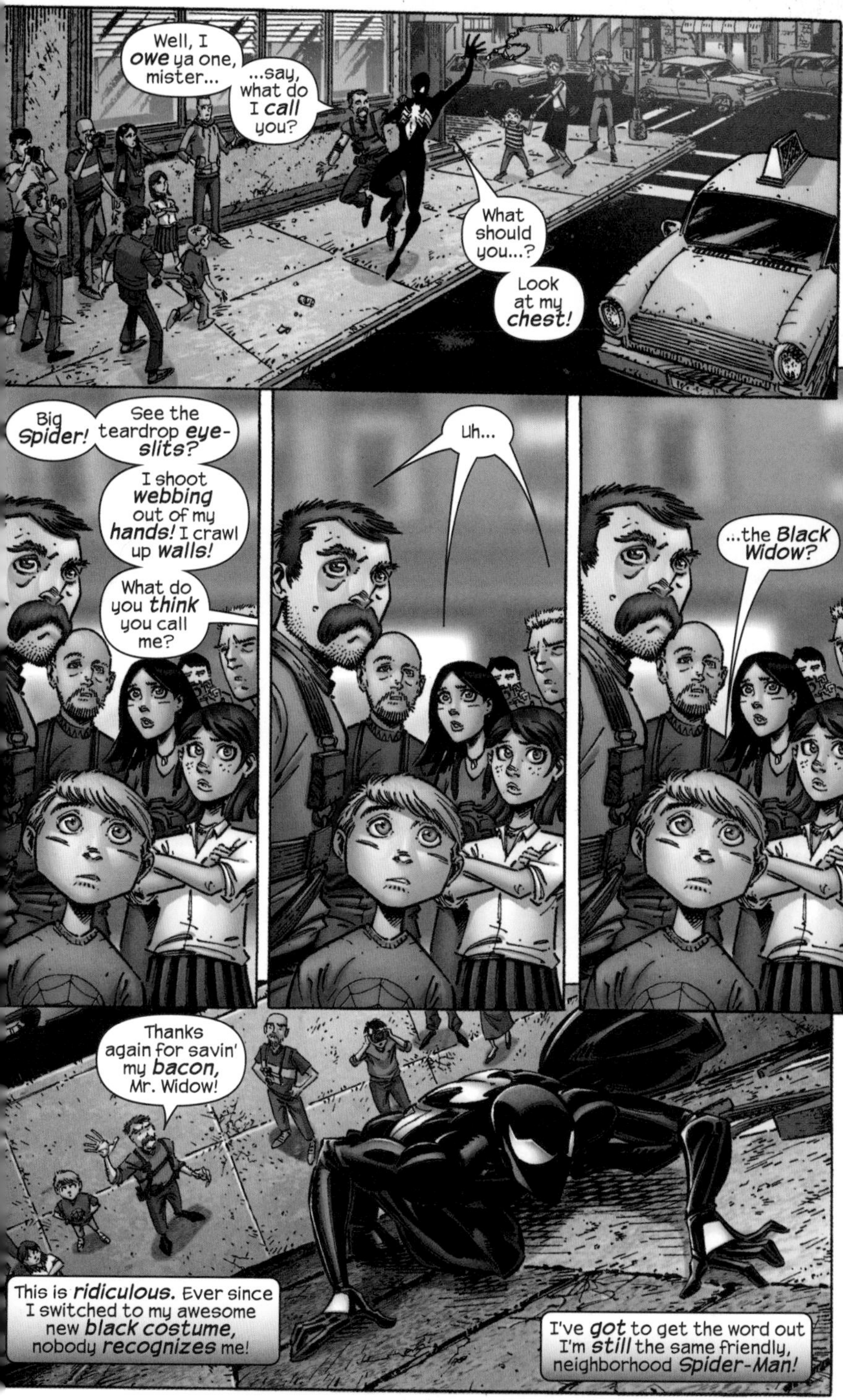

Well, I owe ya one, mister...
...say, what do I call you?
What should you...?
Look at my chest!
Big Spider!
See the teardrop eye-slits?
I shoot webbing out of my hands! I crawl up walls!
What do you think you call me?
Uh...
...the Black Widow?
Thanks again for savin' my bacon, Mr. Widow!
This is ridiculous. Ever since I switched to my awesome new black costume, nobody recognizes me!
I've got to get the word out I'm still the same friendly, neighborhood Spider-Man!

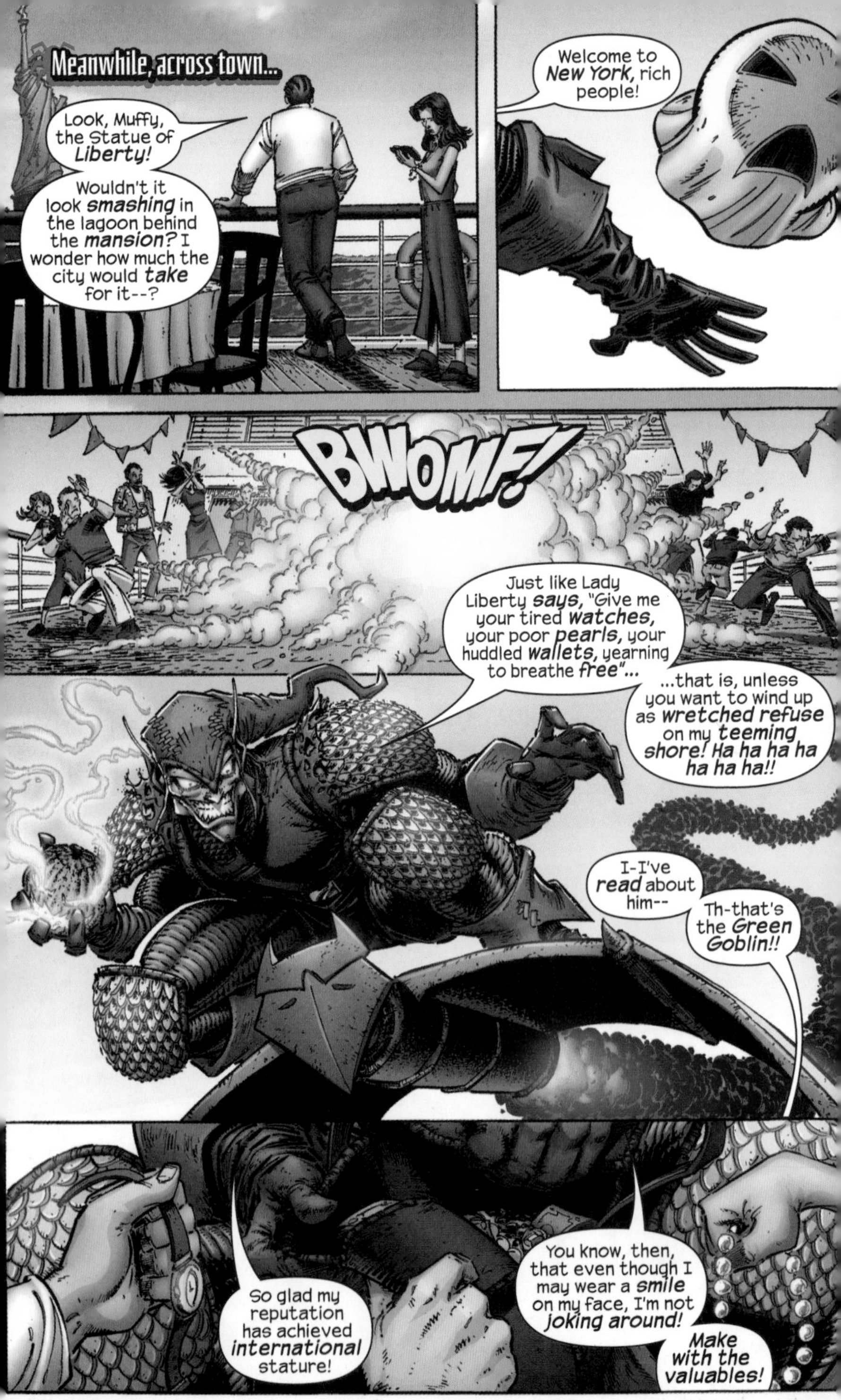

Meanwhile, across town...
Look, Muffy, the Statue of Liberty!
Wouldn't it look smashing in the lagoon behind the mansion? I wonder how much the city would take for it--?
Welcome to New York, rich people!
BWOMF!
Just like Lady Liberty says, "Give me your tired watches, your poor pearls, your huddled wallets, yearning to breathe free"...
...that is, unless you want to wind up as wretched refuse on my teeming shore! Ha ha ha ha ha ha ha!!
I-I've read about him--
Th-that's the Green Goblin!!
So glad my reputation has achieved international stature!
You know, then, that even though I may wear a smile on my face, I'm not joking around!
Make with the valuables!

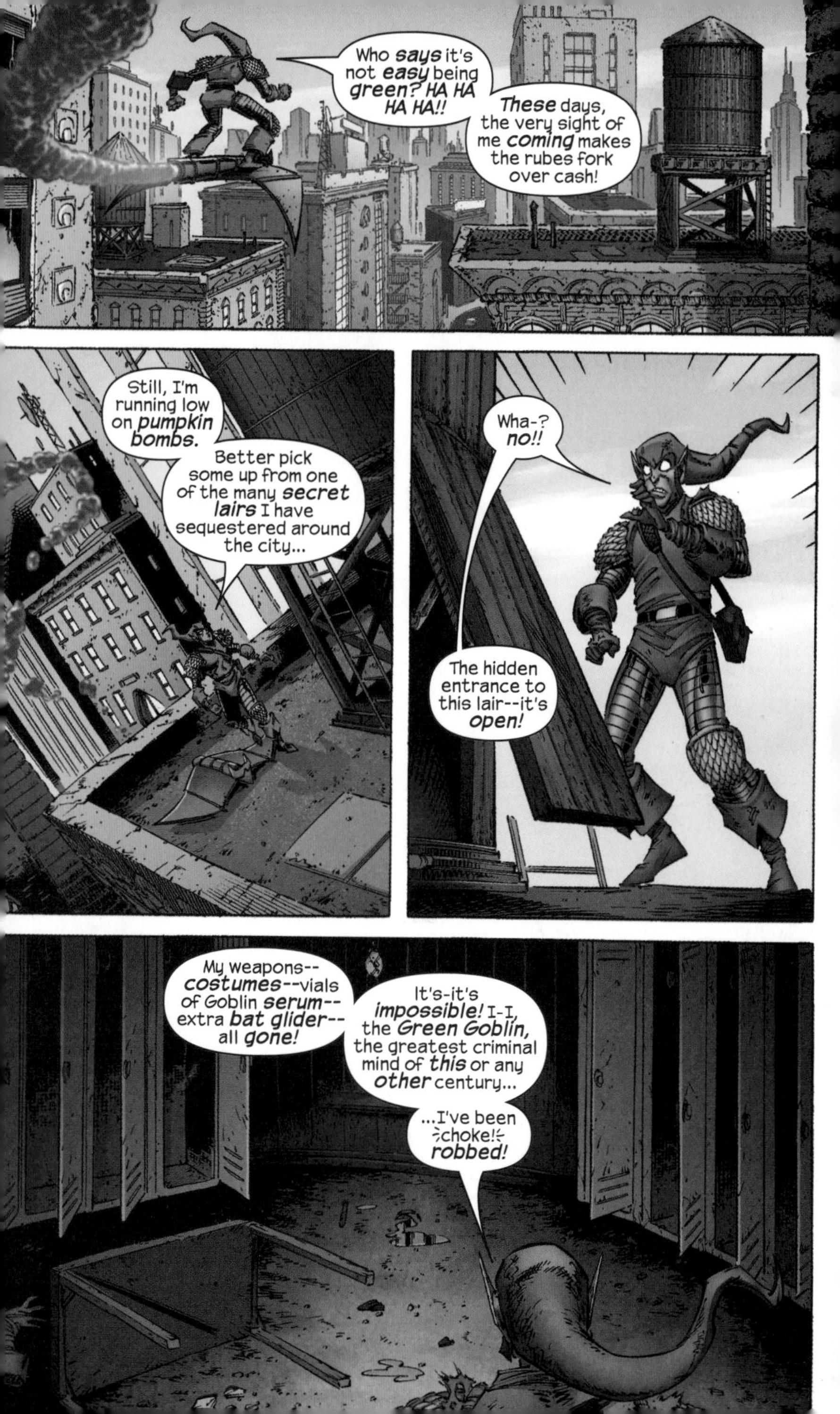
Who says it's not easy being green? HA HA HA HA!!
These days, the very sight of me coming makes the rubes fork over cash!
Still, I'm running low on pumpkin bombs.
Better pick some up from one of the many secret lairs I have sequestered around the city...
Wha-? no!!
The hidden entrance to this lair--it's open!
My weapons--costumes--vials of Goblin serum--extra bat glider--all gone!
It's-it's impossible! I-I, the Green Goblin, the greatest criminal mind of this or any other century...
...I've been ~choke!~ robbed!

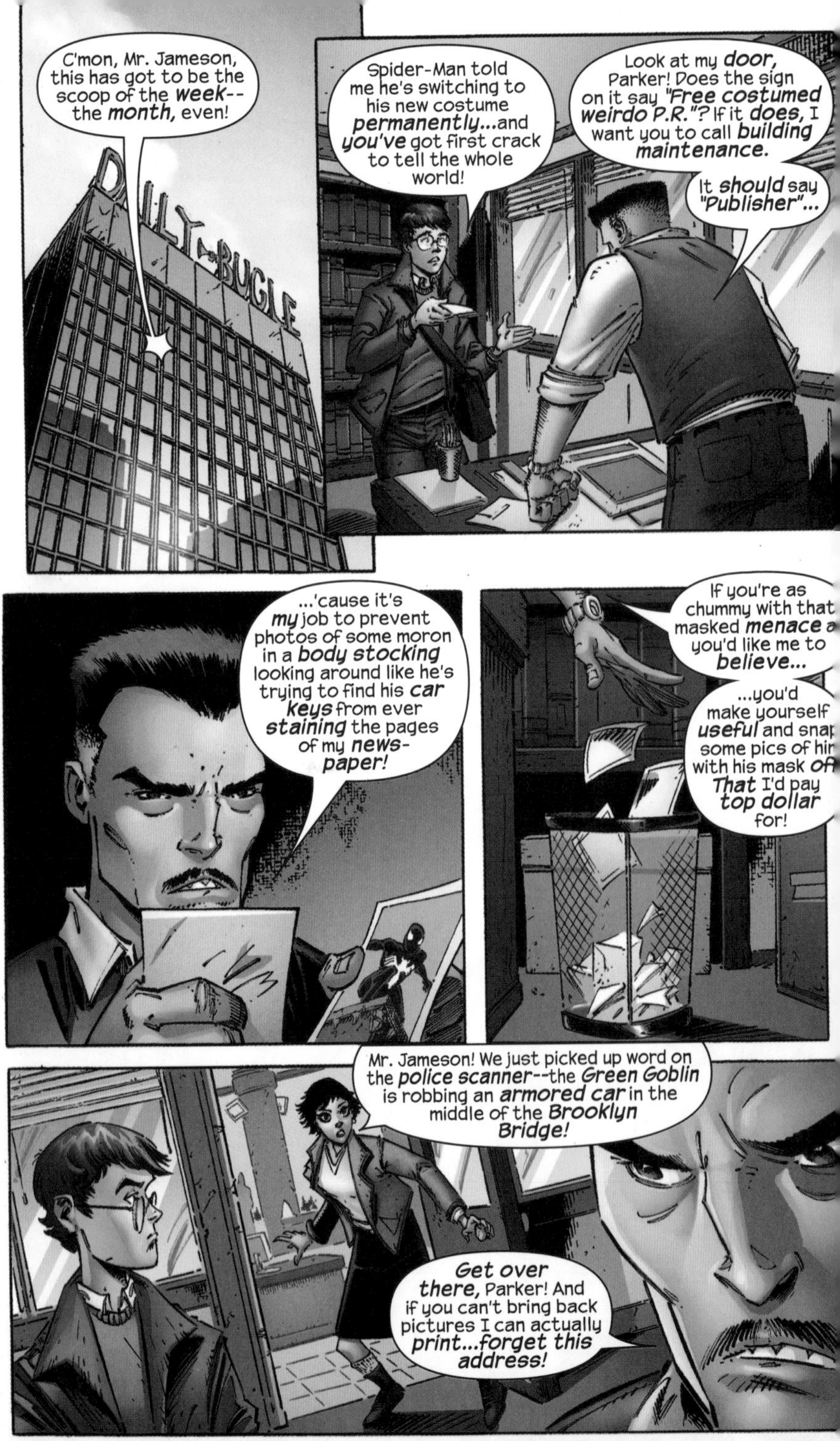

C'mon, Mr. Jameson, this has got to be the scoop of the week-- the month, even!
DAILY BUGLE
Spider-Man told me he's switching to his new costume permanently...and you've got first crack to tell the whole world!
Look at my door, Parker! Does the sign on it say "Free costumed weirdo P.R."? If it does, I want you to call building maintenance.
It should say "Publisher"...
...'cause it's my job to prevent photos of some moron in a body stocking looking around like he's trying to find his car keys from ever staining the pages of my news-paper!
If you're as chummy with that masked menace a you'd like me to believe...
...you'd make yourself useful and snap some pics of hir with his mask of That I'd pay top dollar for!
Mr. Jameson! We just picked up word on the police scanner--the Green Goblin is robbing an armored car in the middle of the Brooklyn Bridge!
Get over there, Parker! And if you can't bring back pictures I can actually print...forget this address!

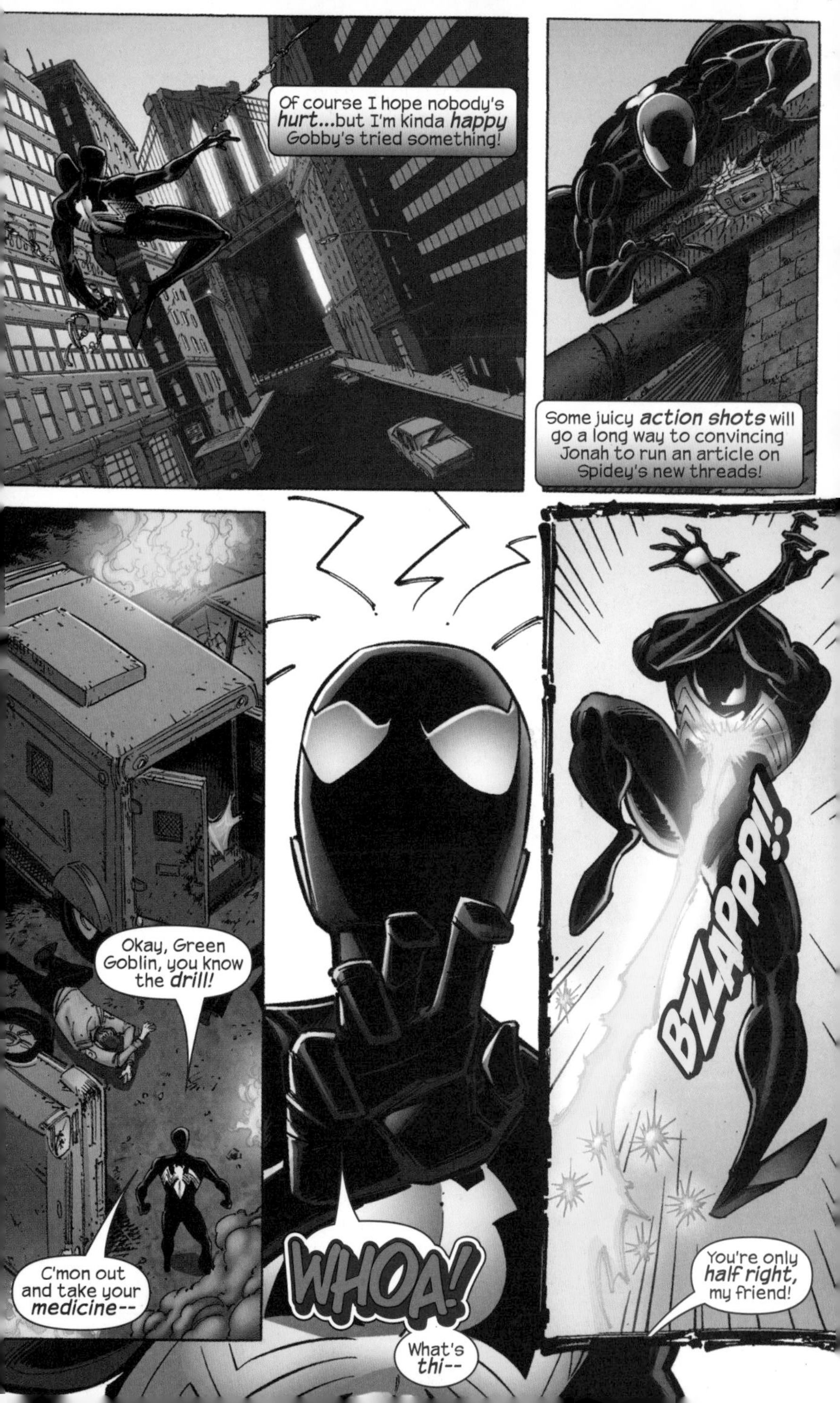

Of course I hope nobody's *hurt*...but I'm kinda *happy* Gobby's tried something!
Some juicy **action shots** will go a long way to convincing Jonah to run an article on Spidey's new threads!
Okay, Green Goblin, you know the *drill!*
C'mon out and take your *medicine*--
WHOA!
What's *thi*--
BZZAPP!!
You're only *half right,* my friend!

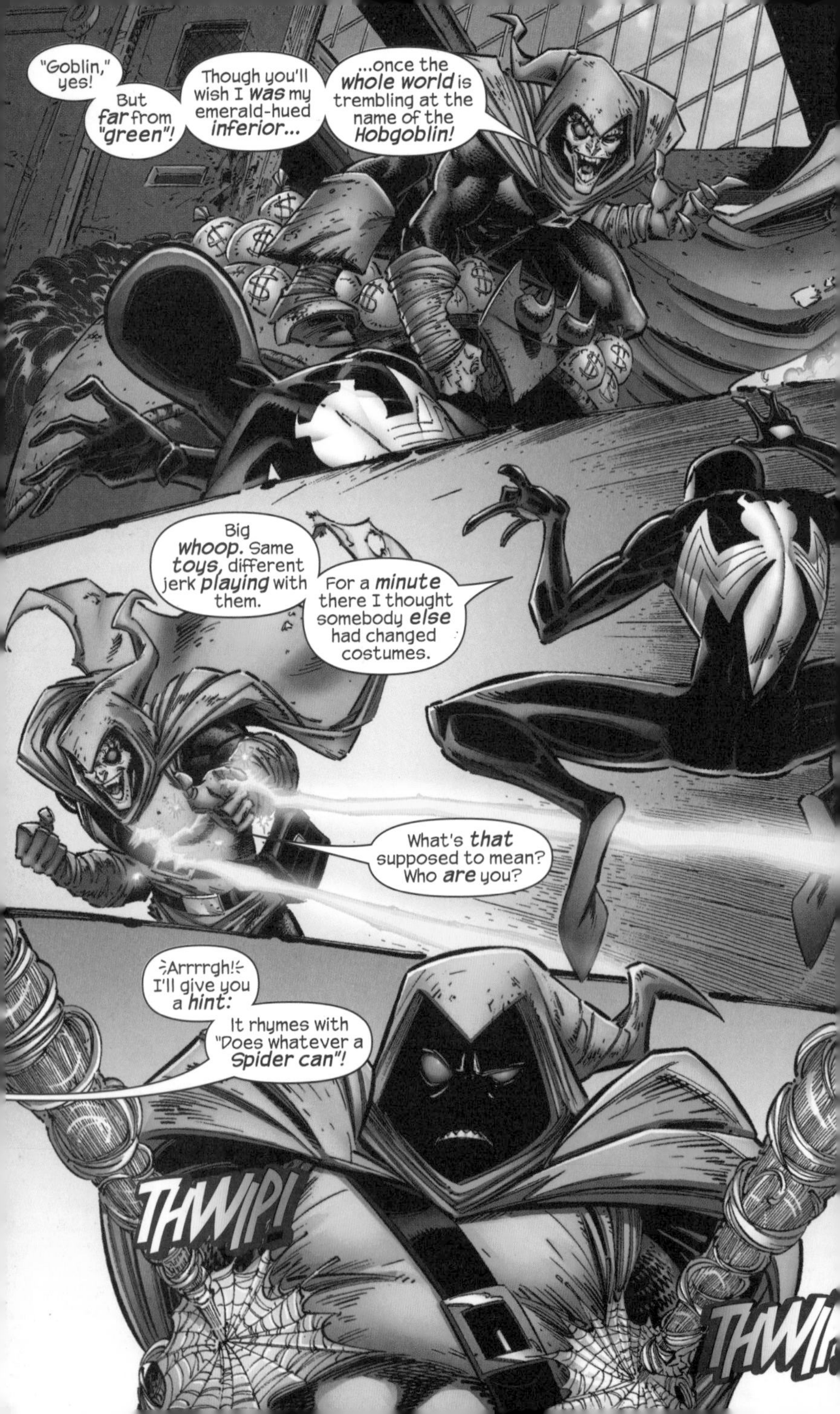
"Goblin," yes!
But far from "green"!
Though you'll wish I was my emerald-hued inferior...
...once the whole world is trembling at the name of the Hobgoblin!
Big whoop. Same toys, different jerk playing with them.
For a minute there I thought somebody else had changed costumes.
What's that supposed to mean? Who are you?
Arrrrgh!
I'll give you a hint:
It rhymes with "Does whatever a Spider can"!
THWIP!
THWI..

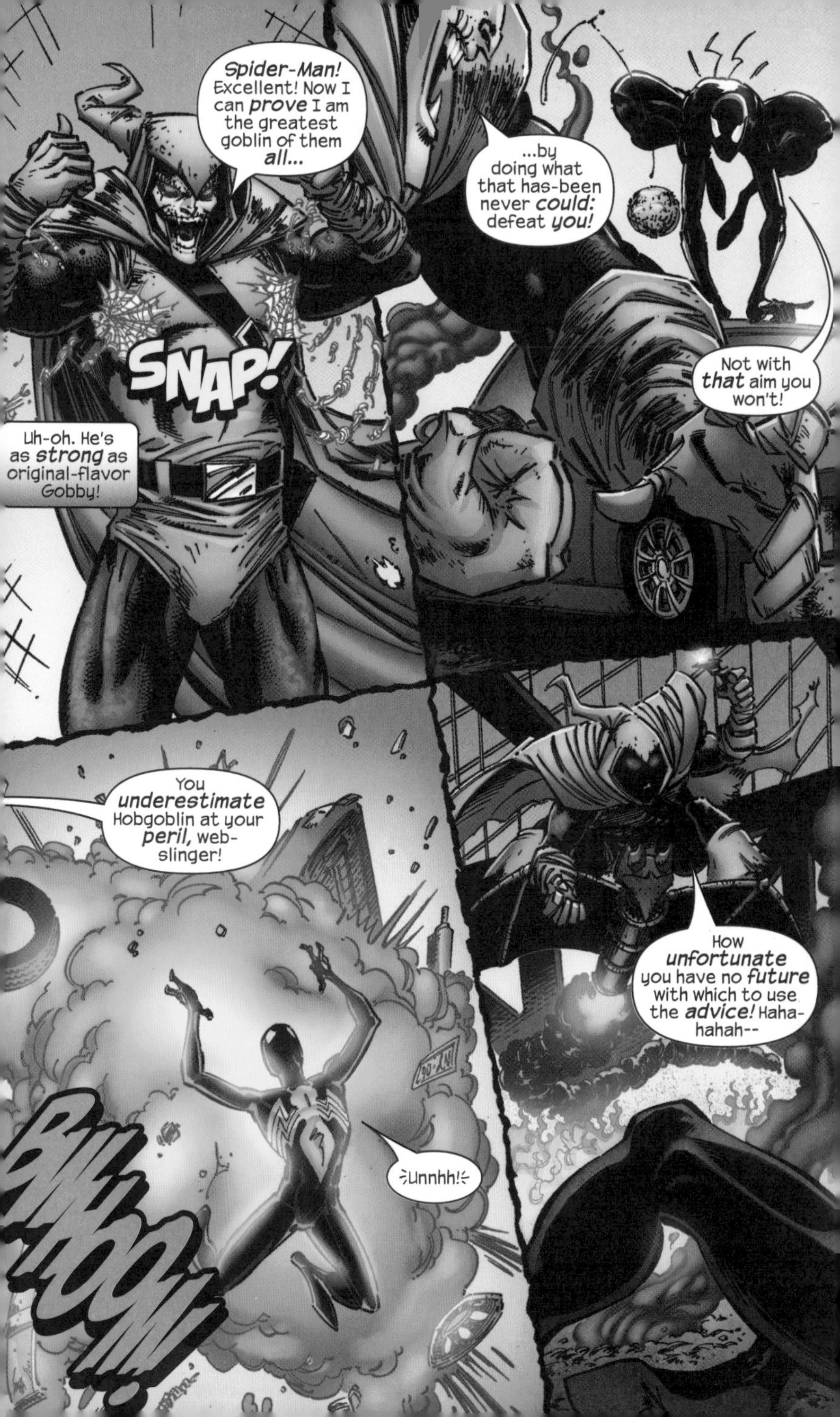
Spider-Man! Excellent! Now I can prove I am the greatest goblin of them all...
...by doing what that has-been never could: defeat you!
SNAP!
Not with that aim you won't!
Uh-oh. He's as strong as original-flavor Gobby!
You underestimate Hobgoblin at your peril, web-slinger!
How unfortunate you have no future with which to use the advice! Haha-hahah--
BHOOM!
Unnhh!

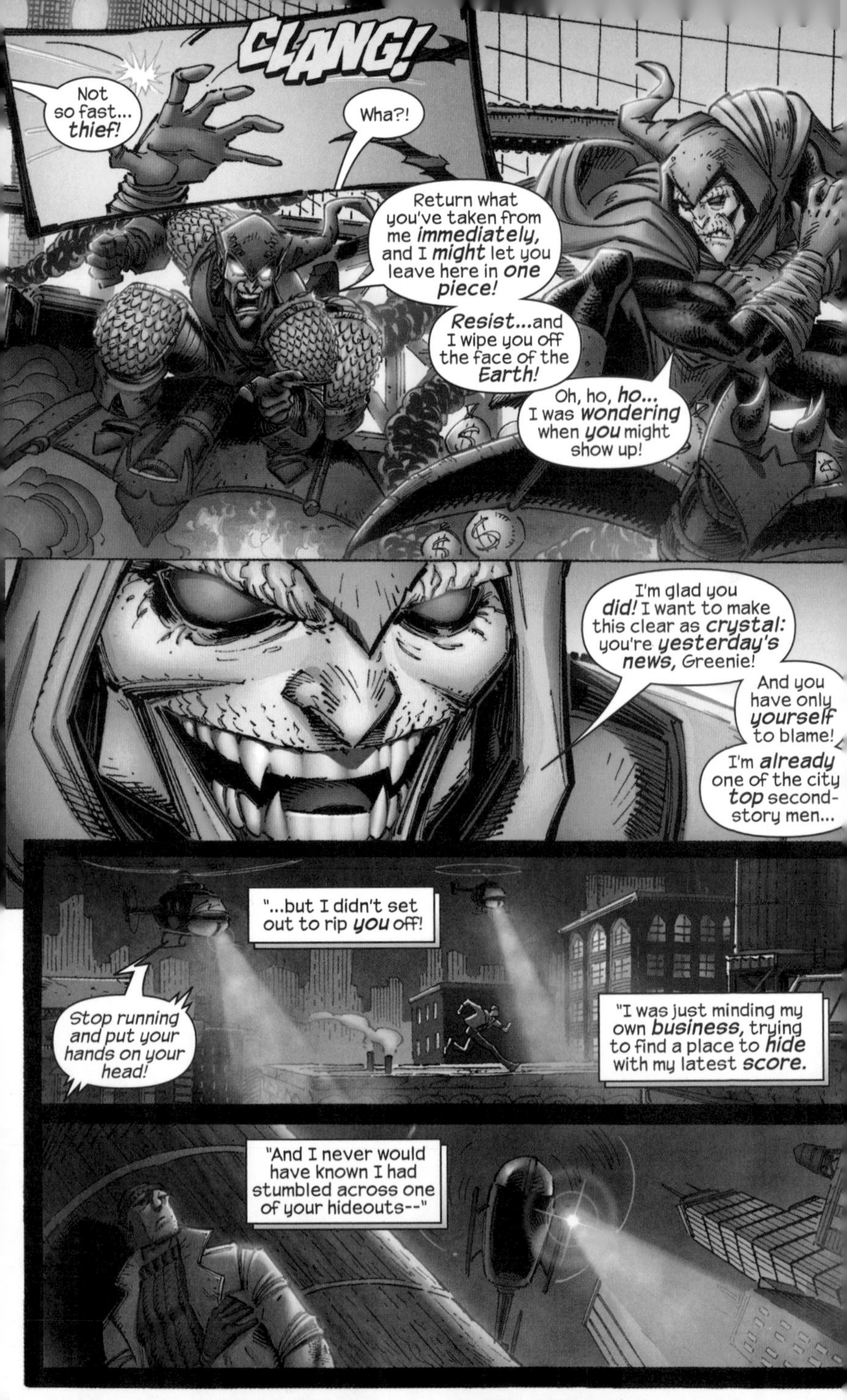
CLANG!
Not so fast... thief!
Wha?!
Return what you've taken from me immediately, and I might let you leave here in one piece!
Resist...and I wipe you off the face of the Earth!
Oh, ho, ho... I was wondering when you might show up!
I'm glad you did! I want to make this clear as crystal: you're yesterday's news, Greenie!
And you have only yourself to blame!
I'm already one of the city top second-story men...
"...but I didn't set out to rip you off!
Stop running and put your hands on your head!
"I was just minding my own business, trying to find a place to hide with my latest score.
"And I never would have known I had stumbled across one of your hideouts--"

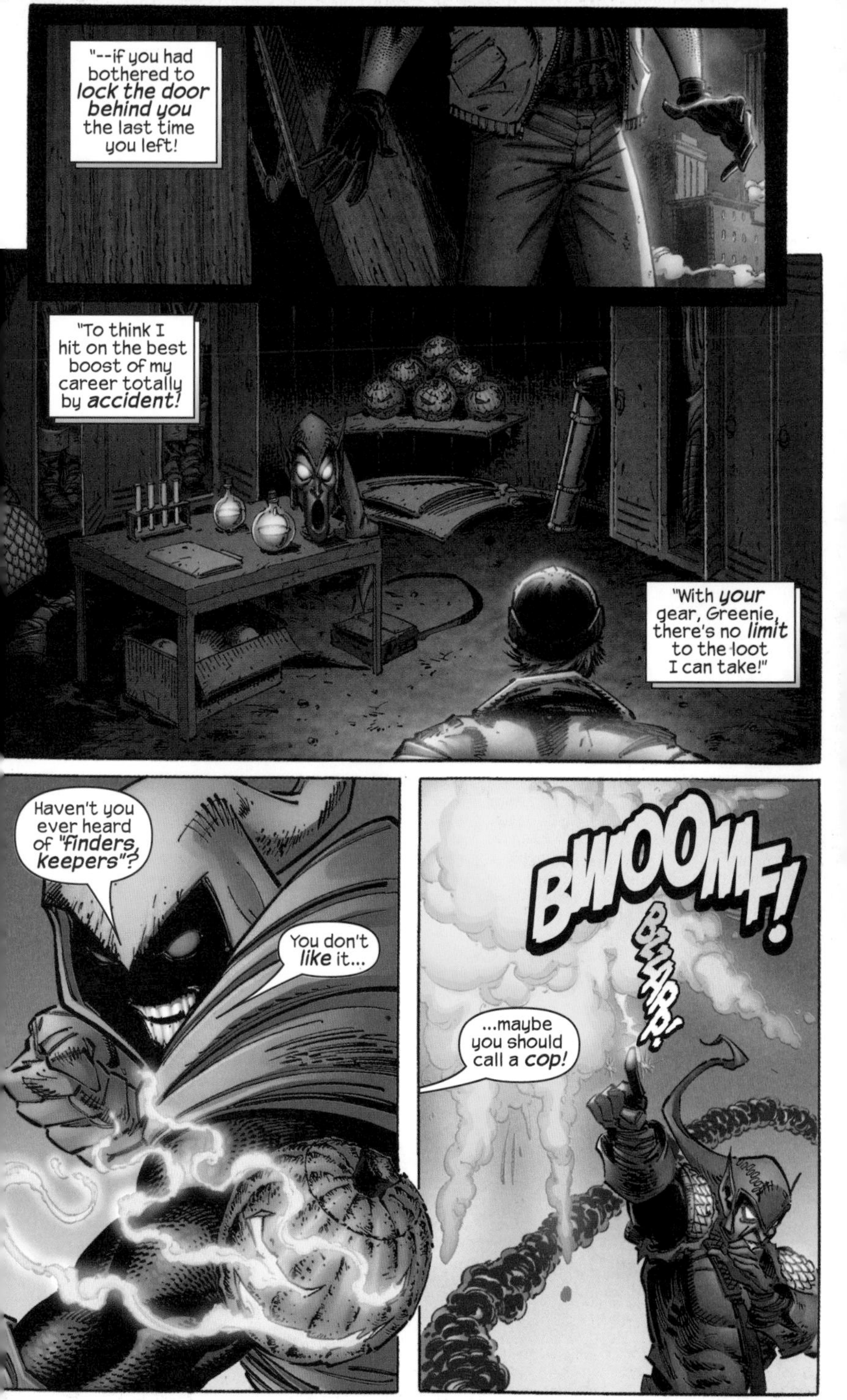
"--if you had bothered to lock the door behind you the last time you left!
"To think I hit on the best boost of my career totally by accident!
"With your gear, Greenie, there's no limit to the loot I can take!"
Haven't you ever heard of "finders, keepers"?
You don't like it...
BWOOMF!
...maybe you should call a cop!

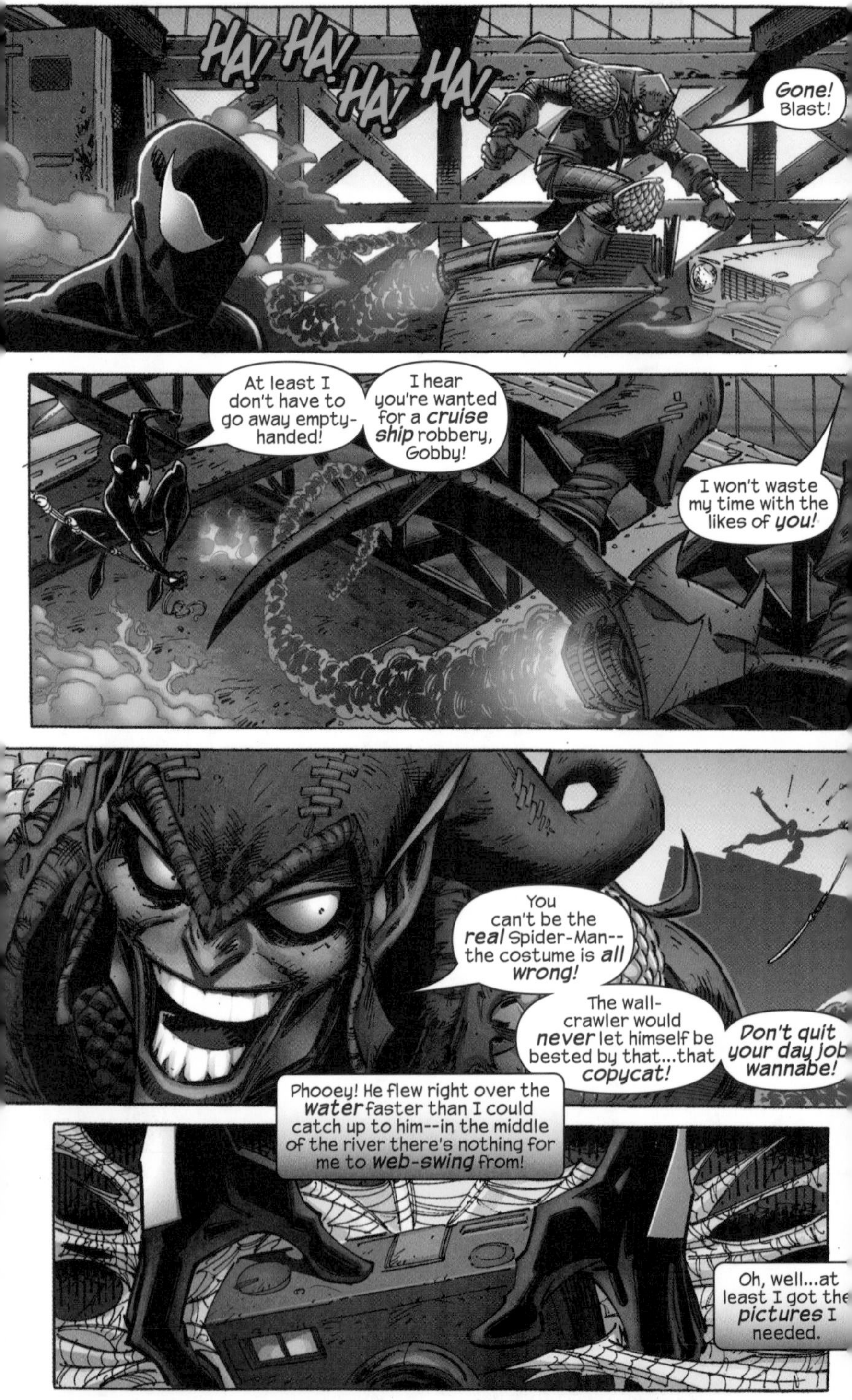
HA! HA! HA! HA!
Gone! Blast!
At least I don't have to go away empty-handed!
I hear you're wanted for a cruise ship robbery, Gobby!
I won't waste my time with the likes of you!
You can't be the real Spider-Man--the costume is all wrong!
The wall-crawler would never let himself be bested by that...that copycat!
Don't quit your day job wannabe!
Phooey! He flew right over the water faster than I could catch up to him--in the middle of the river there's nothing for me to web-swing from!
Oh, well...at least I got the pictures I needed.

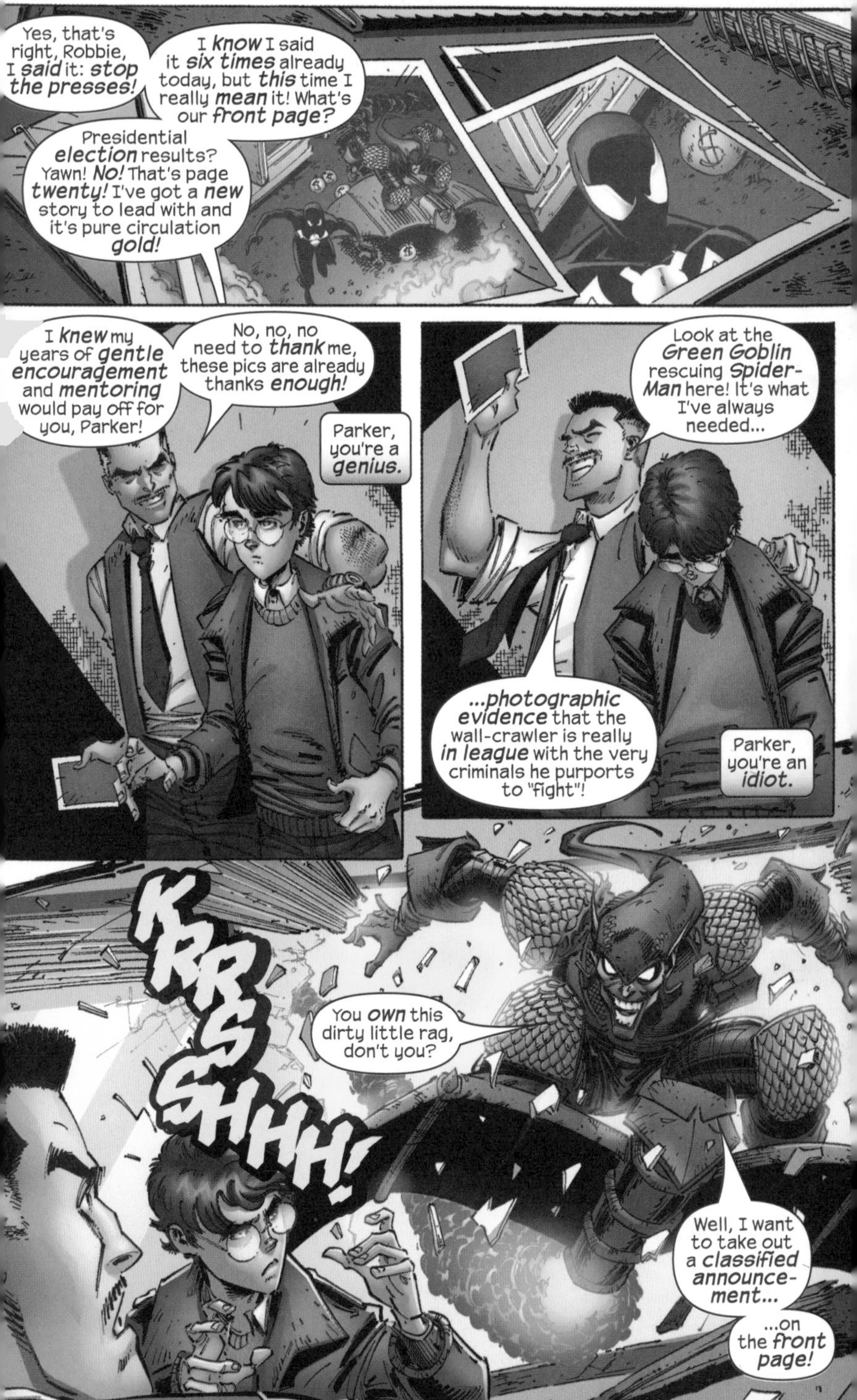
Yes, that's right, Robbie, I said it: stop the presses!
I know I said it six times already today, but this time I really mean it! What's our front page?
Presidential election results? Yawn! No! That's page twenty! I've got a new story to lead with and it's pure circulation gold!
I knew my years of gentle encouragement and mentoring would pay off for you, Parker!
No, no, no need to thank me, these pics are already thanks enough!
Parker, you're a genius.
Look at the Green Goblin rescuing Spider-Man here! It's what I've always needed...
...photographic evidence that the wall-crawler is really in league with the very criminals he purports to "fight"!
Parker, you're an idiot.
KRRSSHHH!
You own this dirty little rag, don't you?
Well, I want to take out a classified announcement...
...on the front page!

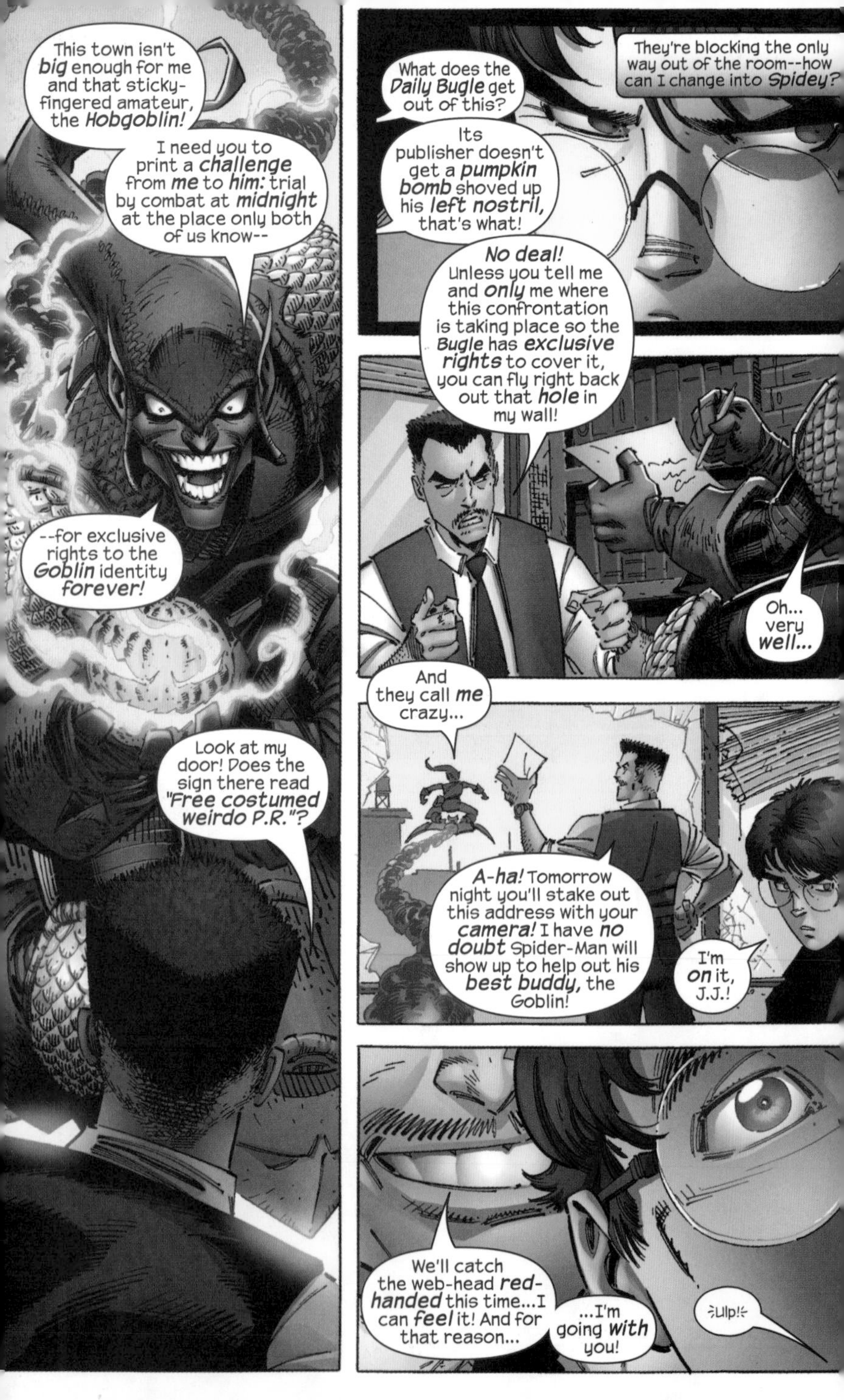
This town isn't big enough for me and that sticky-fingered amateur, the Hobgoblin!
I need you to print a challenge from me to him: trial by combat at midnight at the place only both of us know--
--for exclusive rights to the Goblin identity forever!
Look at my door! Does the sign there read "Free costumed weirdo P.R."?
They're blocking the only way out of the room--how can I change into Spidey?
What does the Daily Bugle get out of this?
Its publisher doesn't get a pumpkin bomb shoved up his left nostril, that's what!
No deal! Unless you tell me and only me where this confrontation is taking place so the Bugle has exclusive rights to cover it, you can fly right back out that hole in my wall!
Oh... very well...
And they call me crazy...
A-ha! Tomorrow night you'll stake out this address with your camera! I have no doubt Spider-Man will show up to help out his best buddy, the Goblin!
I'm on it, J.J.!
We'll catch the web-head red-handed this time...I can feel it! And for that reason...
...I'm going with you!
Ulp!

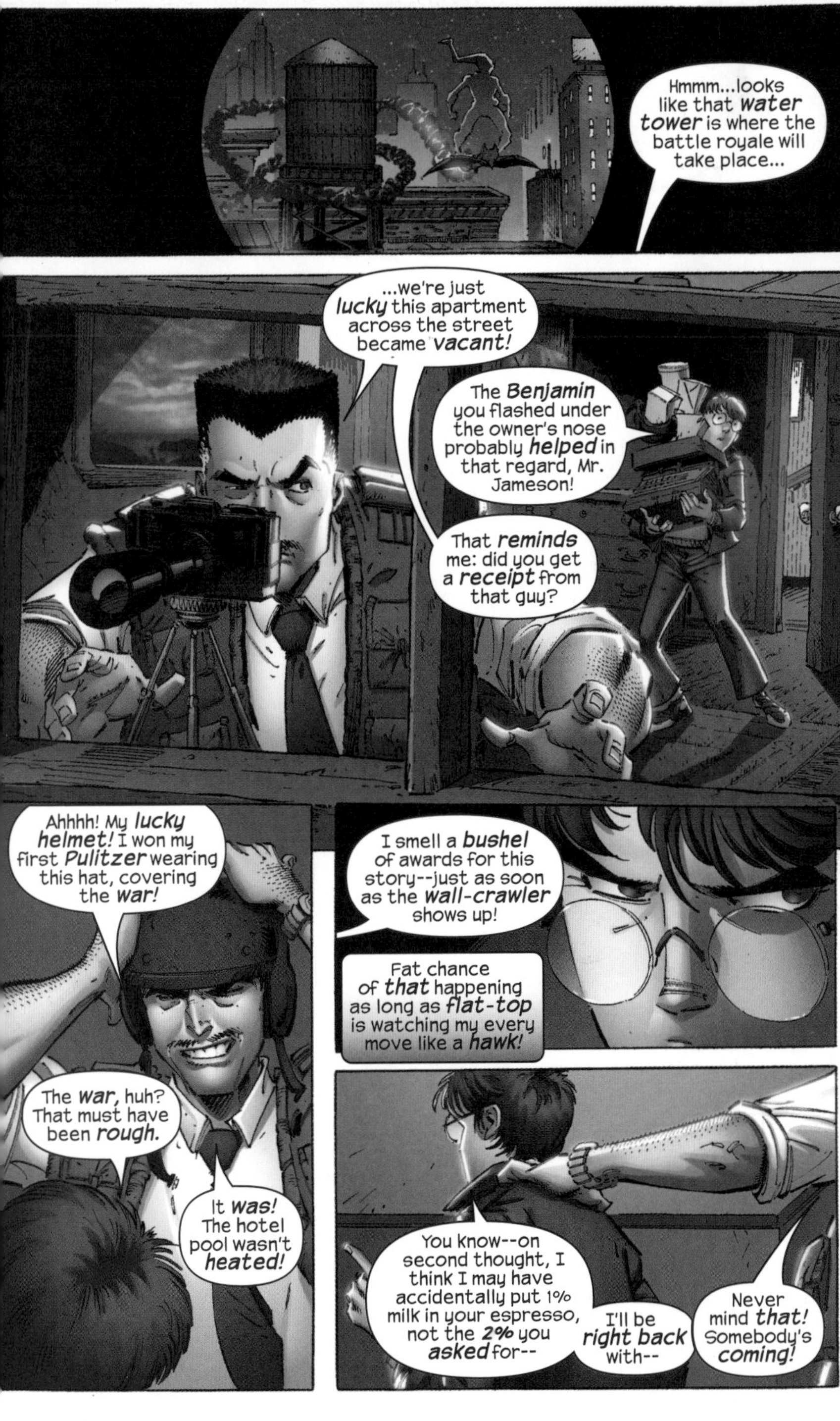

Hmmm...looks like that water tower is where the battle royale will take place...
...we're just lucky this apartment across the street became vacant!
The Benjamin you flashed under the owner's nose probably helped in that regard, Mr. Jameson!
That reminds me: did you get a receipt from that guy?
Ahhhh! My lucky helmet! I won my first Pulitzer wearing this hat, covering the war!
The war, huh? That must have been rough.
It was! The hotel pool wasn't heated!
I smell a bushel of awards for this story--just as soon as the wall-crawler shows up!
Fat chance of that happening as long as flat-top is watching my every move like a hawk!
You know--on second thought, I think I may have accidentally put 1% milk in your espresso, not the 2% you asked for--
I'll be right back with--
Never mind that! Somebody's coming!

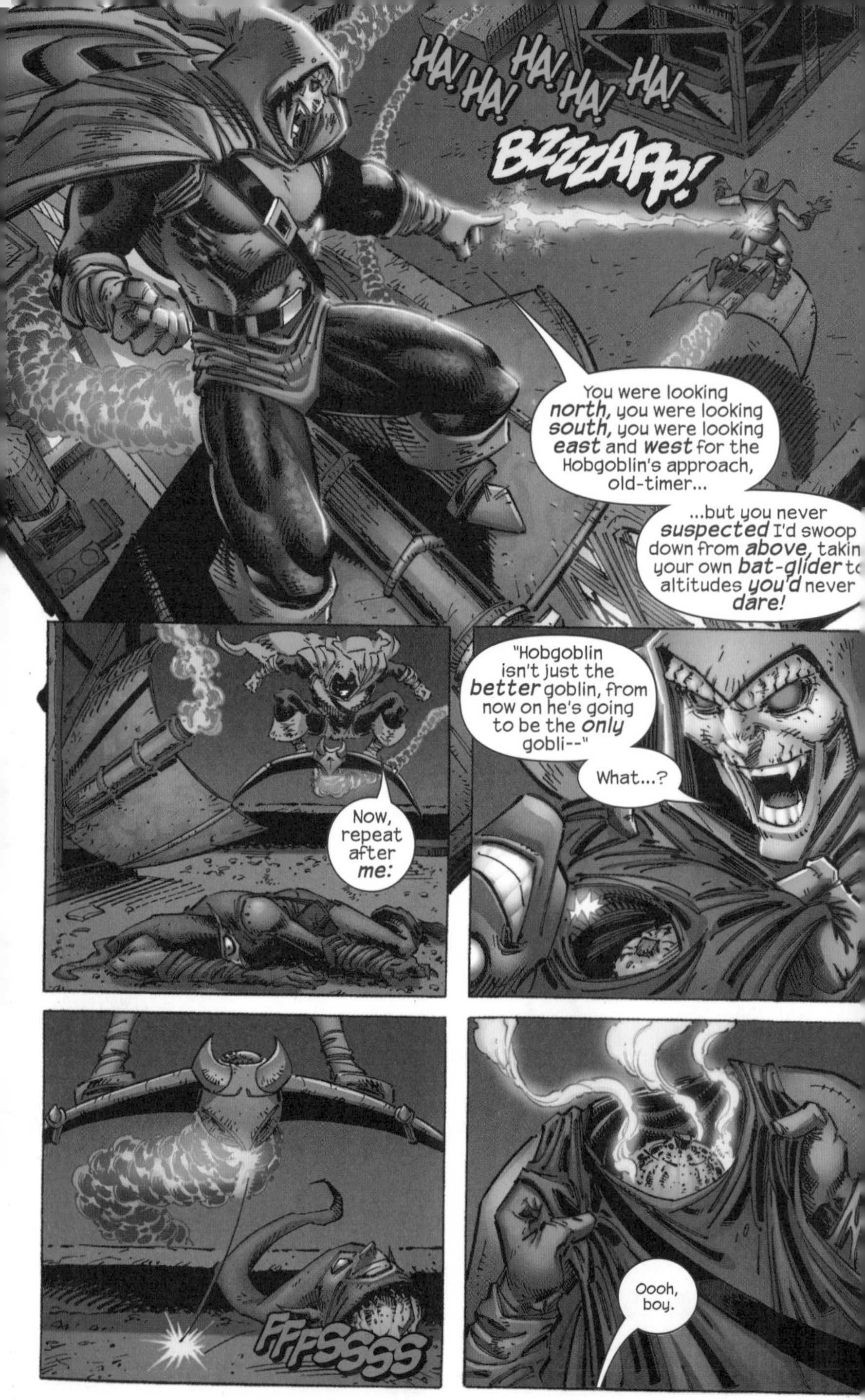
HA! HA! HA! HA! HA!
BZZZAPP!
You were looking north, you were looking south, you were looking east and west for the Hobgoblin's approach, old-timer...
...but you never suspected I'd swoop down from above, takin your own bat-glider t altitudes you'd never dare!
Now, repeat after me:
"Hobgoblin isn't just the better goblin, from now on he's going to be the only gobli--"
What...?
FFFSSSSS
Oooh, boy.

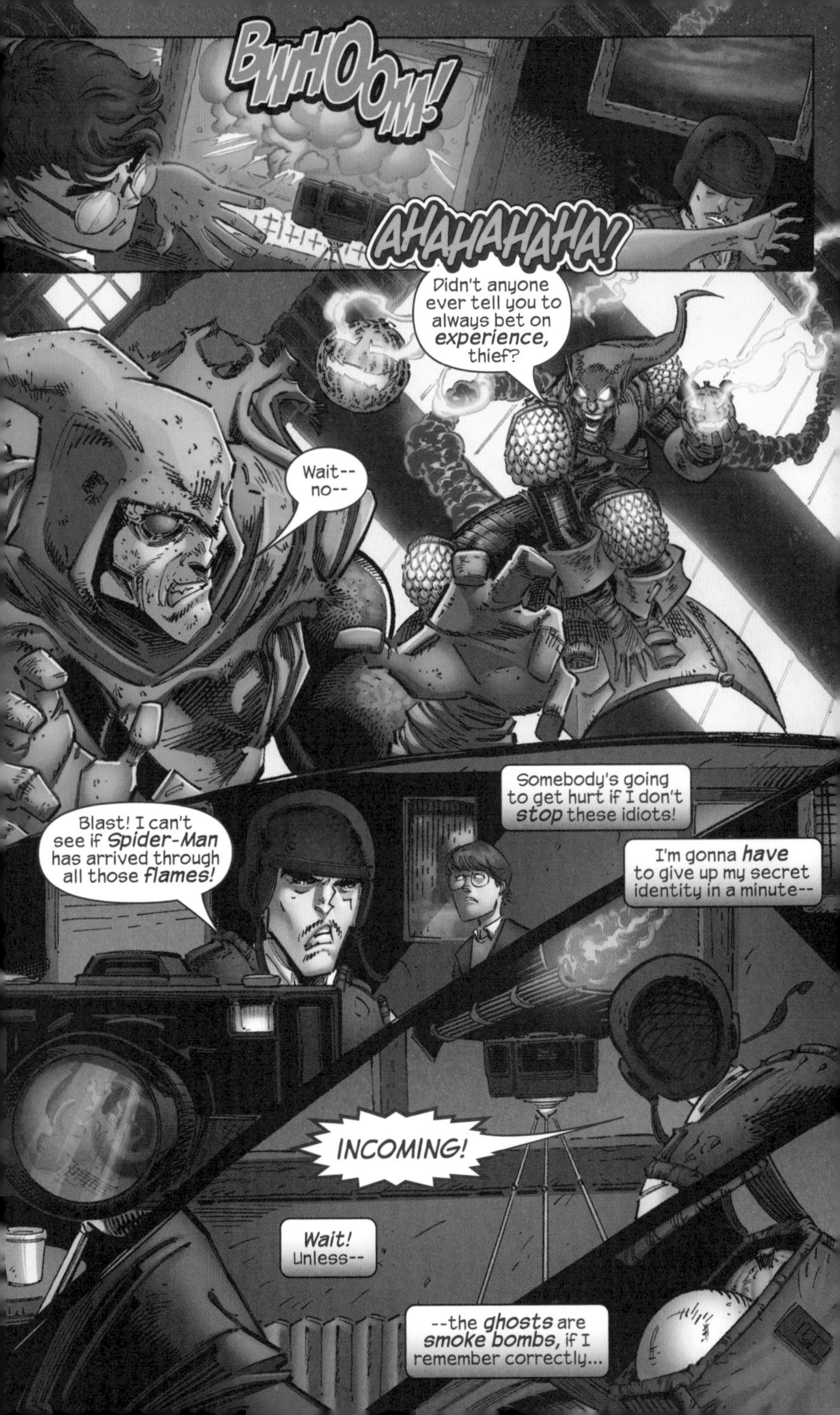
BWHOOM!
AHAHAHAHAHA!
Didn't anyone ever tell you to always bet on *experience,* thief?
Wait-- no--
Somebody's going to get hurt if I don't *stop* these idiots!
Blast! I can't see if *Spider-Man* has arrived through all those *flames!*
I'm gonna *have* to give up my secret identity in a minute--
INCOMING!
Wait! Unless--
--the *ghosts* are *smoke bombs,* if I remember correctly...

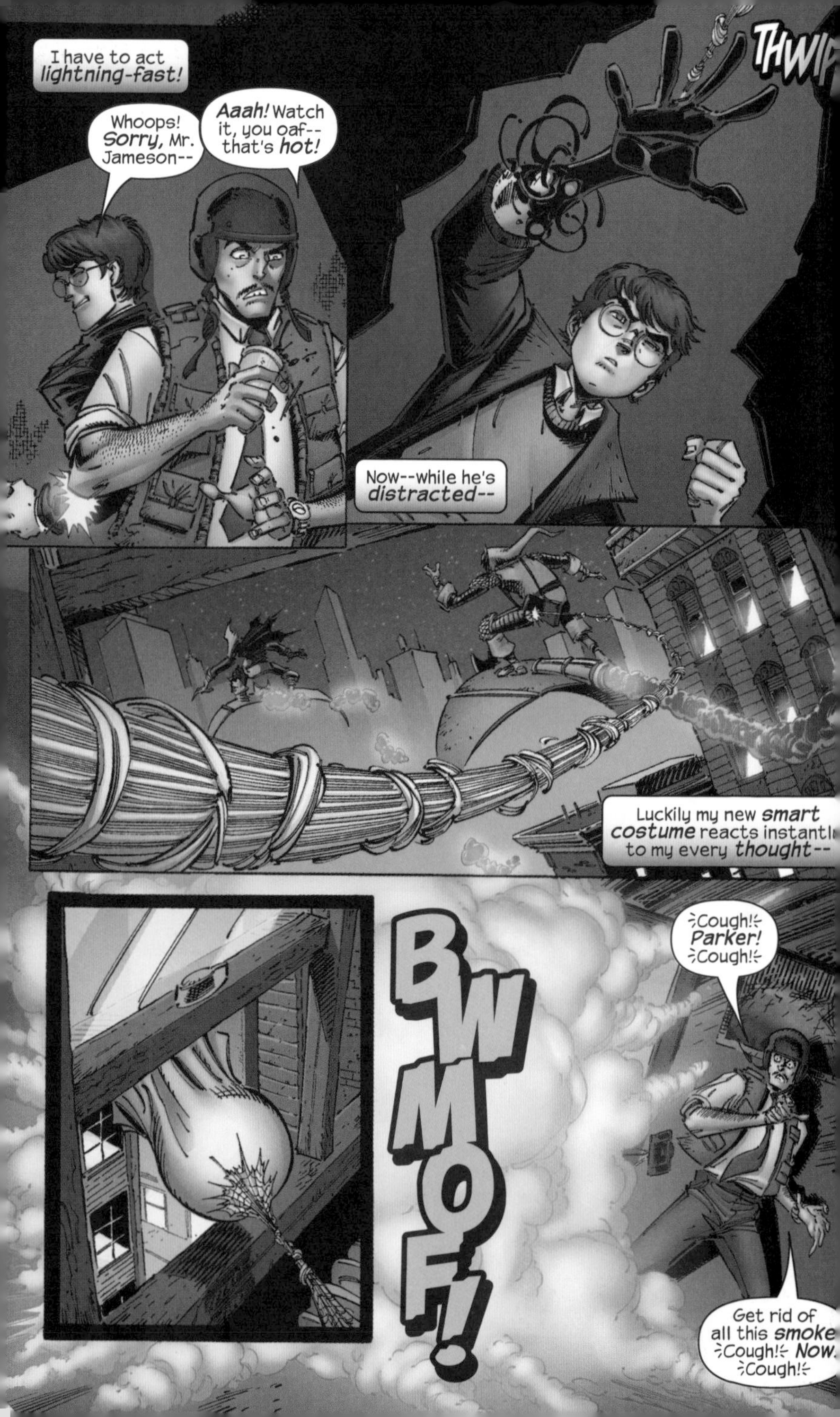
I have to act lightning-fast!
Whoops! Sorry, Mr. Jameson--
Aaah! Watch it, you oaf-- that's hot!
THWIP
Now--while he's distracted--
Luckily my new smart costume reacts instantl to my every thought--
BWMOF!
Cough! Parker! Cough!
Get rid of all this smoke Cough! Now. Cough!

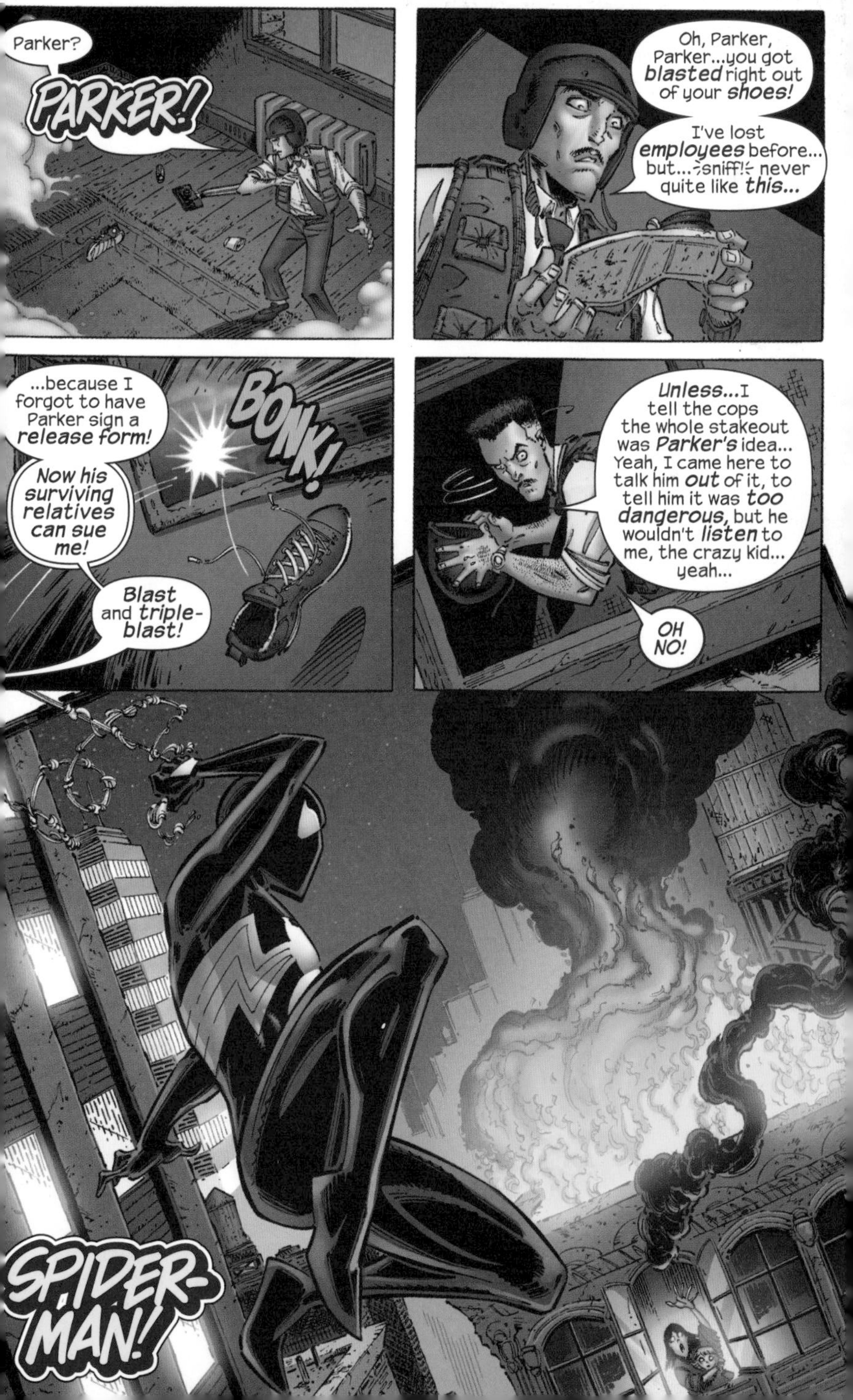
Parker?
PARKER!
Oh, Parker, Parker...you got blasted right out of your shoes!
I've lost employees before... but... sniff! never quite like this...
...because I forgot to have Parker sign a release form!
BONK!
Now his surviving relatives can sue me!
Blast and triple-blast!
Unless...I tell the cops the whole stakeout was Parker's idea... Yeah, I came here to talk him out of it, to tell him it was too dangerous, but he wouldn't listen to me, the crazy kid... yeah...
OH NO!
SPIDER-MAN!

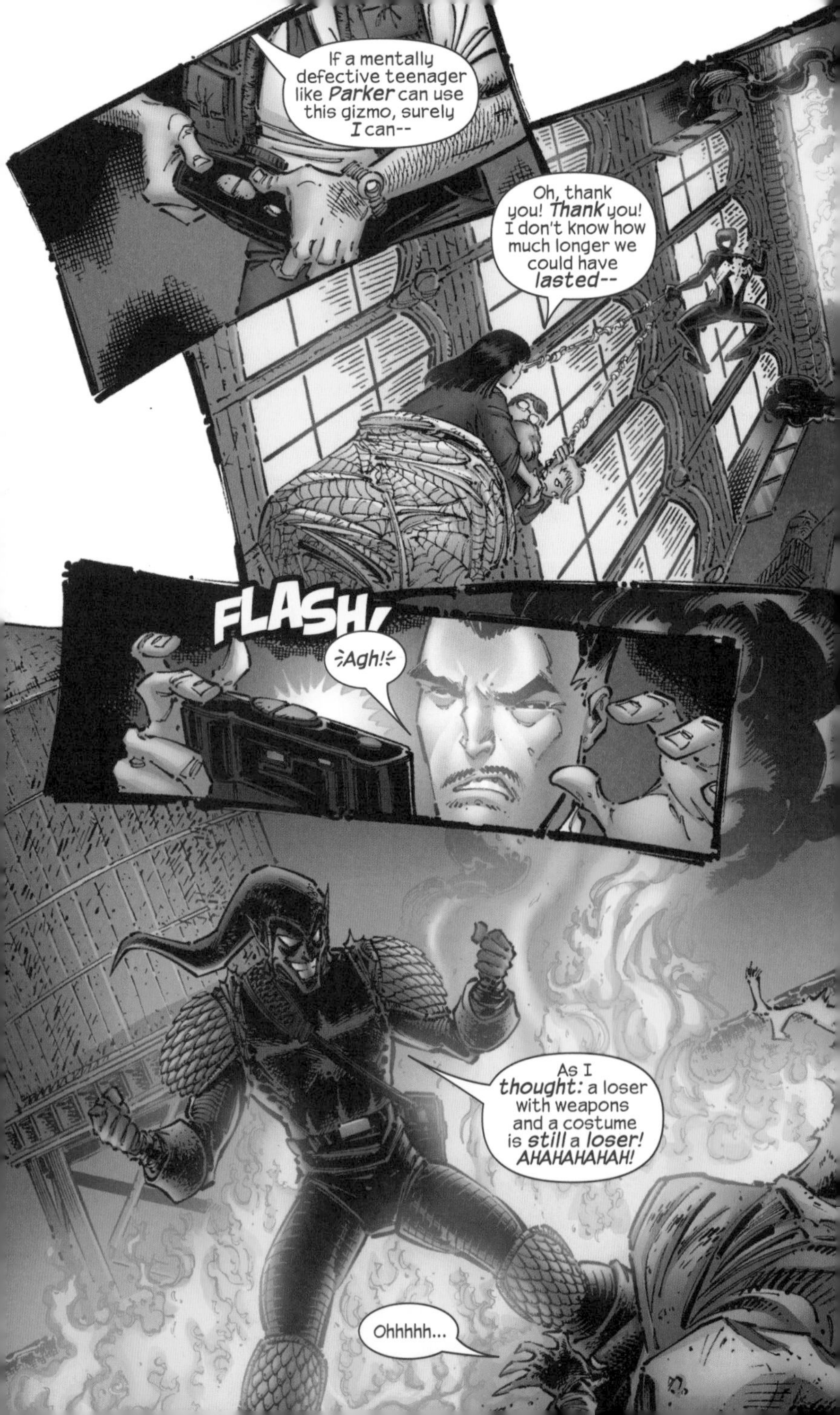
If a mentally defective teenager like *Parker* can use this gizmo, surely *I* can--
Oh, thank you! *Thank* you! I don't know how much longer we could have *lasted*--
FLASH!
Agh!
As I *thought:* a loser with weapons and a costume is *still* a *loser!* AHAHAHAHAH!
Ohhhhh...

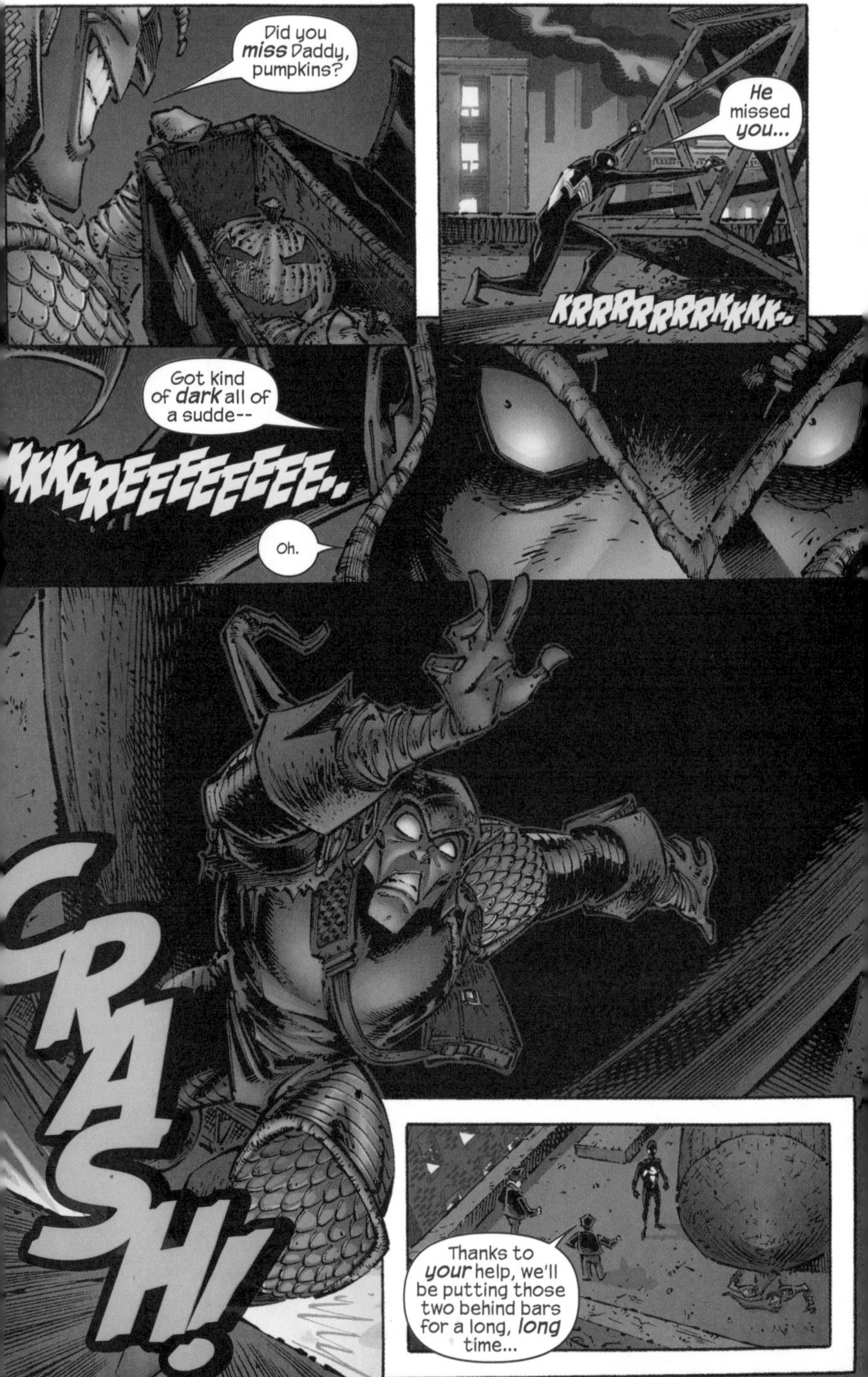
Did you miss Daddy, pumpkins?
He missed you...
KRRRRRRRKKKK-
Got kind of dark all of a sudde--
KKKCREEEEEEEEE-
Oh.
CRASH!
Thanks to your help, we'll be putting those two behind bars for a long, long time...

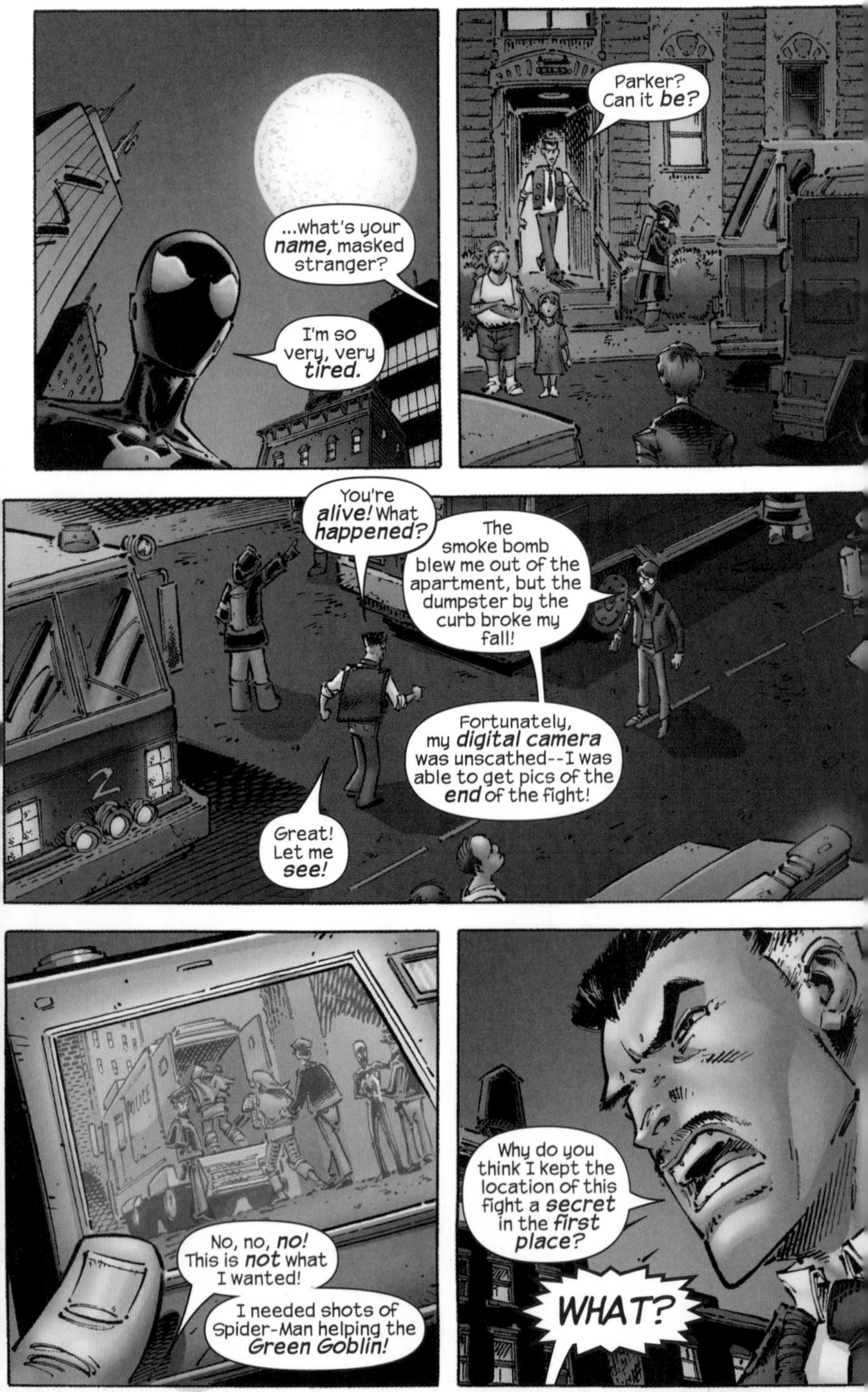
...what's your name, masked stranger?
I'm so very, very tired.
Parker? Can it be?
You're alive! What happened?
The smoke bomb blew me out of the apartment, but the dumpster by the curb broke my fall!
Fortunately, my digital camera was unscathed--I was able to get pics of the end of the fight!
Great! Let me see!
POLICE
No, no, no! This is not what I wanted!
I needed shots of Spider-Man helping the Green Goblin!
Why do you think I kept the location of this fight a secret in the first place?
WHAT?

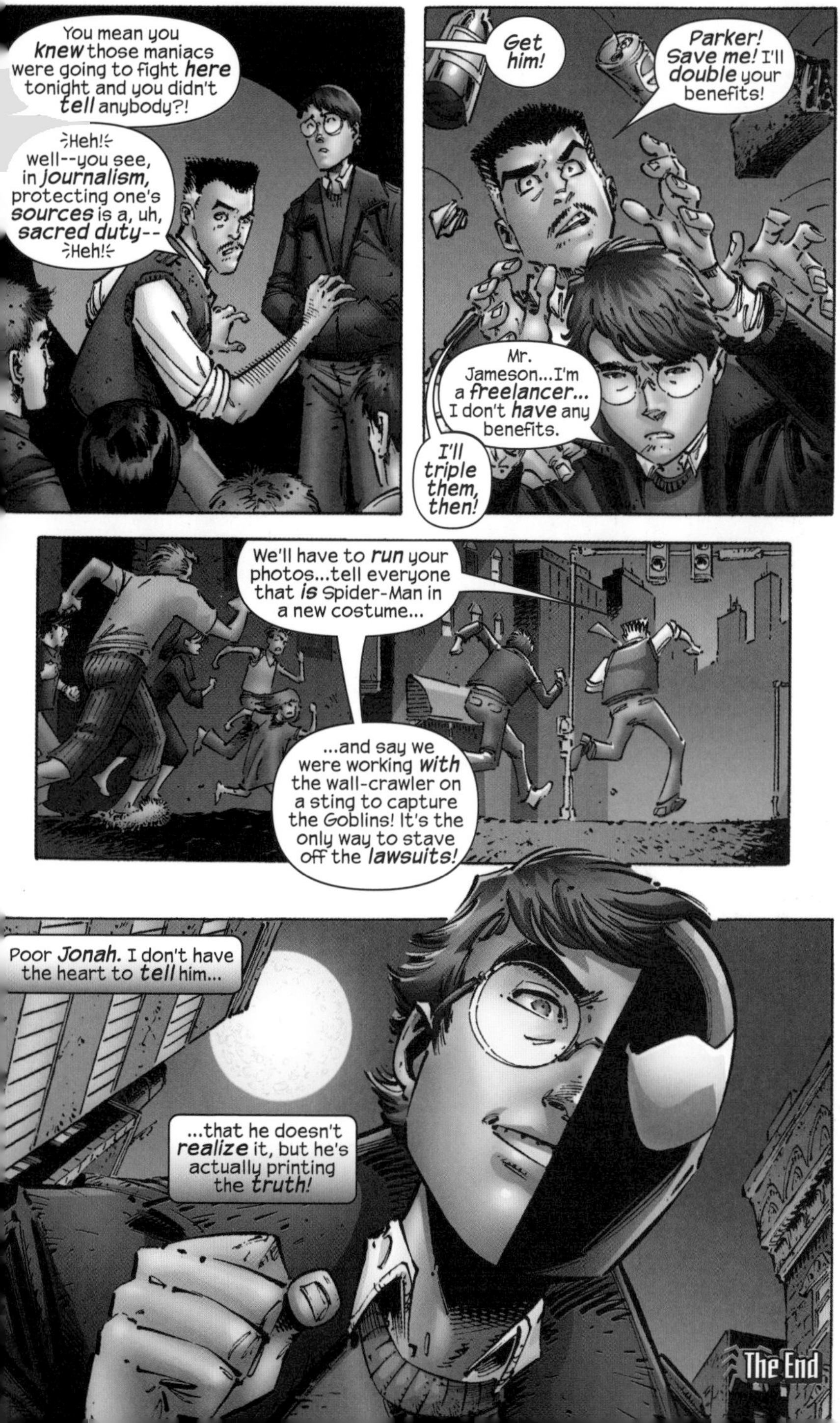

You mean you knew those maniacs were going to fight here tonight and you didn't tell anybody?!
Heh! well--you see, in journalism, protecting one's sources is a, uh, sacred duty-- Heh!
Get him!
Parker! Save me! I'll double your benefits!
Mr. Jameson...I'm a freelancer... I don't have any benefits.
I'll triple them, then!
We'll have to run your photos...tell everyone that is Spider-Man in a new costume...
...and say we were working with the wall-crawler on a sting to capture the Goblins! It's the only way to stave off the lawsuits!
Poor Jonah. I don't have the heart to tell him...
...that he doesn't realize it, but he's actually printing the truth!
The End

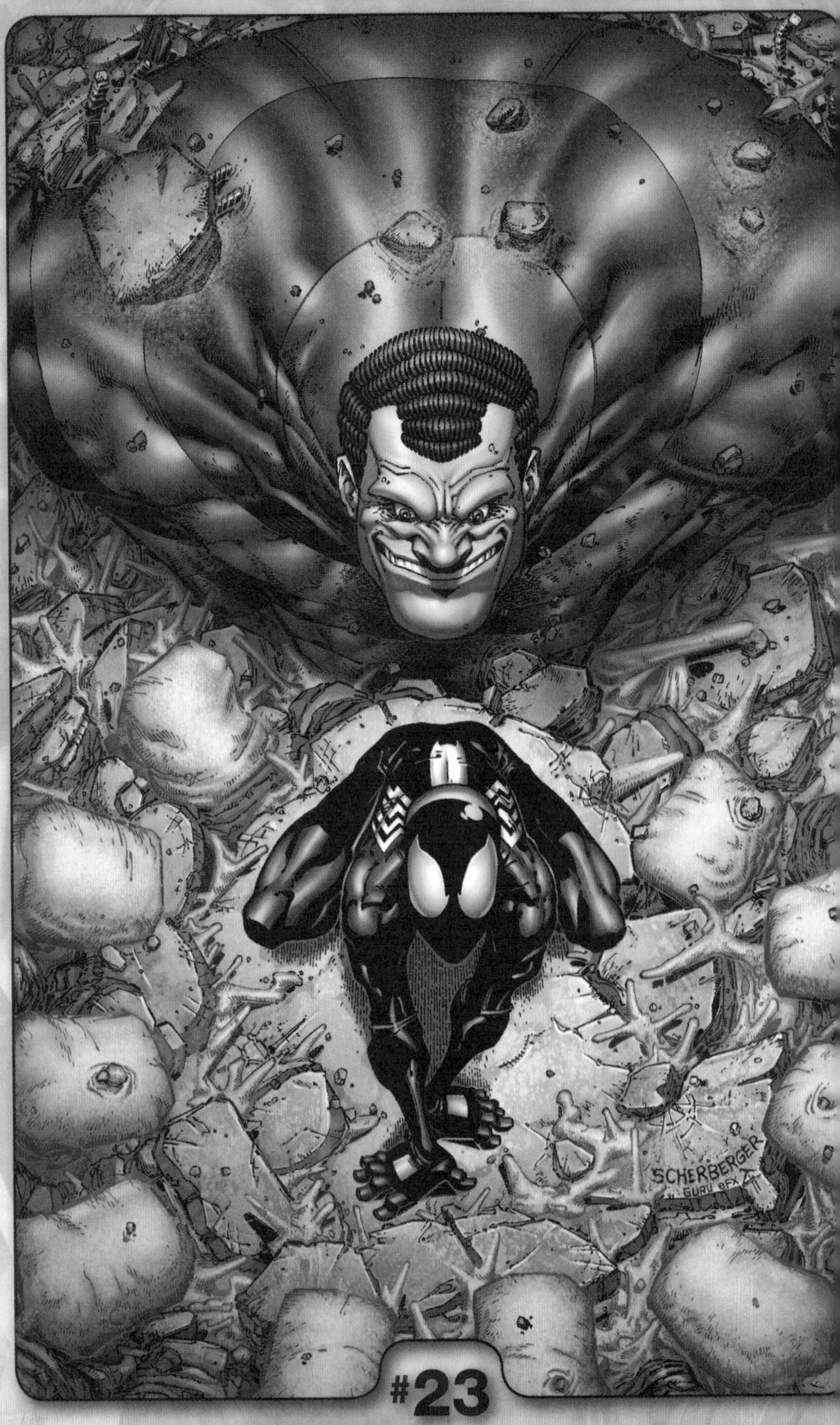
SCHERBERGER
GURU eFX
#23

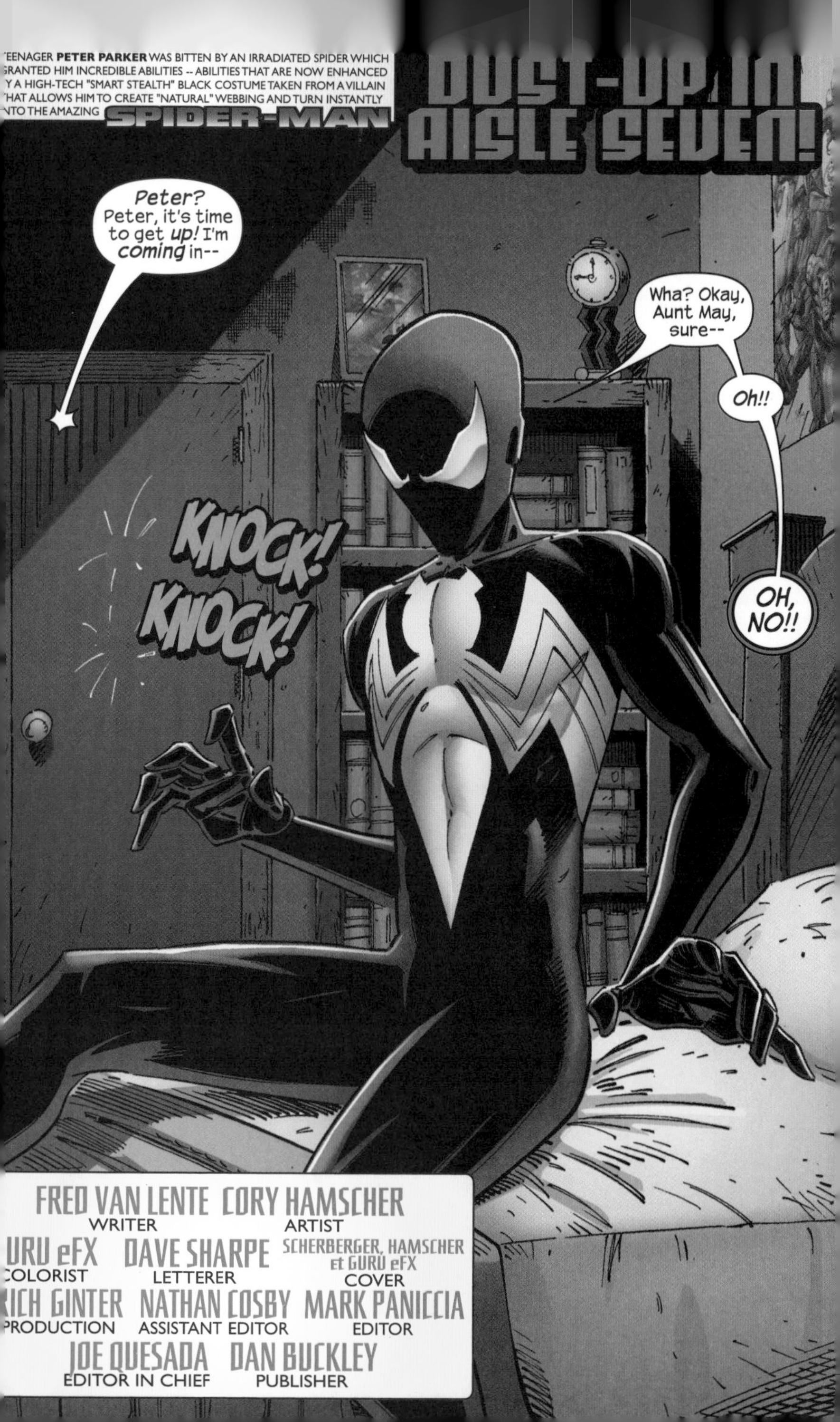
EENAGER PETER PARKER WAS BITTEN BY AN IRRADIATED SPIDER WHICH
RANTED HIM INCREDIBLE ABILITIES -- ABILITIES THAT ARE NOW ENHANCED
Y A HIGH-TECH "SMART STEALTH" BLACK COSTUME TAKEN FROM A VILLAIN
HAT ALLOWS HIM TO CREATE "NATURAL" WEBBING AND TURN INSTANTLY
NTO THE AMAZING SPIDER-MAN
DUST-UP IN AISLE SEVEN!
Peter? Peter, it's time to get up! I'm coming in--
KNOCK! KNOCK!
Wha? Okay, Aunt May, sure--
Oh!!
OH, NO!!
FRED VAN LENTE WRITER
CORY HAMSCHER ARTIST
URU eFX OLORIST
DAVE SHARPE LETTERER
SCHERBERGER, HAMSCHER et GURU eFX COVER
ICH GINTER RODUCTION
NATHAN COSBY ASSISTANT EDITOR
MARK PANICCIA EDITOR
JOE QUESADA EDITOR IN CHIEF
DAN BUCKLEY PUBLISHER

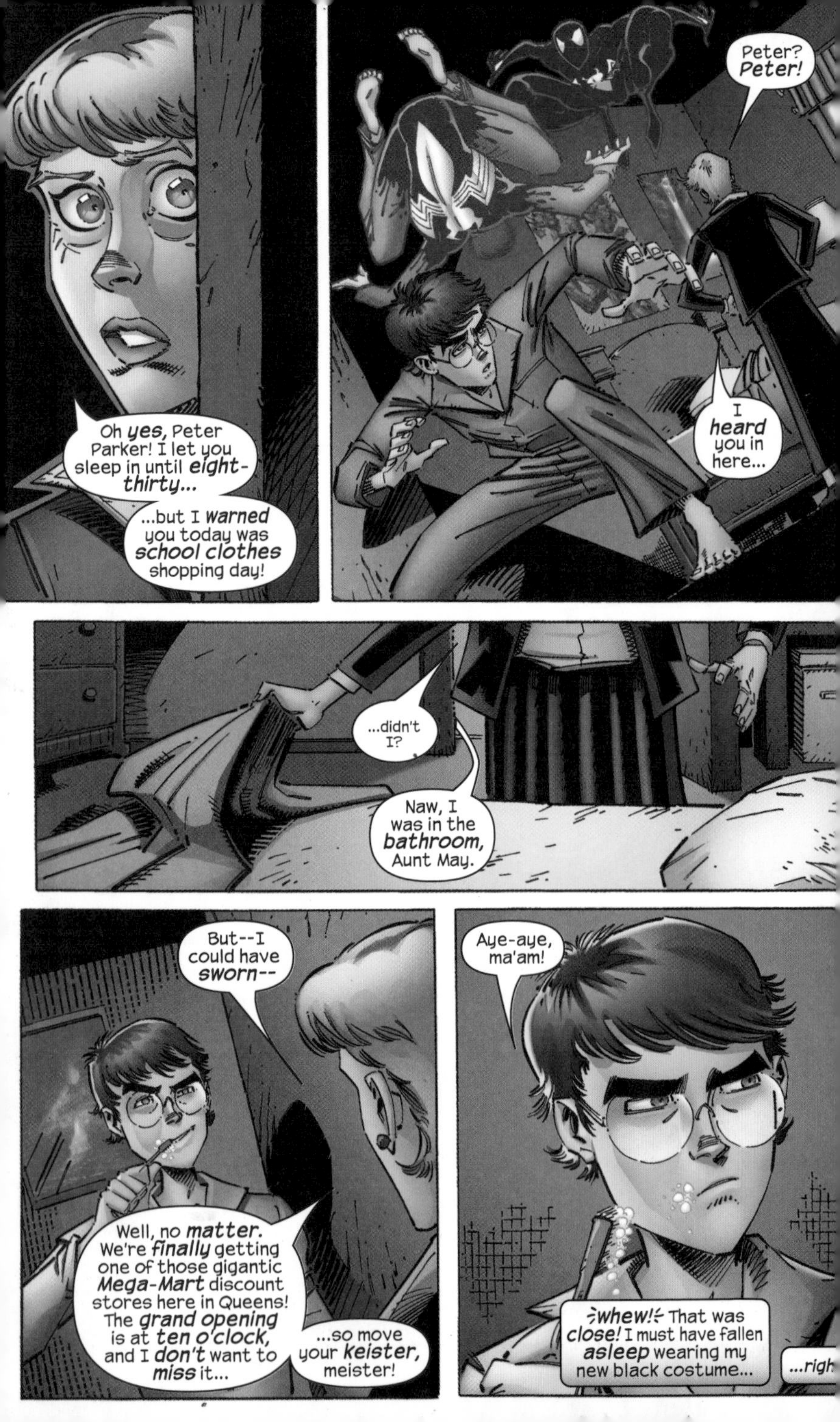
Oh yes, Peter Parker! I let you sleep in until eight-thirty...
...but I warned you today was school clothes shopping day!
Peter? Peter!
I heard you in here...
...didn't I?
Naw, I was in the bathroom, Aunt May.
But--I could have sworn--
Well, no matter. We're finally getting one of those gigantic Mega-Mart discount stores here in Queens! The grand opening is at ten o'clock, and I don't want to miss it...
...so move your keister, meister!
Aye-aye, ma'am!
whew! That was close! I must have fallen asleep wearing my new black costume...

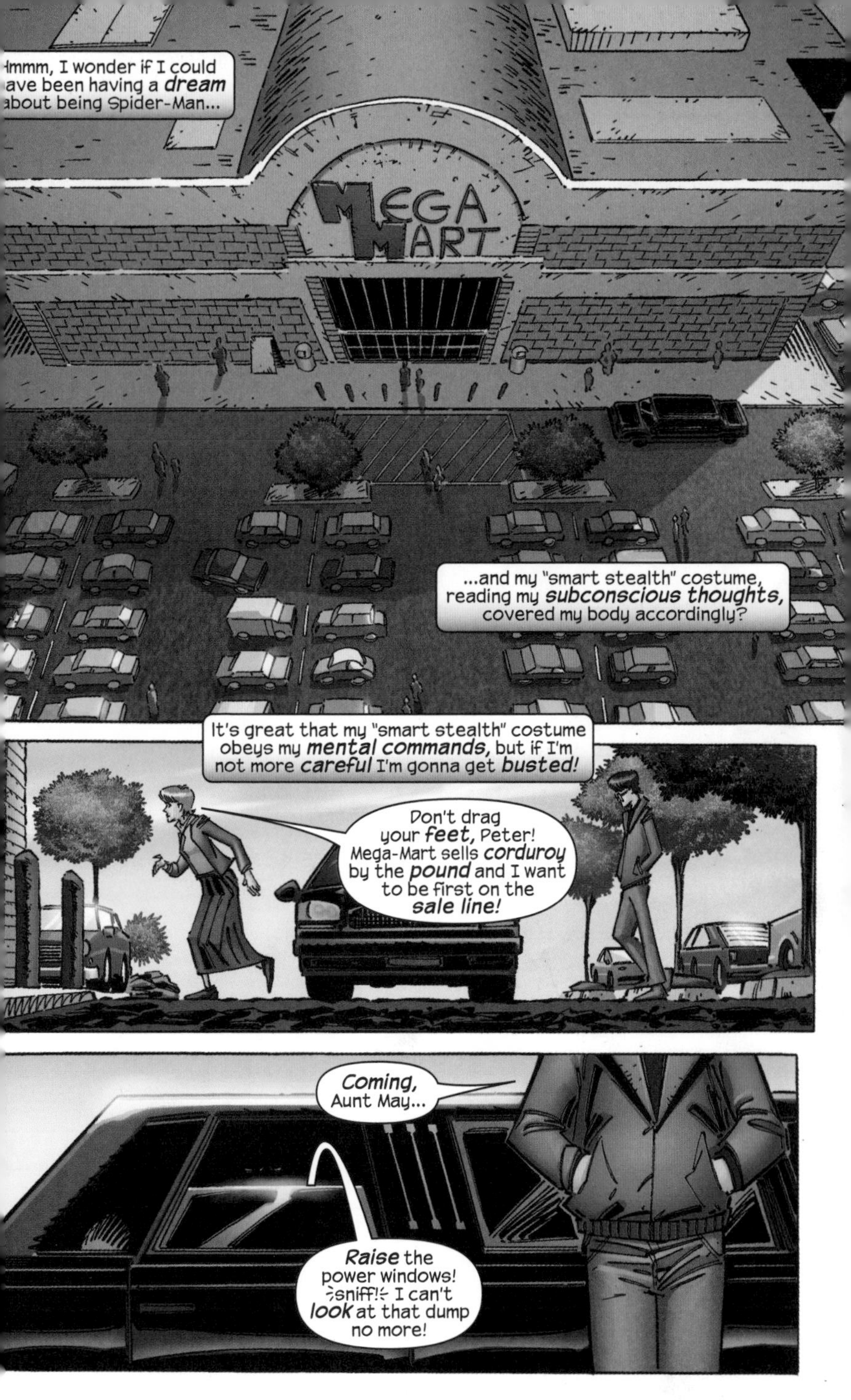
mmm, I wonder if I could ave been having a dream bout being Spider-Man...
MEGA MART
...and my "smart stealth" costume, reading my subconscious thoughts, covered my body accordingly?
It's great that my "smart stealth" costume obeys my mental commands, but if I'm not more careful I'm gonna get busted!
Don't drag your feet, Peter! Mega-Mart sells corduroy by the pound and I want to be first on the sale line!
Coming, Aunt May...
Raise the power windows! *sniff!* I can't look at that dump no more!

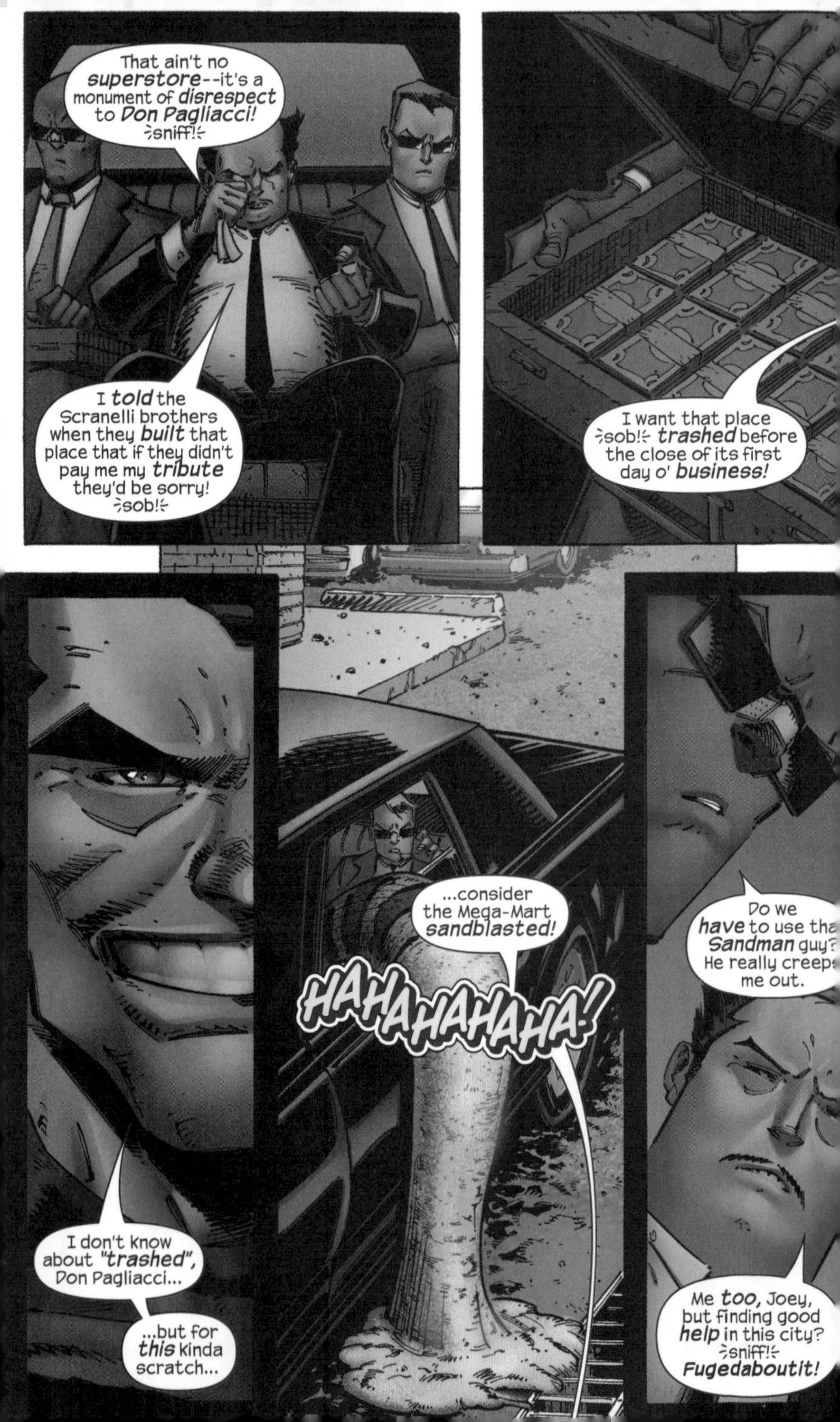
That ain't no superstore--it's a monument of disrespect to Don Pagliacci! sniff!
I told the Scranelli brothers when they built that place that if they didn't pay me my tribute they'd be sorry! sob!
I want that place sob! trashed before the close of its first day o' business!
I don't know about "trashed", Don Pagliacci...
...but for this kinda scratch...
...consider the Mega-Mart sandblasted!
HAHAHAHAHAHA!
Do we have to use tha Sandman guy? He really creeps me out.
Me too, Joey, but finding good help in this city? sniff! Fugedaboutit!

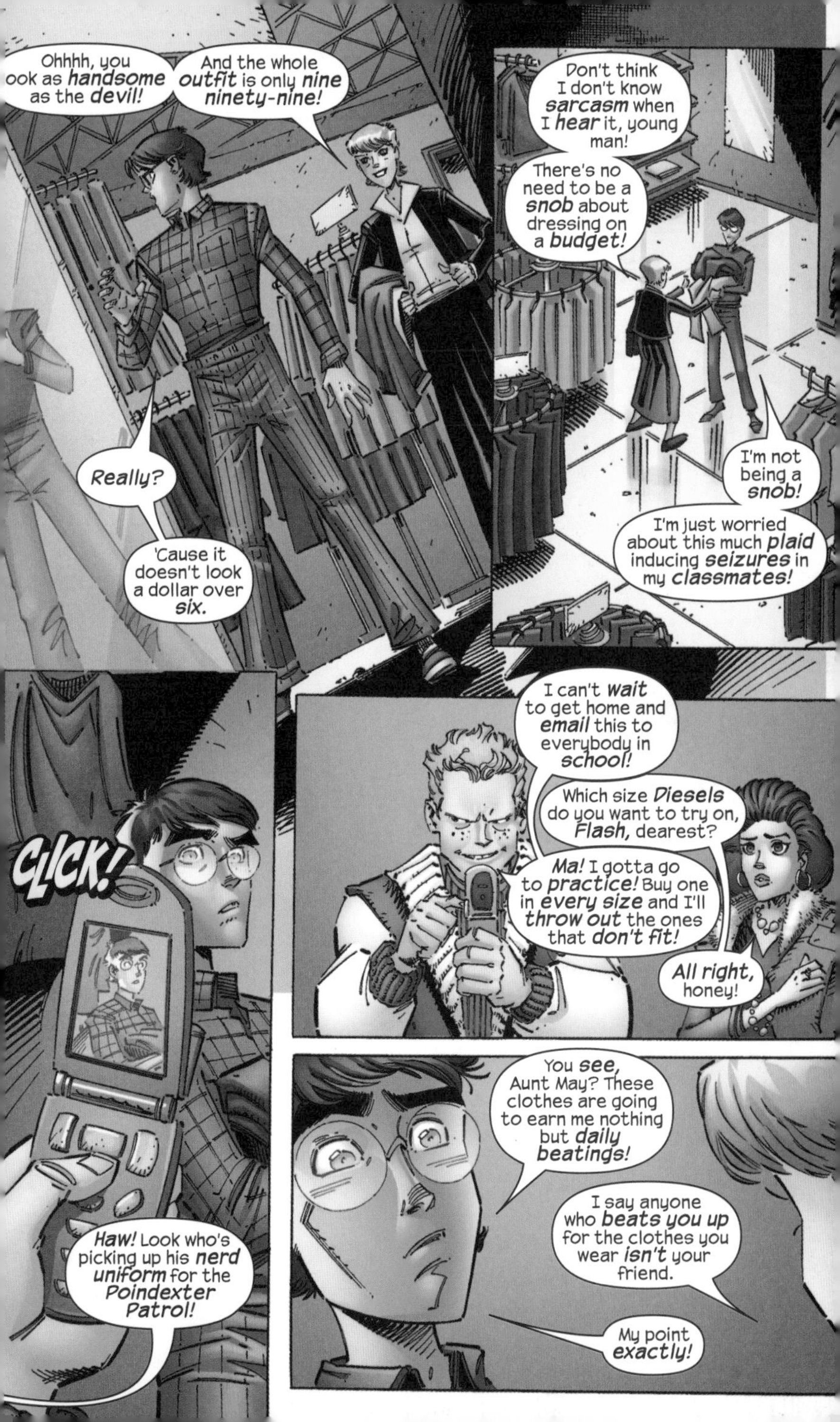

Ohhhh, you ook as handsome as the devil!
And the whole outfit is only nine ninety-nine!
Really?
'Cause it doesn't look a dollar over six.
Don't think I don't know sarcasm when I hear it, young man!
There's no need to be a snob about dressing on a budget!
I'm not being a snob!
I'm just worried about this much plaid inducing seizures in my classmates!
CLICK!
I can't wait to get home and email this to everybody in school!
Which size Diesels do you want to try on, Flash, dearest?
Ma! I gotta go to practice! Buy one in every size and I'll throw out the ones that don't fit!
All right, honey!
Haw! Look who's picking up his nerd uniform for the Poindexter Patrol!
You see, Aunt May? These clothes are going to earn me nothing but daily beatings!
I say anyone who beats you up for the clothes you wear isn't your friend.
My point exactly!

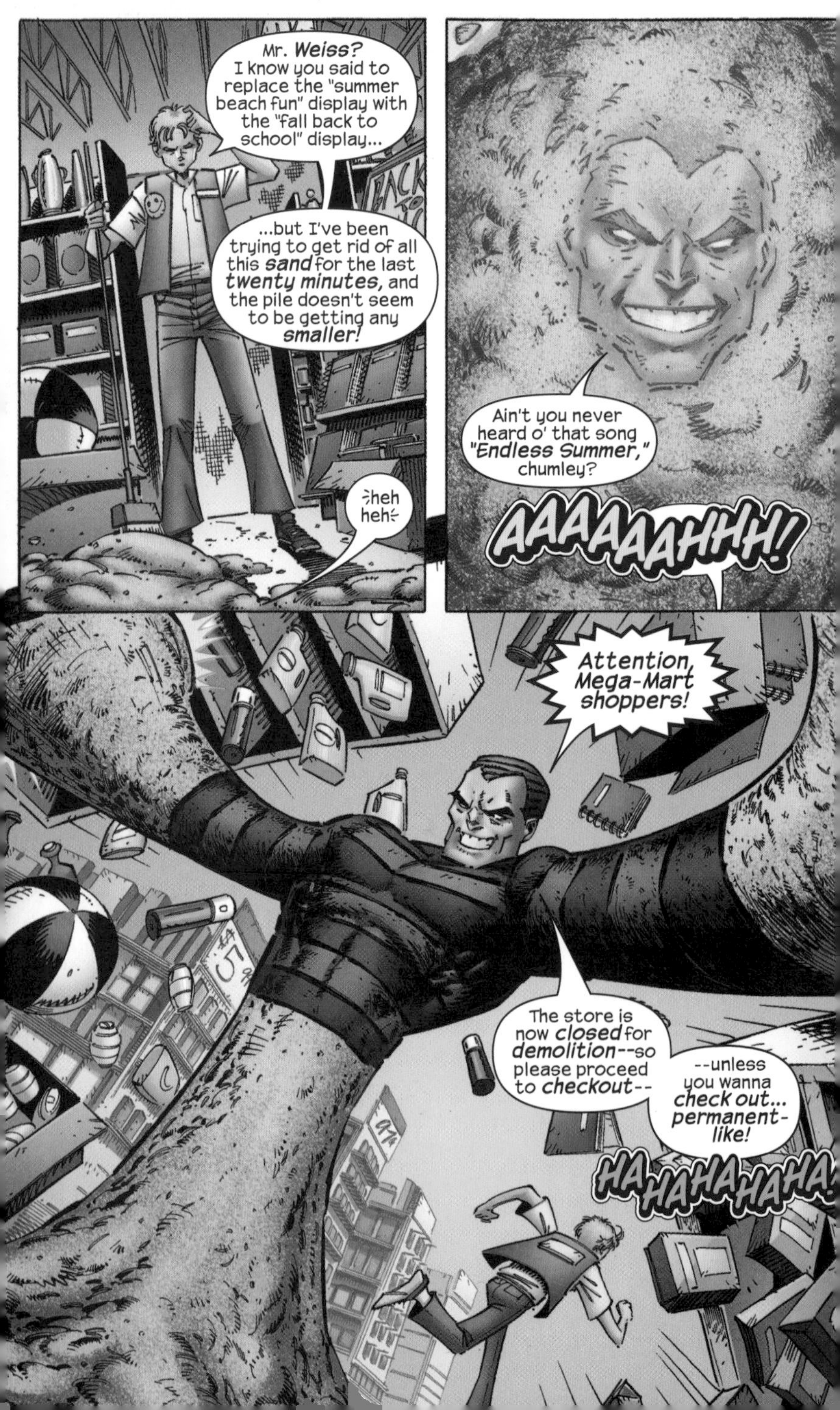
Mr. Weiss? I know you said to replace the "summer beach fun" display with the "fall back to school" display...
...but I've been trying to get rid of all this sand for the last twenty minutes, and the pile doesn't seem to be getting any smaller!
heh heh
Ain't you never heard o' that song "Endless Summer," chumley?
AAAAAAHHH!
Attention, Mega-Mart shoppers!
The store is now closed for demolition--so please proceed to checkout--
--unless you wanna check out... permanent-like!
HAHAHAHAHAHA!

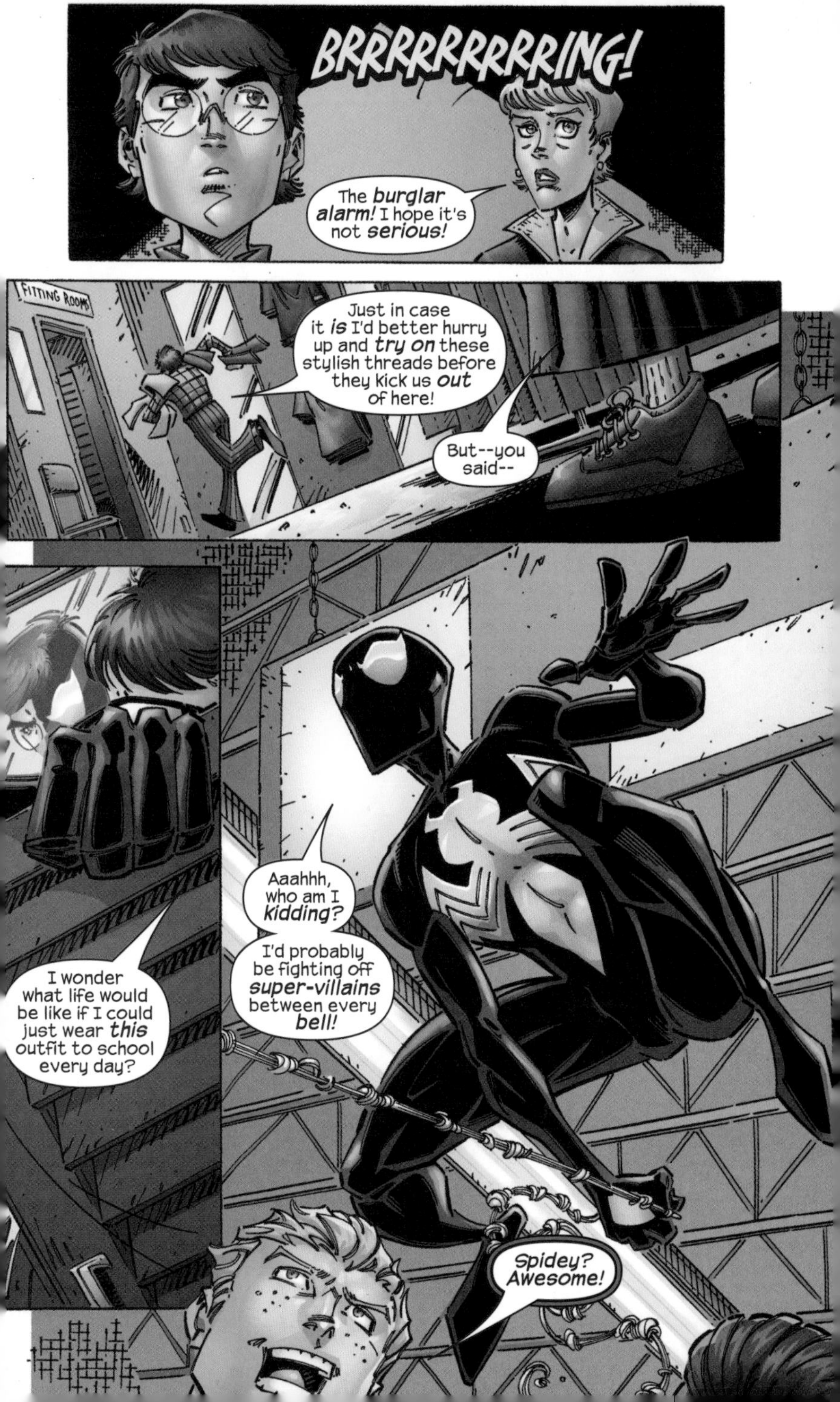
BRRRRRRRRRING!
The burglar alarm! I hope it's not serious!
FITTING ROOMS
Just in case it is I'd better hurry up and try on these stylish threads before they kick us out of here!
But--you said--
I wonder what life would be like if I could just wear this outfit to school every day?
Aaahhh, who am I kidding?
I'd probably be fighting off super-villains between every bell!
Spidey? Awesome!

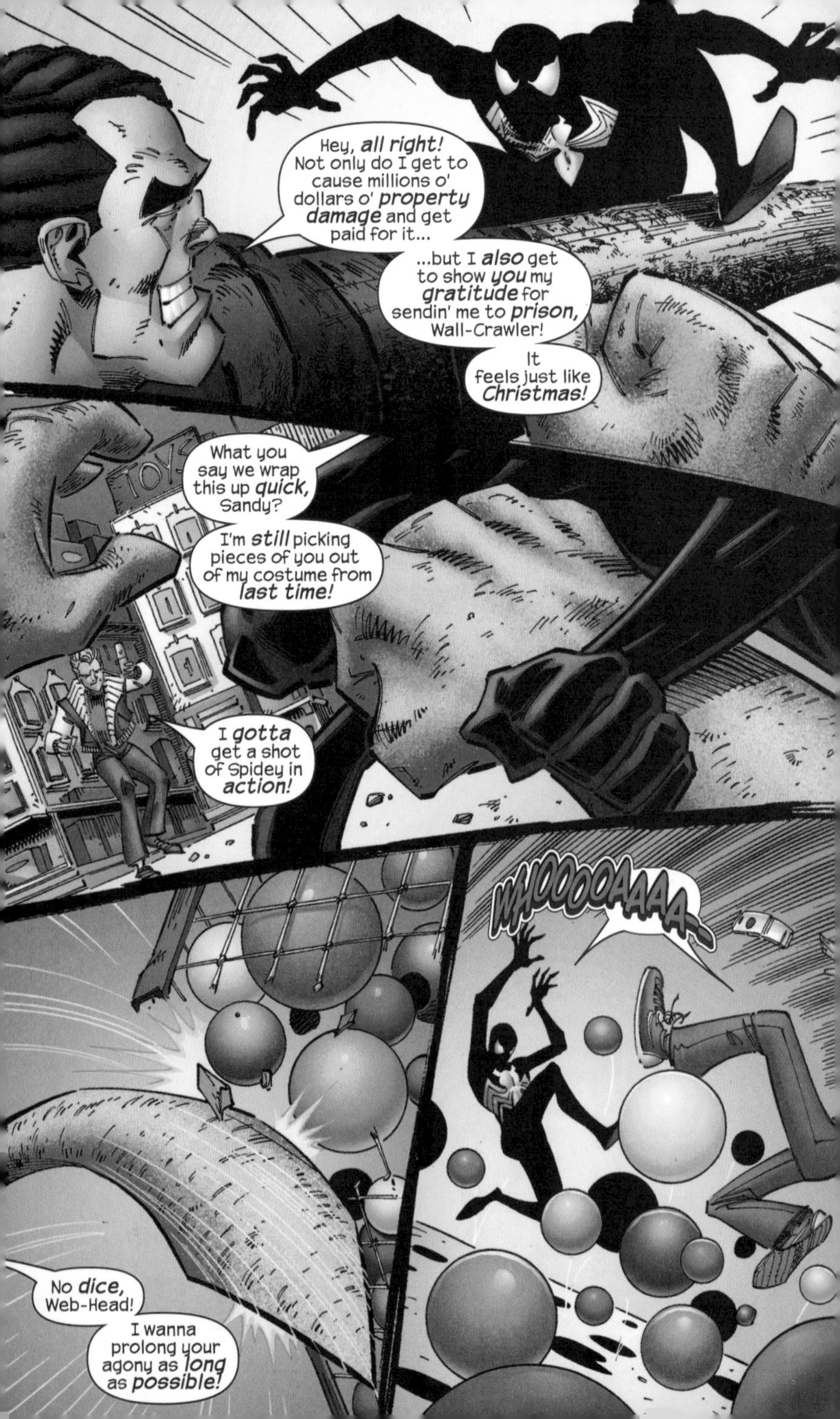
Hey, all right! Not only do I get to cause millions o' dollars o' property damage and get paid for it...
...but I also get to show you my gratitude for sendin' me to prison, Wall-Crawler!
It feels just like Christmas!
TOYS
What you say we wrap this up quick, Sandy?
I'm still picking pieces of you out of my costume from last time!
I gotta get a shot of Spidey in action!
No dice, Web-Head!
I wanna prolong your agony as long as possible!
WHOOOOAAAA--

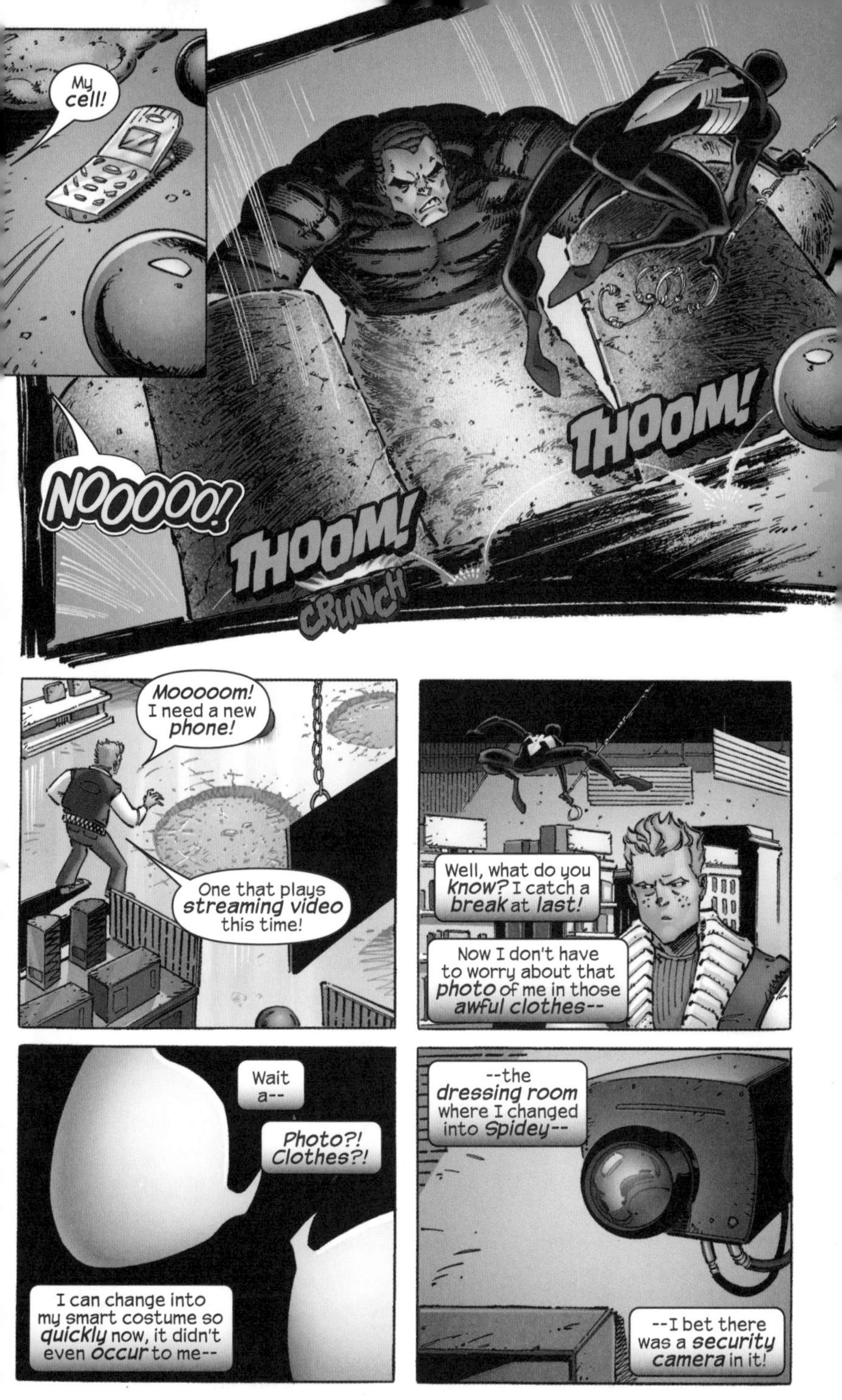
My cell!
NOOOOO!
THOOM!
CRUNCH
THOOM!
Mooooom! I need a new phone!
One that plays streaming video this time!
Well, what do you know? I catch a break at last!
Now I don't have to worry about that photo of me in those awful clothes--
Wait a--
Photo?! Clothes?!
I can change into my smart costume so quickly now, it didn't even occur to me--
--the dressing room where I changed into Spidey--
--I bet there was a security camera in it!

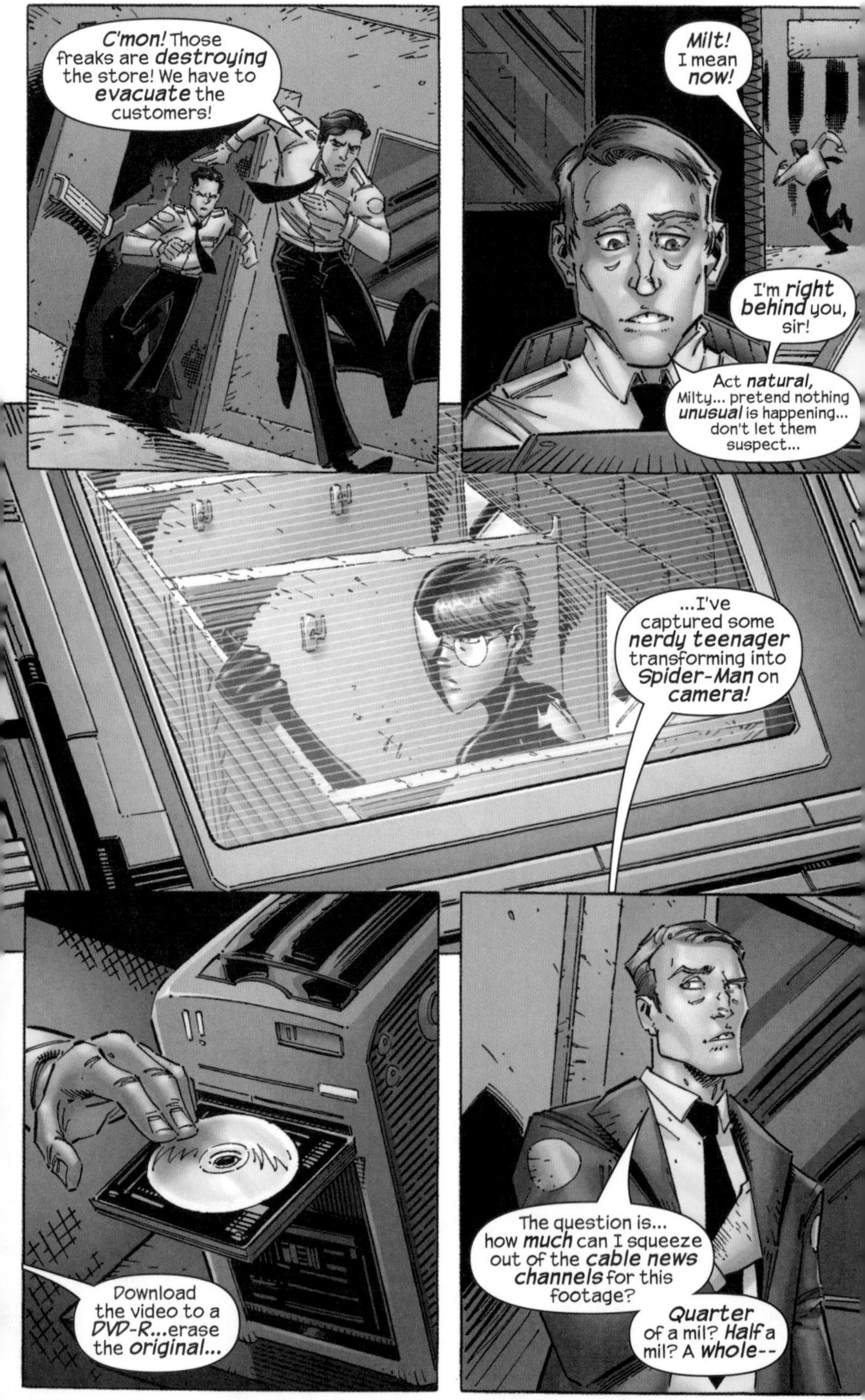
C'mon! Those freaks are destroying the store! We have to evacuate the customers!
Milt! I mean now!
I'm right behind you, sir!
Act natural, Milty... pretend nothing unusual is happening... don't let them suspect...
...I've captured some nerdy teenager transforming into Spider-Man on camera!
Download the video to a DVD-R...erase the original...
The question is... how much can I squeeze out of the cable news channels for this footage?
Quarter of a mil? Half a mil? A whole--

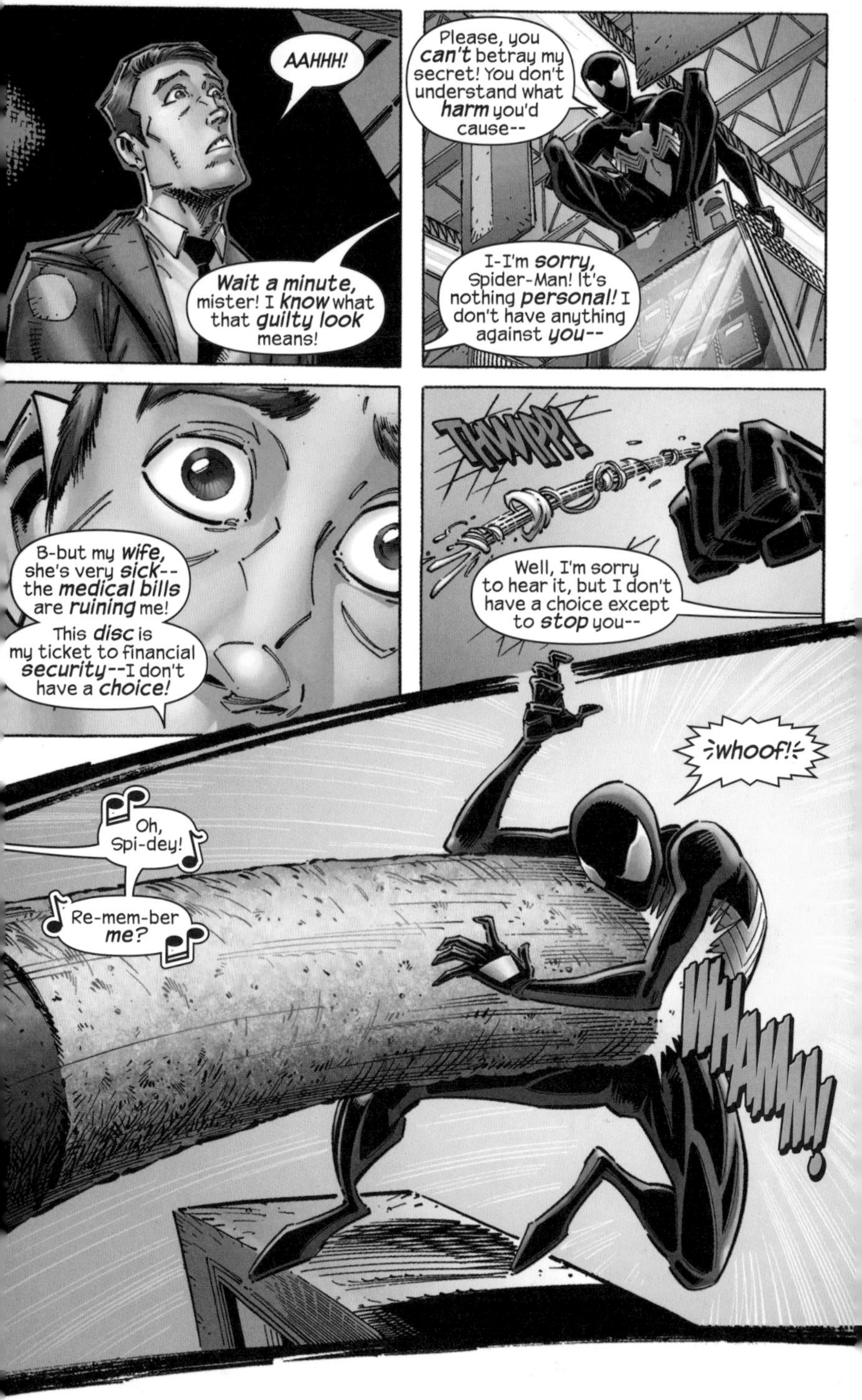
AAHHH!
Wait a minute, mister! I KNOW what that guilty look means!
Please, you can't betray my secret! You don't understand what harm you'd cause--
I-I'm sorry, Spider-Man! It's nothing personal! I don't have anything against you--
B-but my wife, she's very sick-- the medical bills are ruining me!
This disc is my ticket to financial security--I don't have a choice!
THWIPP!
Well, I'm sorry to hear it, but I don't have a choice except to stop you--
whoof!
Oh, Spi-dey!
Re-mem-ber me?
WHAMM!

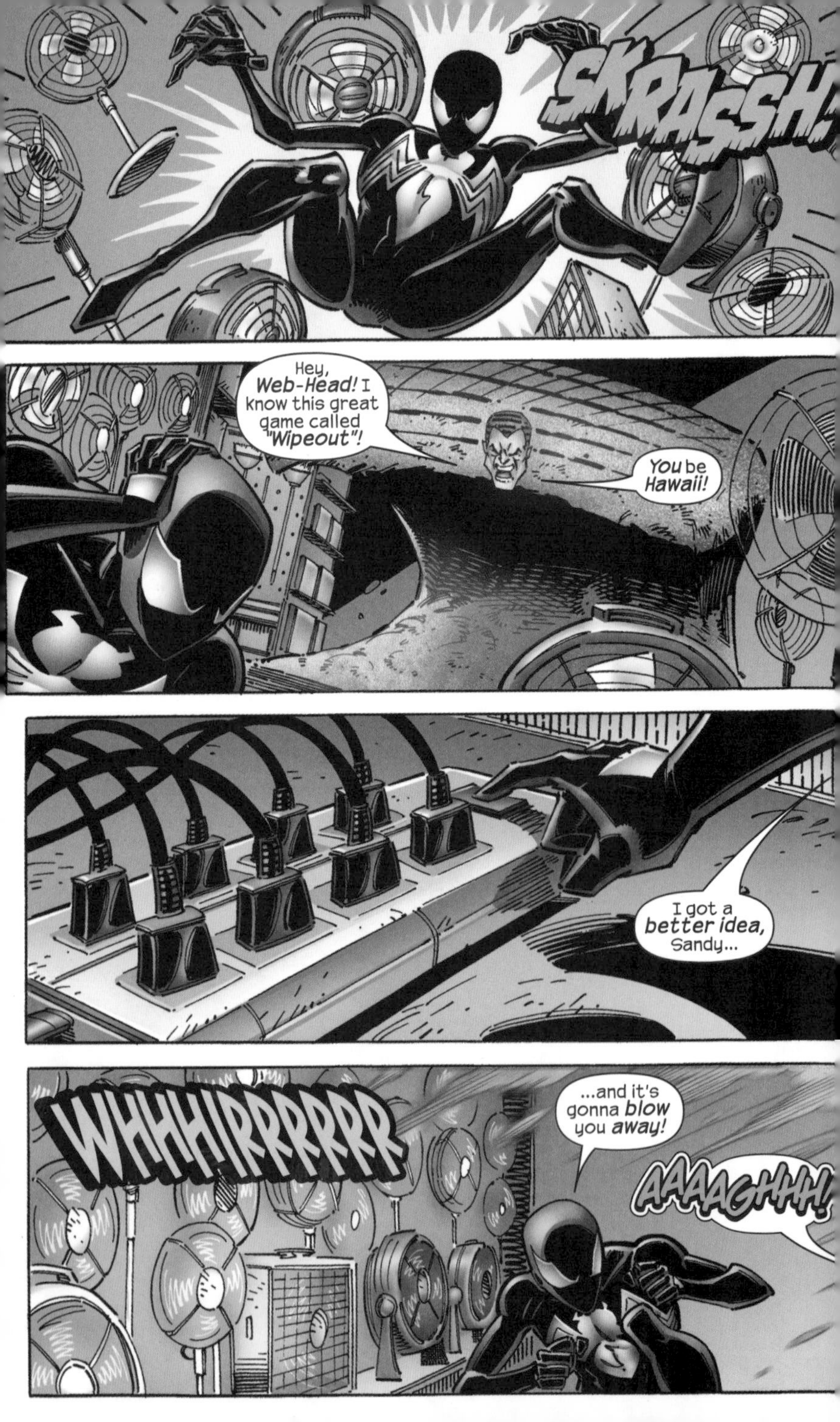
SKRASSH!
Hey, Web-Head! I know this great game called "Wipeout"!
You be Hawaii!
I got a better idea, Sandy...
WHHHIRRRRRR
...and it's gonna blow you away!
AAAAGHHH!

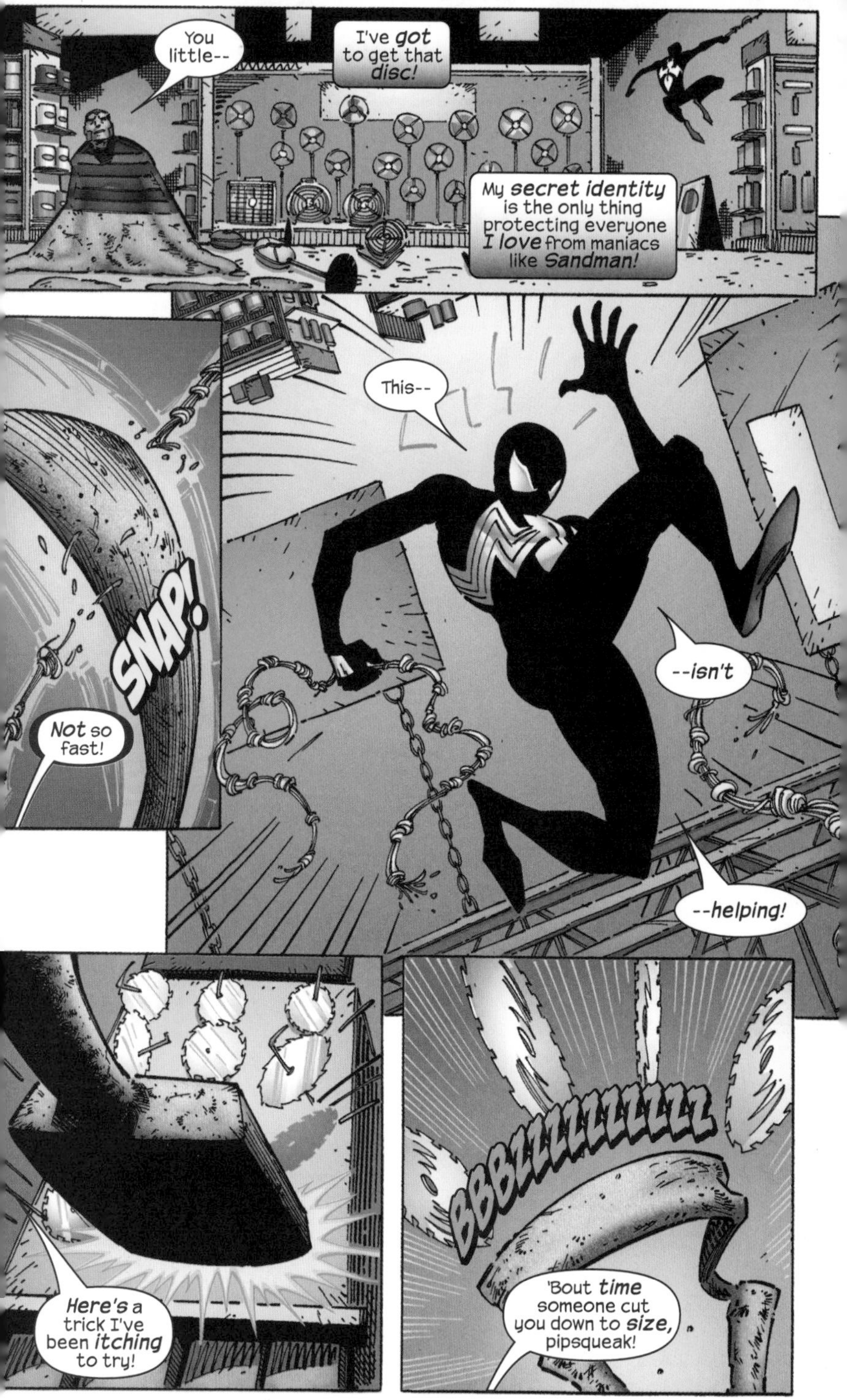
You little--
I've got to get that disc!
My secret identity is the only thing protecting everyone I love from maniacs like Sandman!
This--
SNAP!
Not so fast!
--isn't
--helping!
Here's a trick I've been itching to try!
BBBZZZZZZZZZZ
'Bout time someone cut you down to size, pipsqueak!

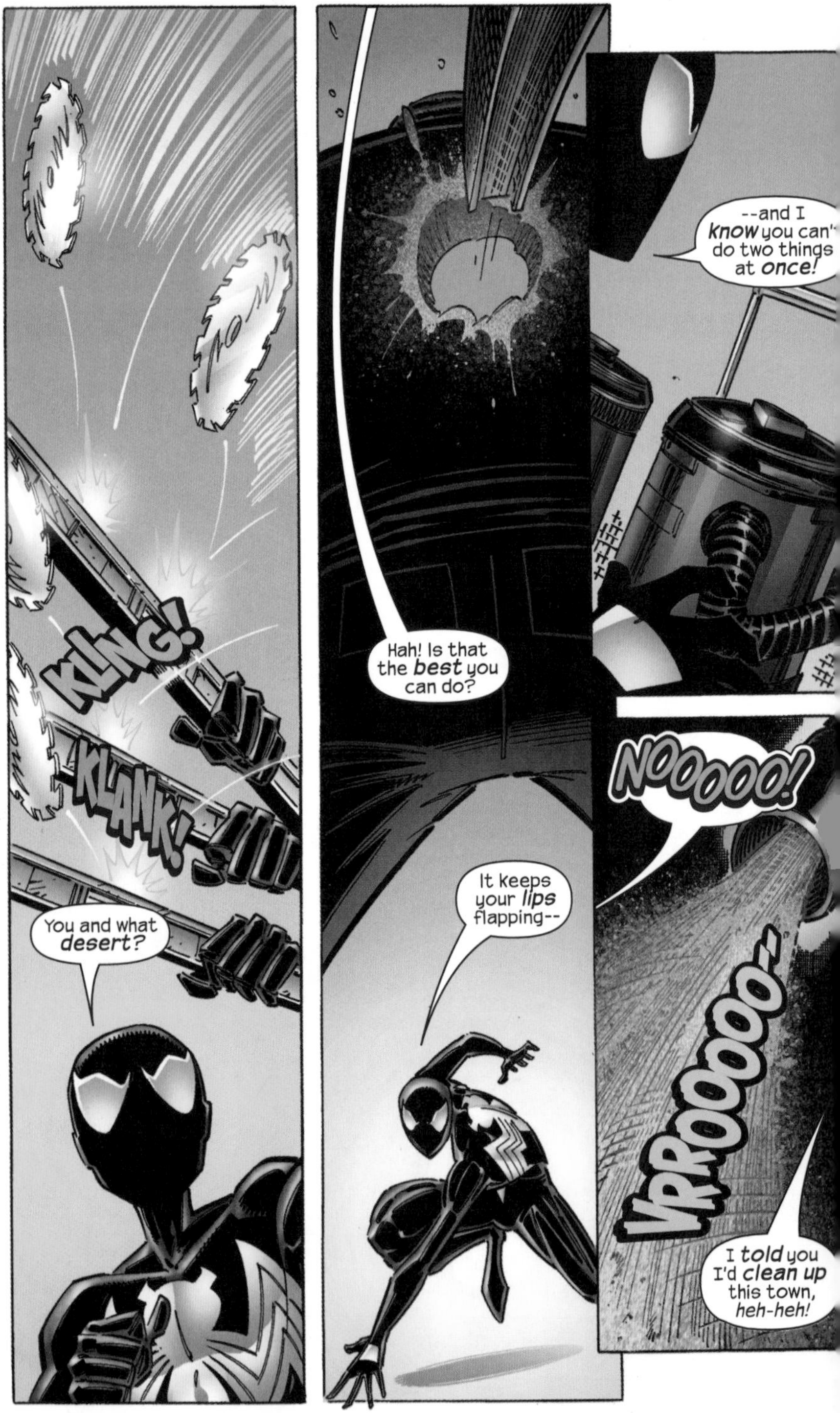
KLING!
KLANK!
You and what desert?
Hah! Is that the best you can do?
It keeps your lips flapping--
--and I know you can't do two things at once!
NOOOOOO!
VRROOOOO-
I told you I'd clean up this town, heh-heh!

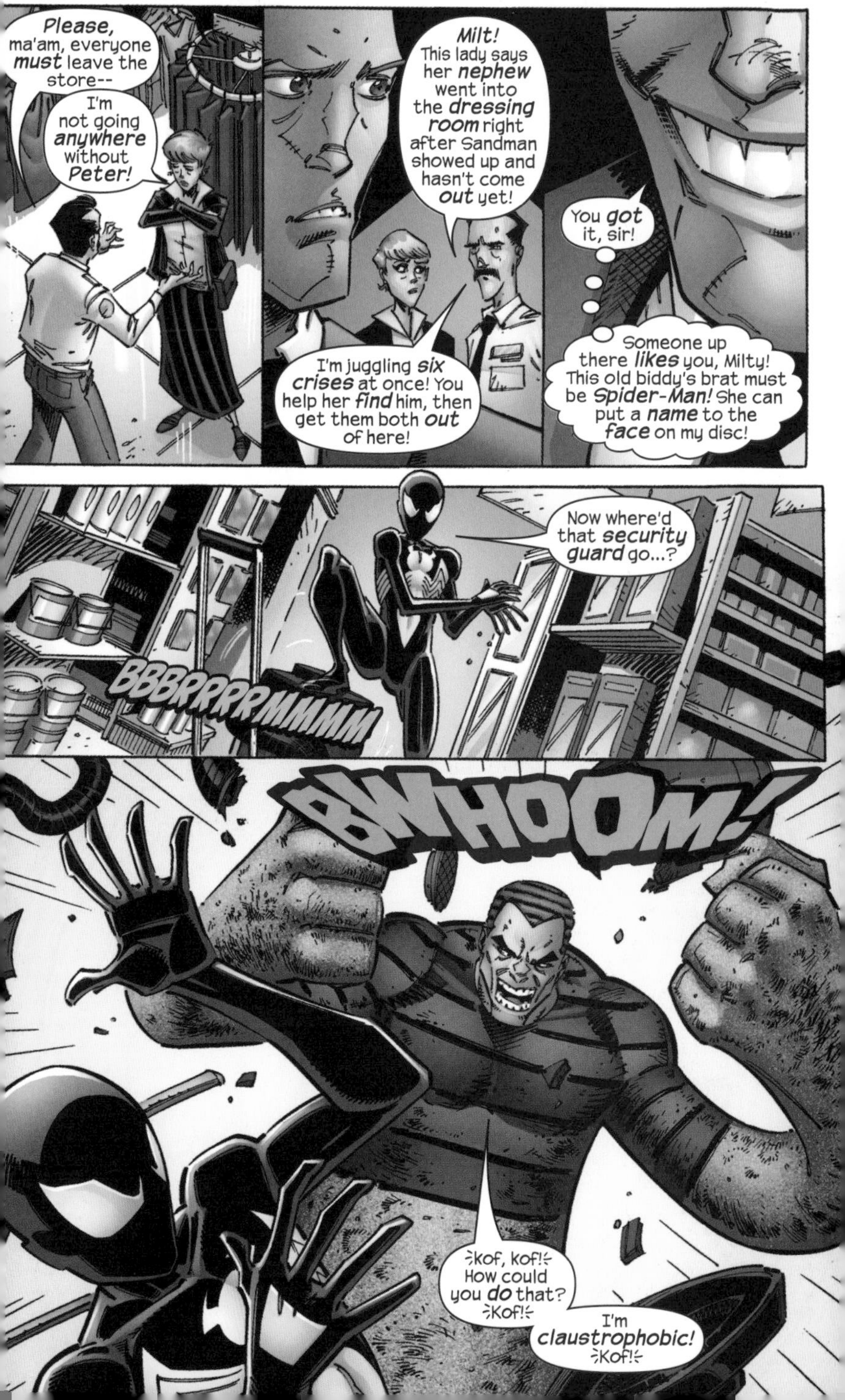
Please, ma'am, everyone must leave the store--
I'm not going anywhere without Peter!
Milt! This lady says her nephew went into the dressing room right after Sandman showed up and hasn't come out yet!
I'm juggling six crises at once! You help her find him, then get them both out of here!
You got it, sir!
Someone up there likes you, Milty! This old biddy's brat must be Spider-Man! She can put a name to the face on my disc!
Now where'd that security guard go...?
BBBRRRRRMMMMM
BWHOOM!
kof, kof! How could you do that? Kof!
I'm claustrophobic! Kof!

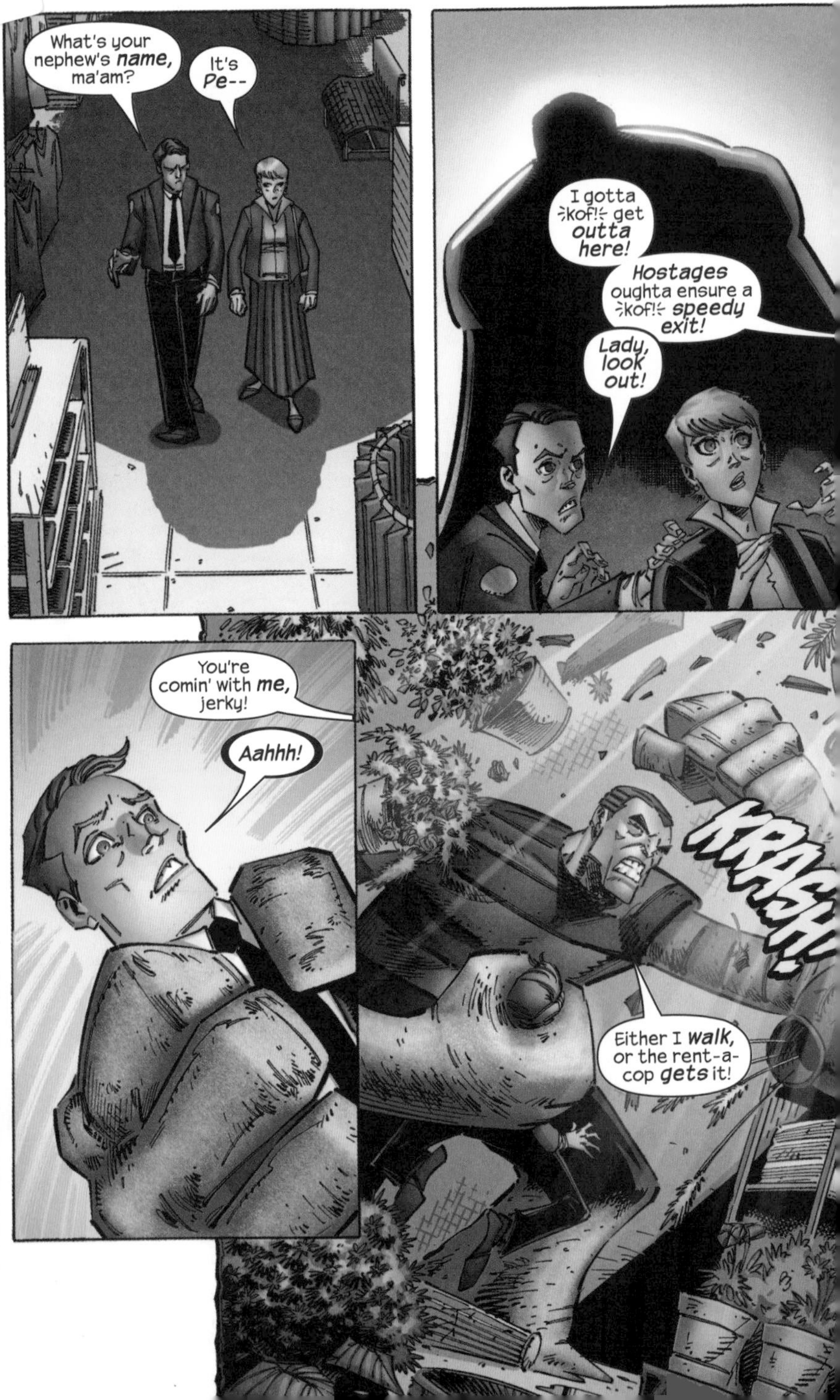
What's your nephew's name, ma'am?
It's Pe--
I gotta ⁝kof!⁝ get outta here!
Hostages oughta ensure a ⁝kof!⁝ speedy exit!
Lady, look out!
You're comin' with me, jerky!
Aahhh!
KRASH!
Either I walk, or the rent-a-cop gets it!

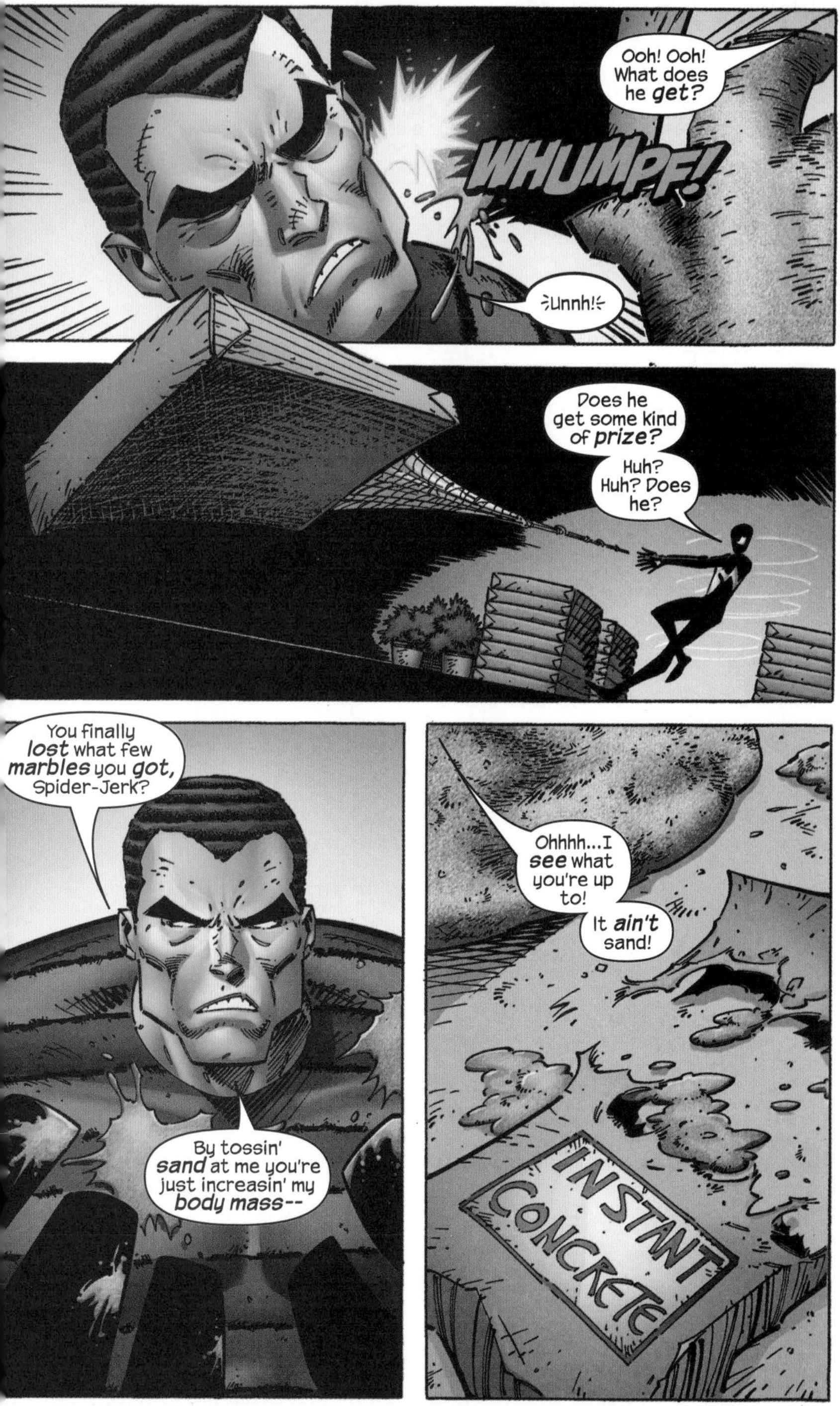
Ooh! Ooh! What does he get?
WHUMPF!
Unnh!
Does he get some kind of prize?
Huh? Huh? Does he?
You finally lost what few marbles you got, Spider-Jerk?
By tossin' sand at me you're just increasin' my body mass--
Ohhhh...I see what you're up to!
It ain't sand!
INSTANT CONCRETE

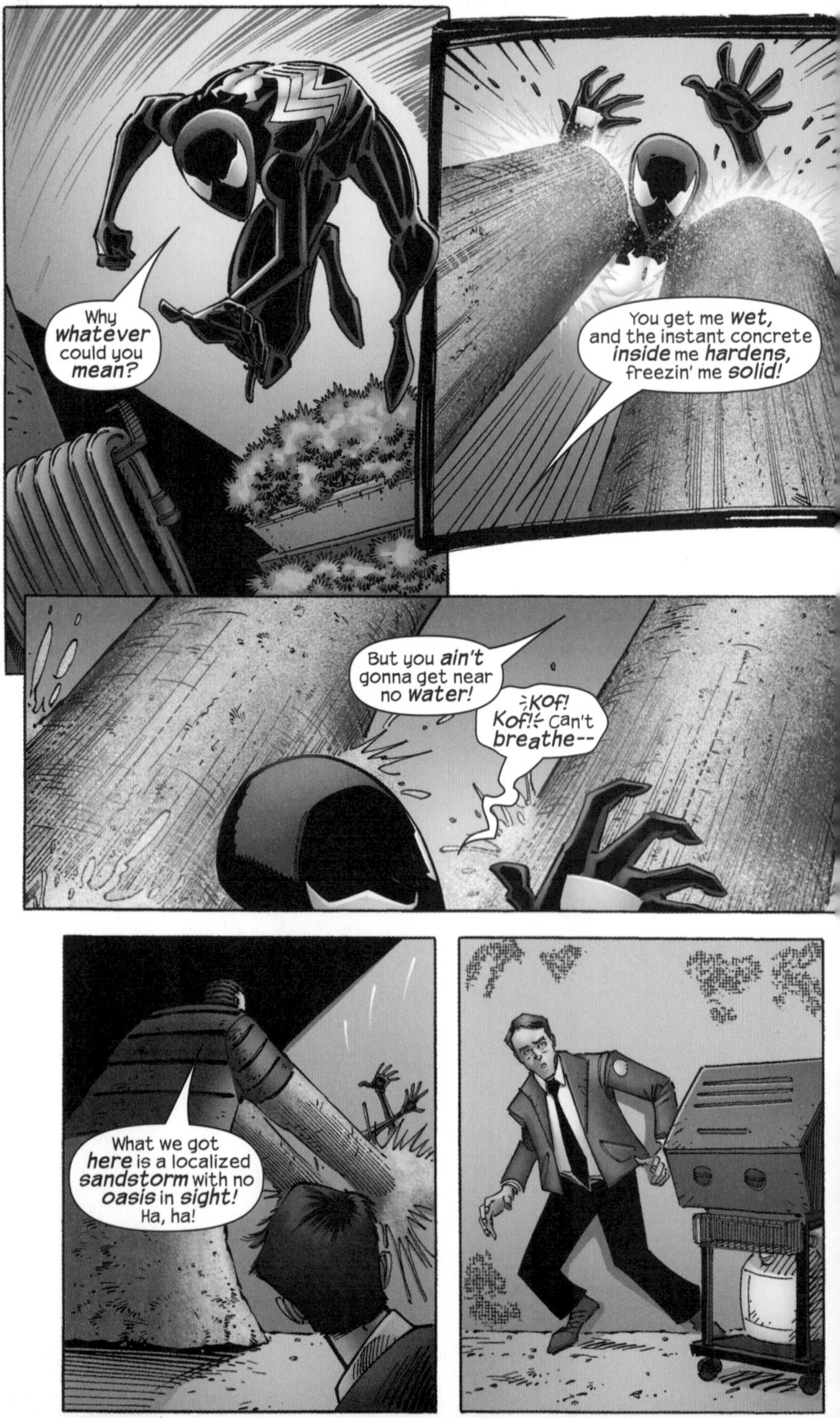

Why *whatever* could you *mean?*
You get me *wet,* and the instant concrete *inside* me *hardens,* freezin' me *solid!*
But you *ain't* gonna get near no *water!*
KOF! KOF! Can't *breathe--*
What we got *here* is a localized *sandstorm* with no *oasis* in *sight!* Ha, ha!

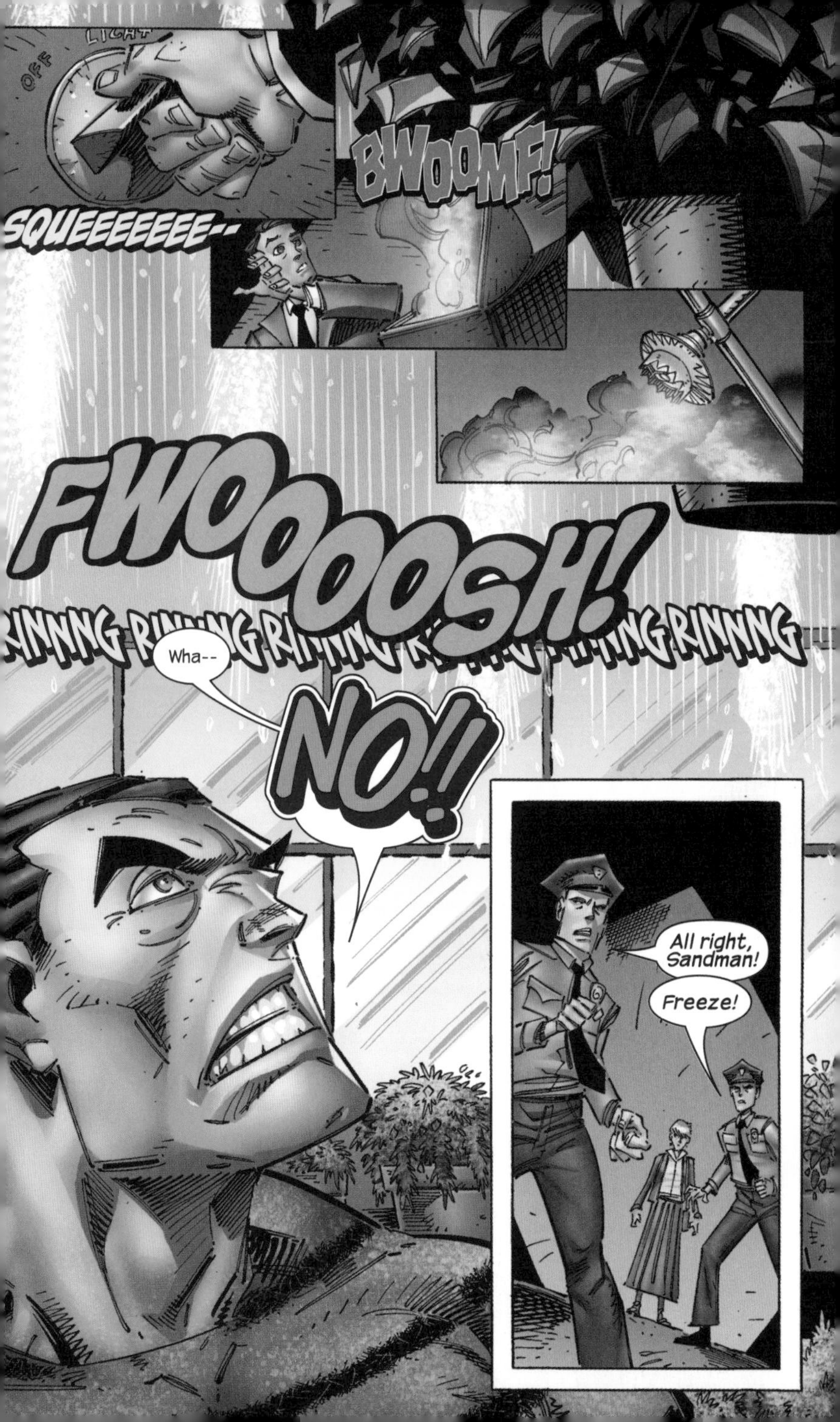
LIGHT
OFF
BWOOMF!
SQUEEEEEEEE--
FWOOOOSH!
RINNNG RINNNG RINNNG RINNNG
Wha--
NO!!
All right, Sandman!
Freeze!

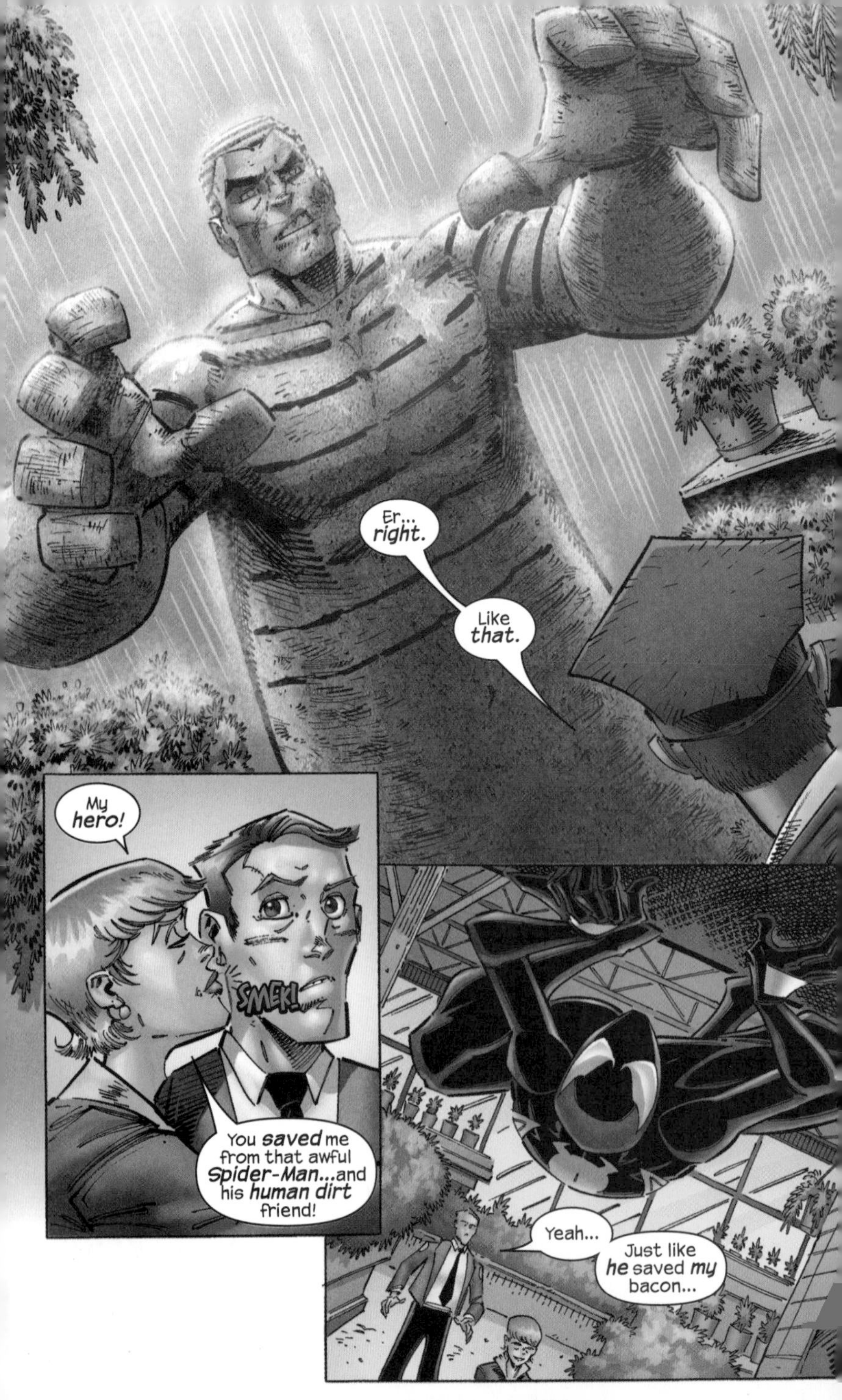

Er... right.
Like that.
My hero!
SMEK!
You saved me from that awful Spider-Man...and his human dirt friend!
Yeah...
Just like he saved my bacon...

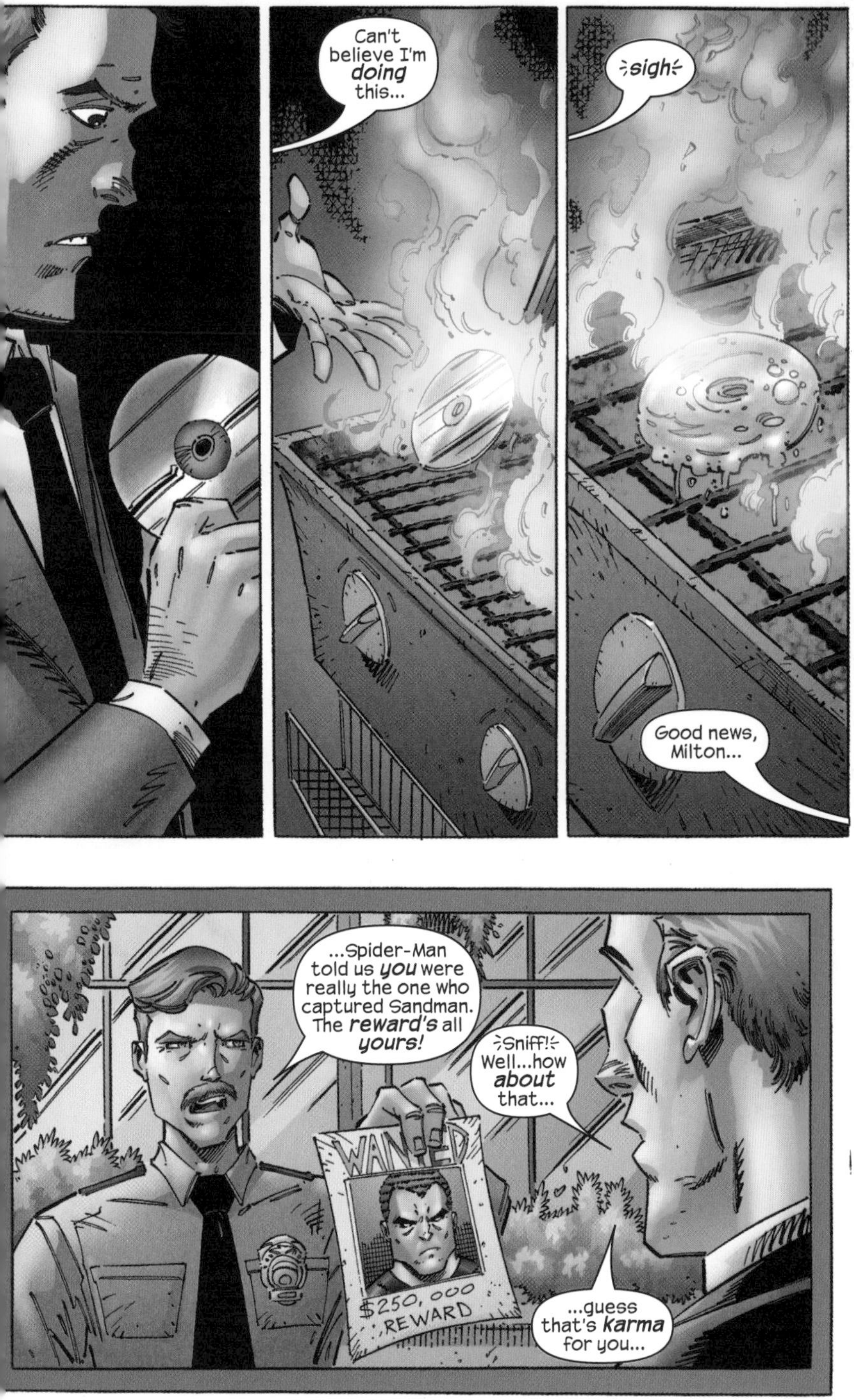
Can't believe I'm doing this...
sigh
Good news, Milton...
...Spider-Man told us you were really the one who captured Sandman. The reward's all yours!
Sniff! Well...how about that...
WANTED
$250,000 REWARD
...guess that's karma for you...

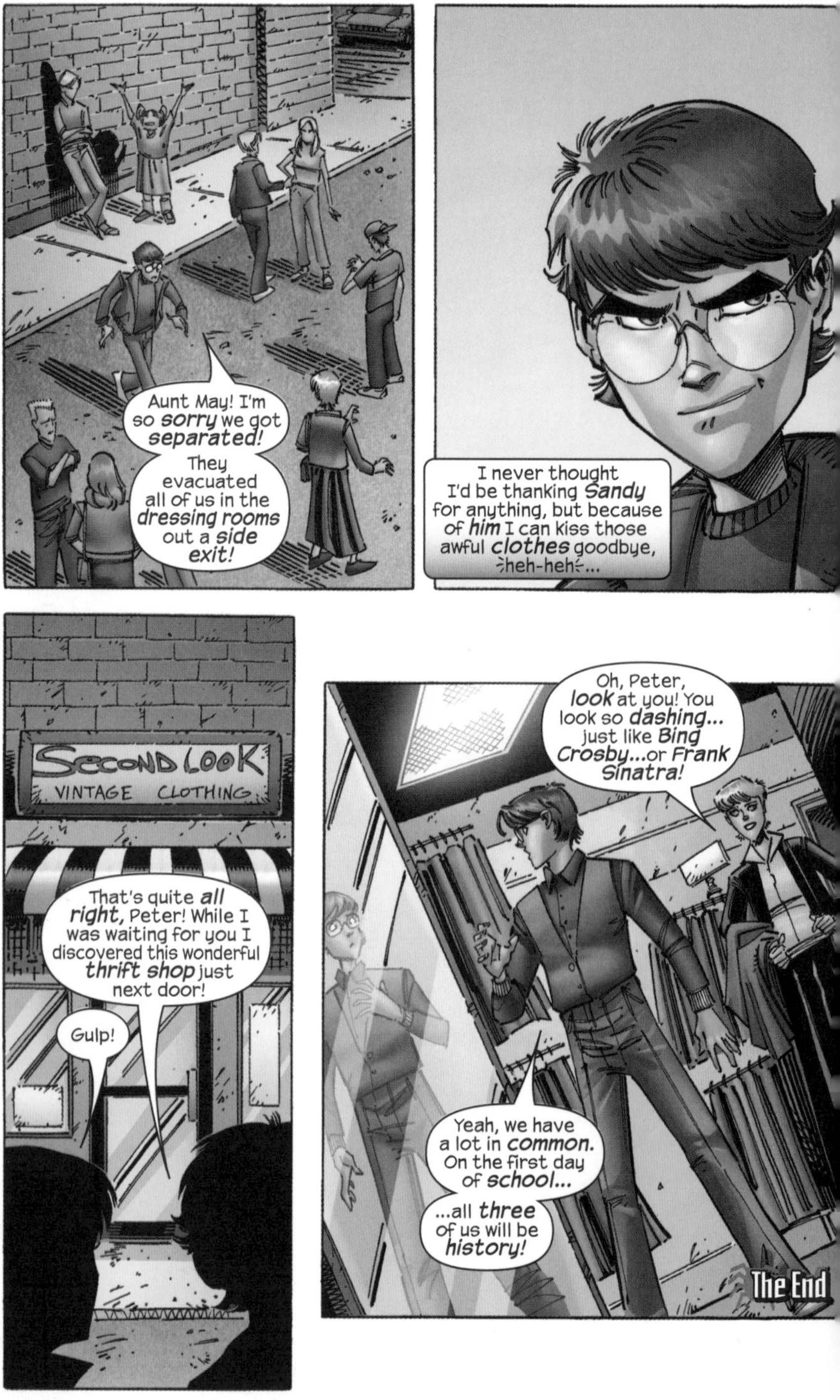
Aunt May! I'm so sorry we got separated!
They evacuated all of us in the dressing rooms out a side exit!
I never thought I'd be thanking Sandy for anything, but because of him I can kiss those awful clothes goodbye, heh-heh...
SECOND LOOK
VINTAGE CLOTHING
That's quite all right, Peter! While I was waiting for you I discovered this wonderful thrift shop just next door!
Gulp!
Oh, Peter, look at you! You look so dashing... just like Bing Crosby...or Frank Sinatra!
Yeah, we have a lot in common. On the first day of school...
...all three of us will be history!
The End

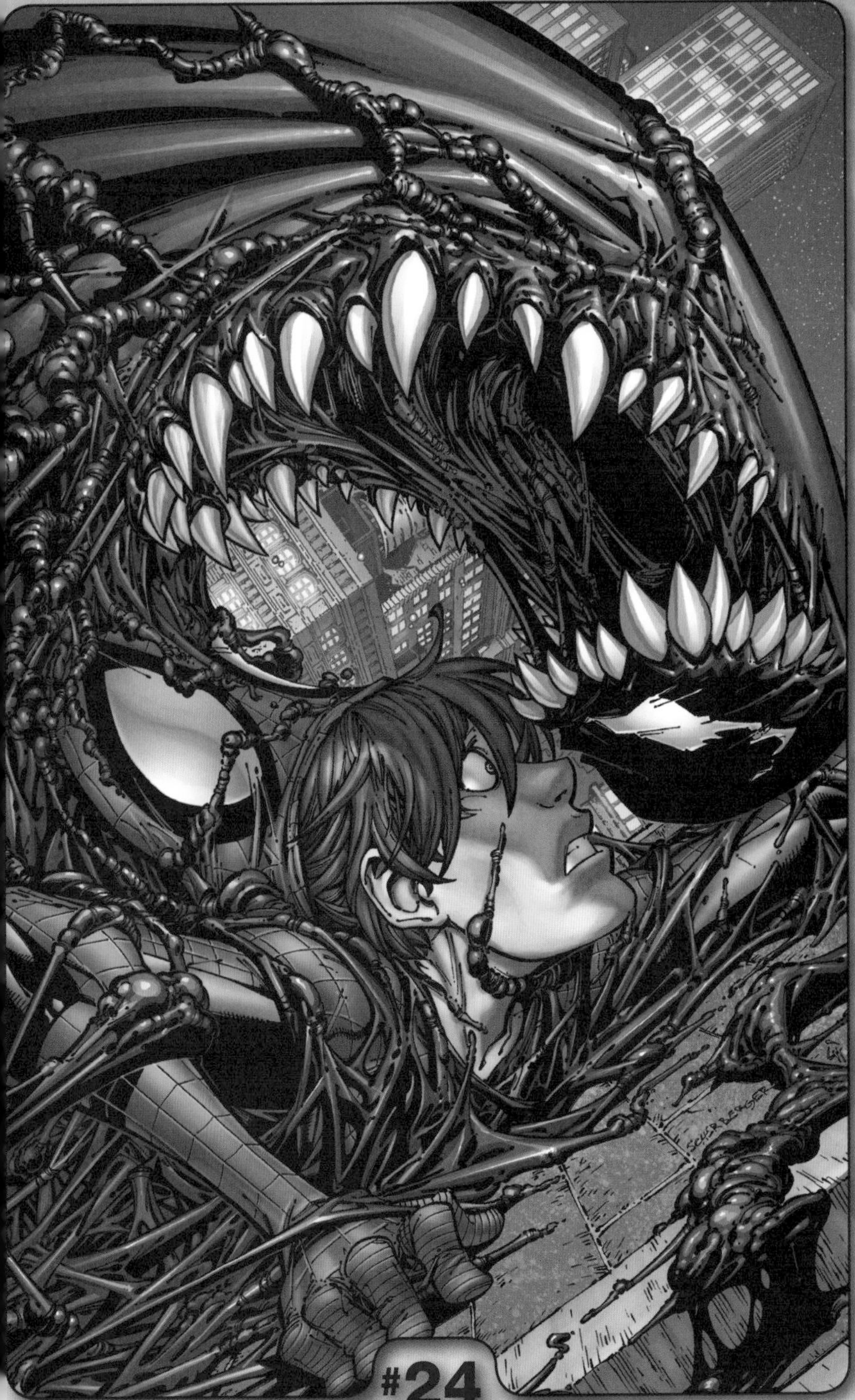

#24

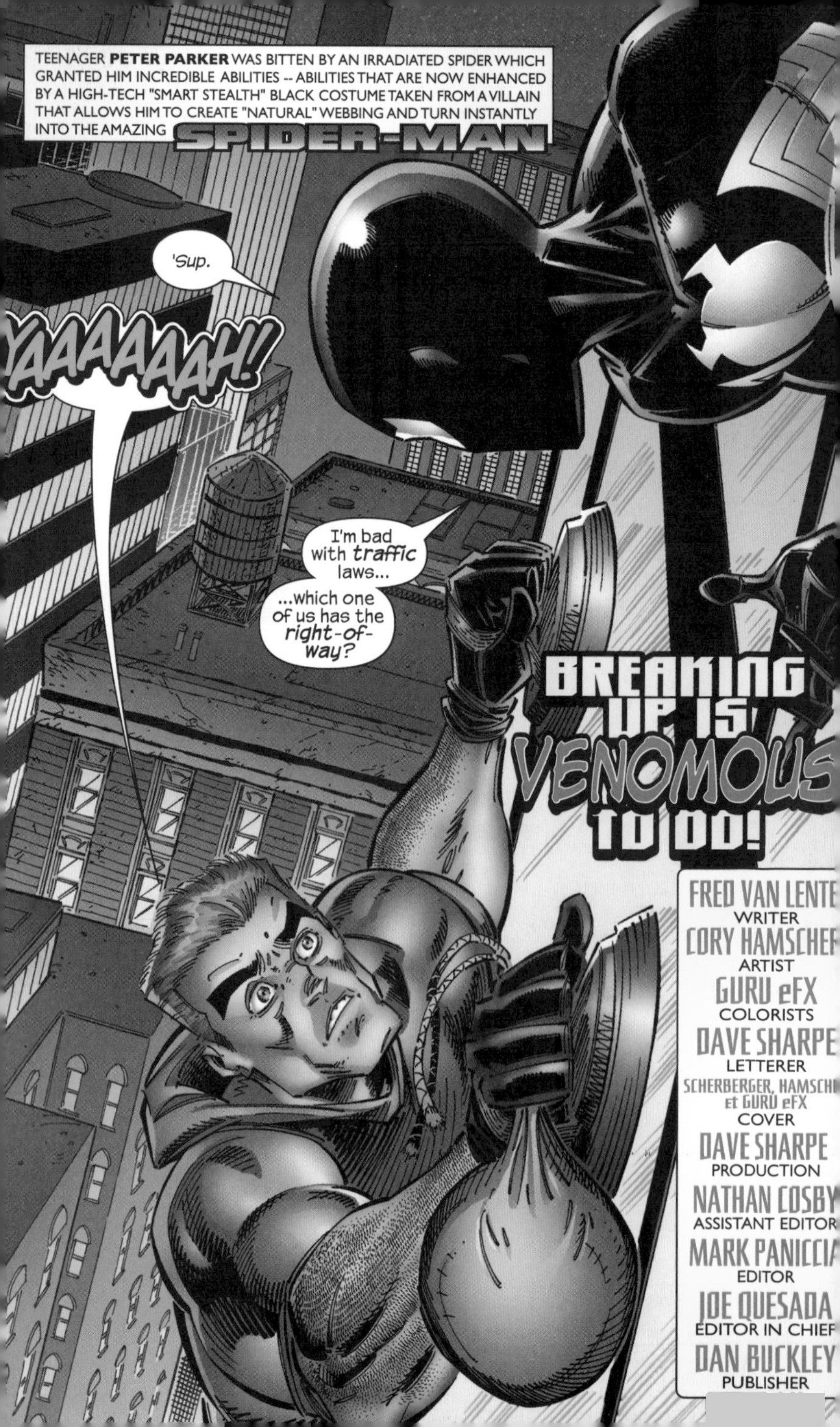

TEENAGER PETER PARKER WAS BITTEN BY AN IRRADIATED SPIDER WHICH GRANTED HIM INCREDIBLE ABILITIES -- ABILITIES THAT ARE NOW ENHANCED BY A HIGH-TECH "SMART STEALTH" BLACK COSTUME TAKEN FROM A VILLAIN THAT ALLOWS HIM TO CREATE "NATURAL" WEBBING AND TURN INSTANTLY INTO THE AMAZING SPIDER-MAN
'Sup.
YAAAAAAH!!
I'm bad with traffic laws...
...which one of us has the right-of-way?
BREAKING UP IS VENOMOUS TO DO!
FRED VAN LENTE WRITER
CORY HAMSCHER ARTIST
GURU eFX COLORISTS
DAVE SHARPE LETTERER
SCHERBERGER, HAMSCHER et GURU eFX COVER
DAVE SHARPE PRODUCTION
NATHAN COSBY ASSISTANT EDITOR
MARK PANICCIA EDITOR
JOE QUESADA EDITOR IN CHIEF
DAN BUCKLEY PUBLISHER

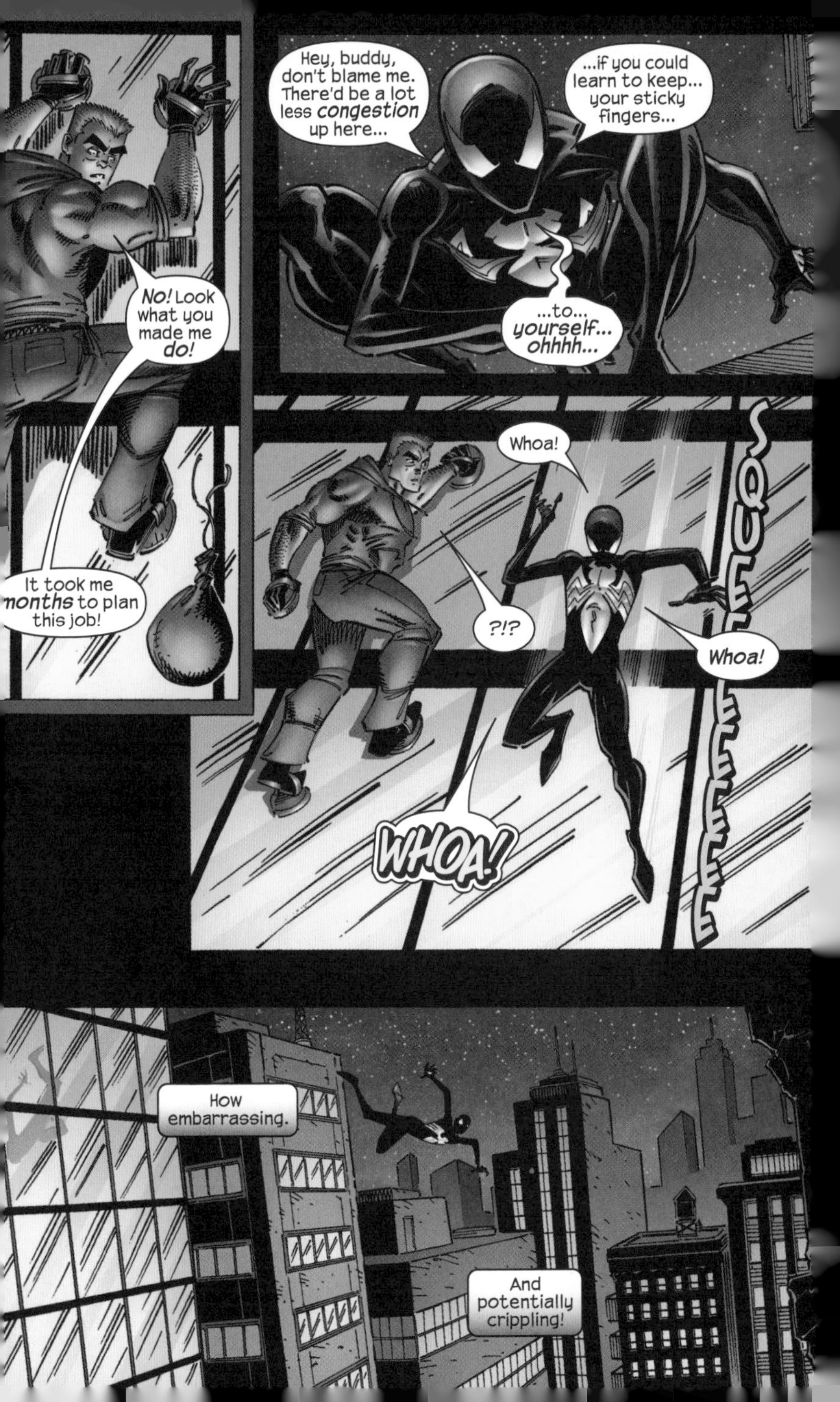
No! Look what you made me do!
It took me months to plan this job!
Hey, buddy, don't blame me. There'd be a lot less congestion up here...
...if you could learn to keep... your sticky fingers...
...to... yourself... ohhhh...
Whoa!
?!?
Whoa!
WHOA!
How embarrassing.
And potentially crippling!

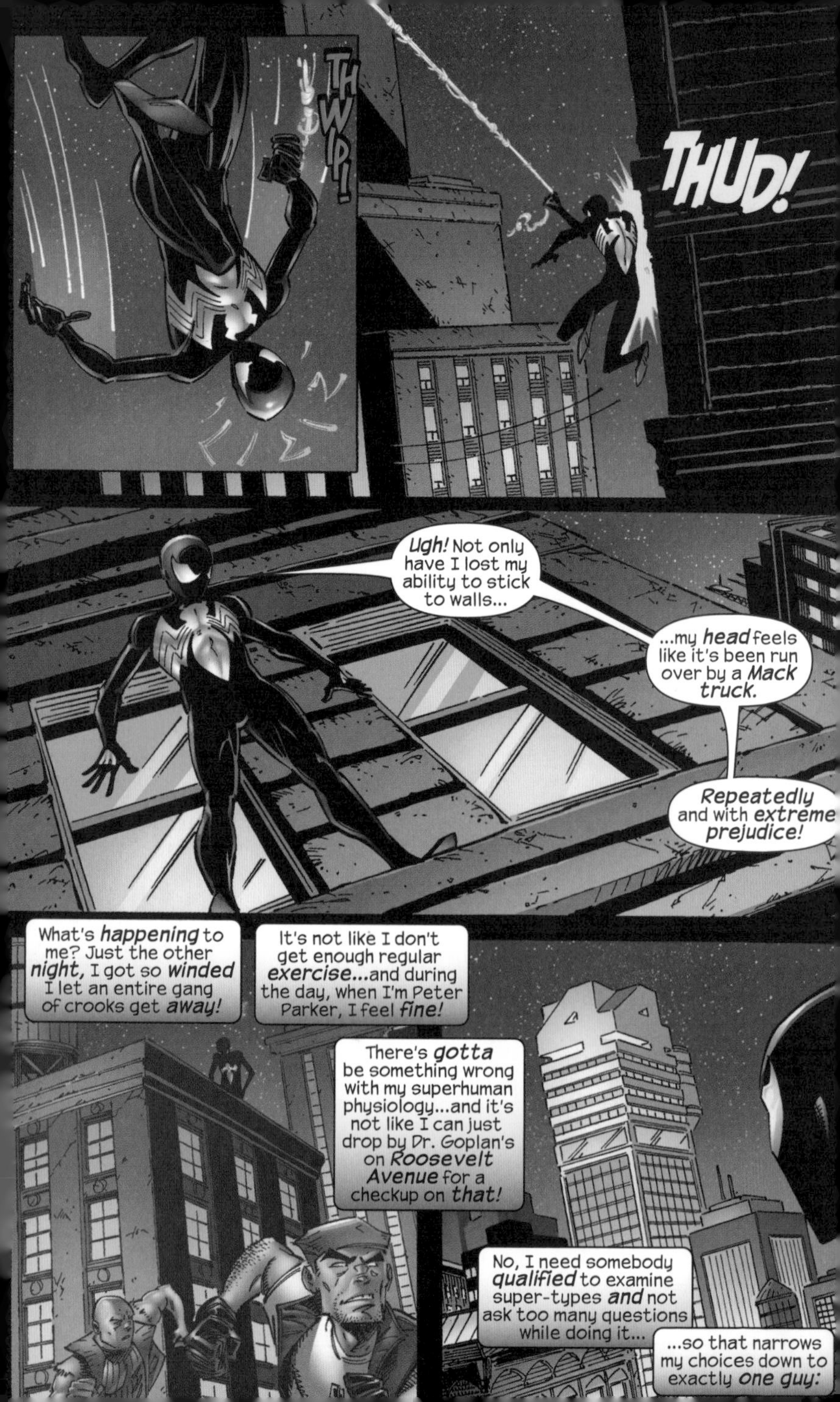
THWIP!
THUD!
Ugh! Not only have I lost my ability to stick to walls...
...my head feels like it's been run over by a Mack truck.
Repeatedly and with extreme prejudice!
What's happening to me? Just the other night, I got so winded I let an entire gang of crooks get away!
It's not like I don't get enough regular exercise...and during the day, when I'm Peter Parker, I feel fine!
There's gotta be something wrong with my superhuman physiology...and it's not like I can just drop by Dr. Goplan's on Roosevelt Avenue for a checkup on that!
No, I need somebody qualified to examine super-types and not ask too many questions while doing it...
...so that narrows my choices down to exactly one guy:

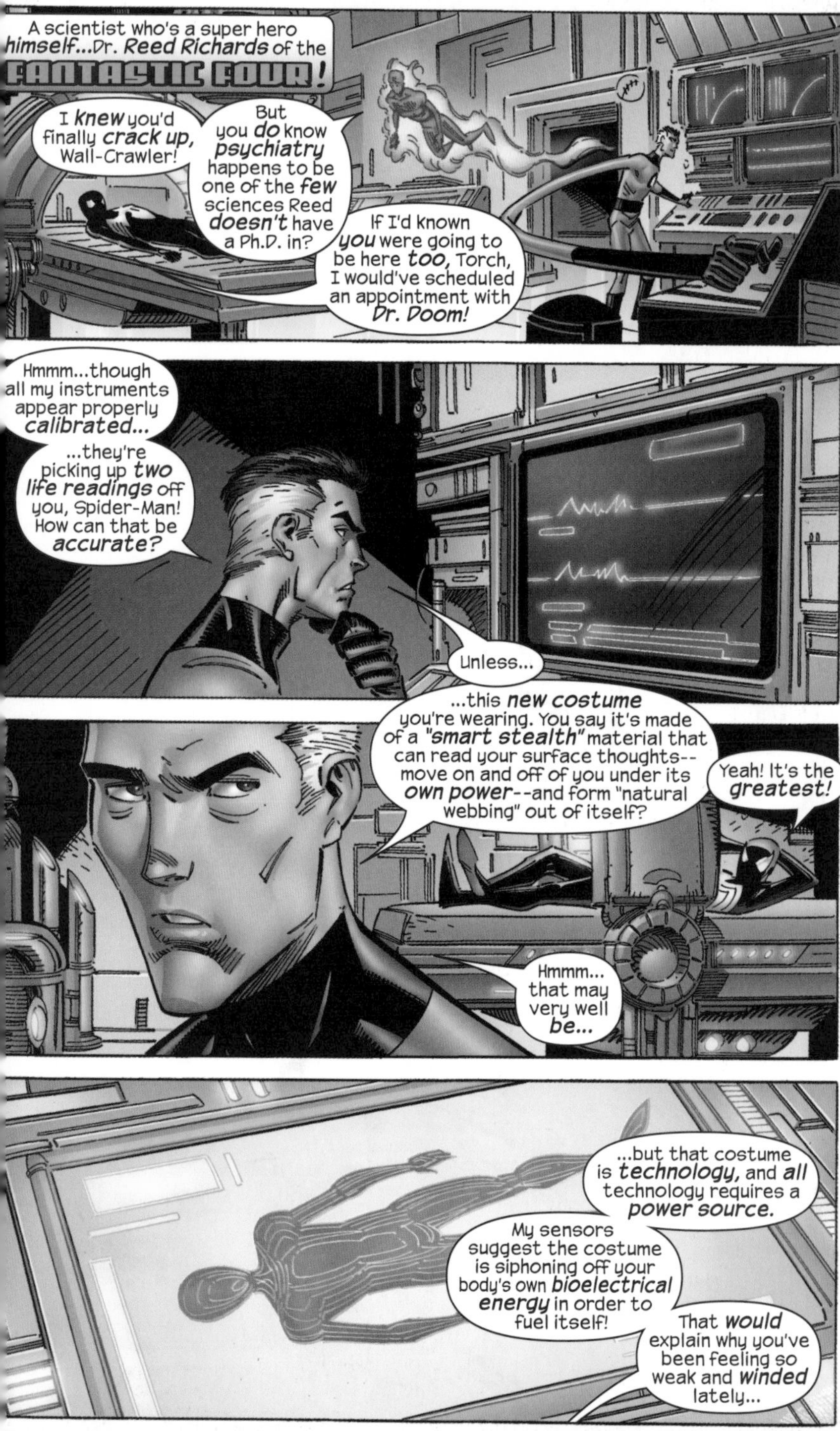

A scientist who's a super hero himself...Dr. Reed Richards of the FANTASTIC FOUR!
I knew you'd finally crack up, Wall-Crawler!
But you do know psychiatry happens to be one of the few sciences Reed doesn't have a Ph.D. in?
If I'd known you were going to be here too, Torch, I would've scheduled an appointment with Dr. Doom!
Hmmm...though all my instruments appear properly calibrated...
...they're picking up two life readings off you, Spider-Man! How can that be accurate?
Unless...
...this new costume you're wearing. You say it's made of a "smart stealth" material that can read your surface thoughts--move on and off of you under its own power--and form "natural webbing" out of itself?
Yeah! It's the greatest!
Hmmm... that may very well be...
...but that costume is technology, and all technology requires a power source.
My sensors suggest the costume is siphoning off your body's own bioelectrical energy in order to fuel itself!
That would explain why you've been feeling so weak and winded lately...

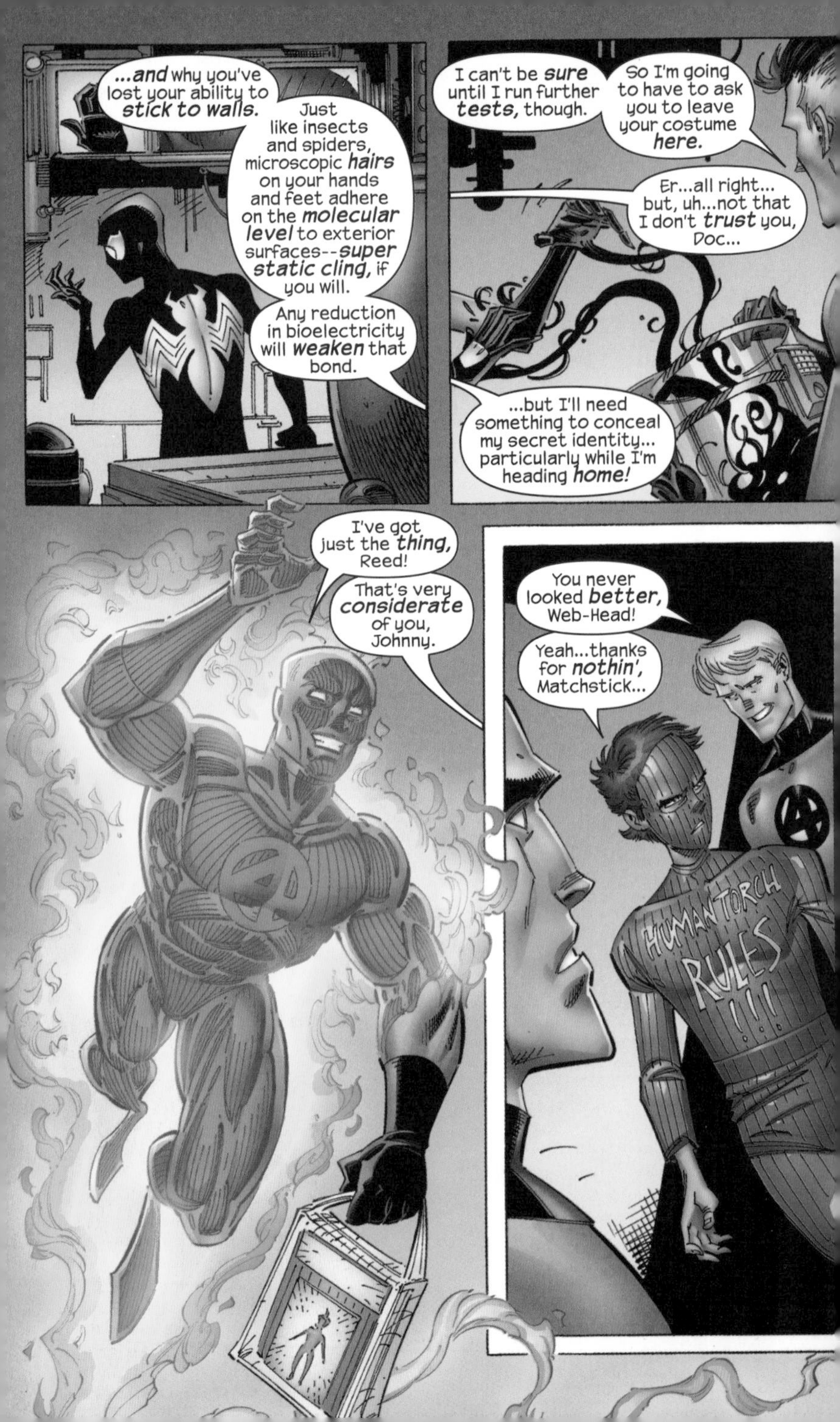
...and why you've lost your ability to stick to walls.
Just like insects and spiders, microscopic hairs on your hands and feet adhere on the molecular level to exterior surfaces--super static cling, if you will.
Any reduction in bioelectricity will weaken that bond.
I can't be sure until I run further tests, though.
So I'm going to have to ask you to leave your costume here.
Er...all right... but, uh...not that I don't trust you, Doc...
...but I'll need something to conceal my secret identity... particularly while I'm heading home!
I've got just the thing, Reed!
That's very considerate of you, Johnny.
You never looked better, Web-Head!
Yeah...thanks for nothin', Matchstick...
HUMAN TORCH RULES !!!

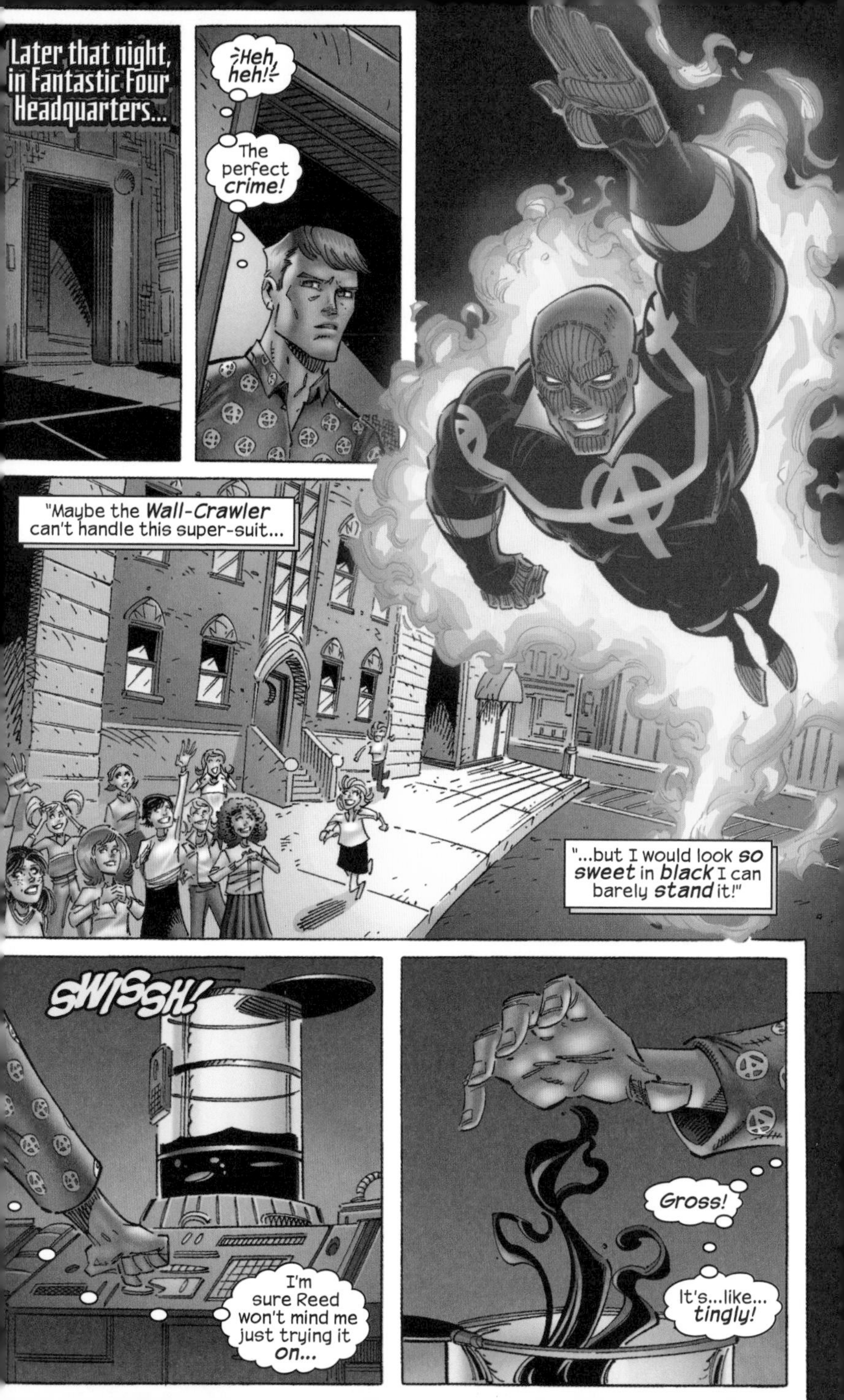
Later that night, in Fantastic Four Headquarters...
Heh, heh!
The perfect crime!
"Maybe the Wall-Crawler can't handle this super-suit...
"...but I would look so sweet in black I can barely stand it!"
SWISSH!
I'm sure Reed won't mind me just trying it on...
Gross!
It's...like... tingly!

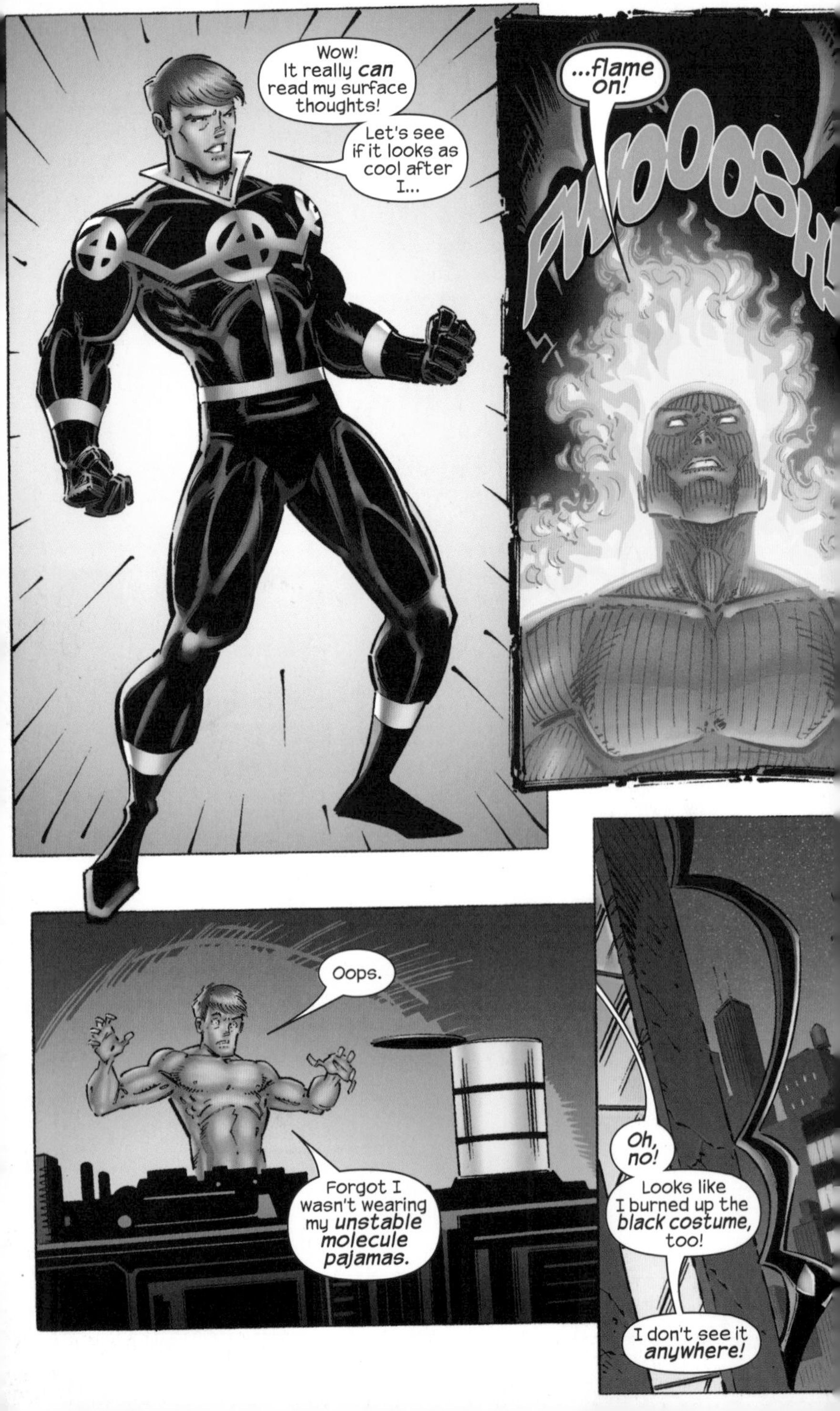

Wow! It really *can* read my surface thoughts!
Let's see if it looks as cool after I...
...*flame on!*
FWOOOOSH
Oops.
Forgot I wasn't wearing my *unstable molecule pajamas.*
Oh, no!
Looks like I burned up the *black costume,* too!
I don't see it *anywhere!*

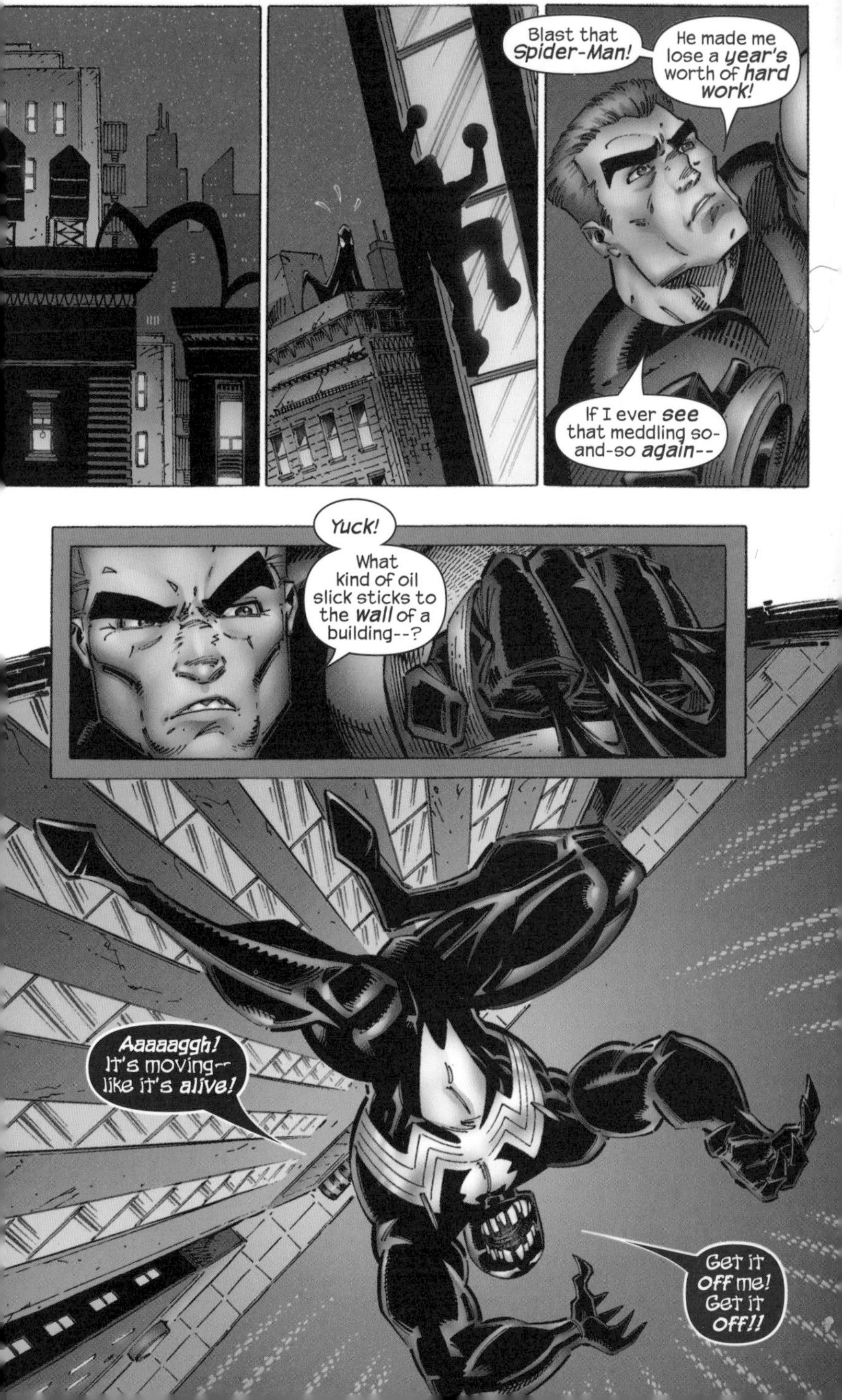
Blast that Spider-Man!
He made me lose a year's worth of hard work!
If I ever see that meddling so-and-so again--
Yuck!
What kind of oil slick sticks to the wall of a building--?
Aaaaaggh! It's moving-- like it's alive!
Get it off me! Get it off!!

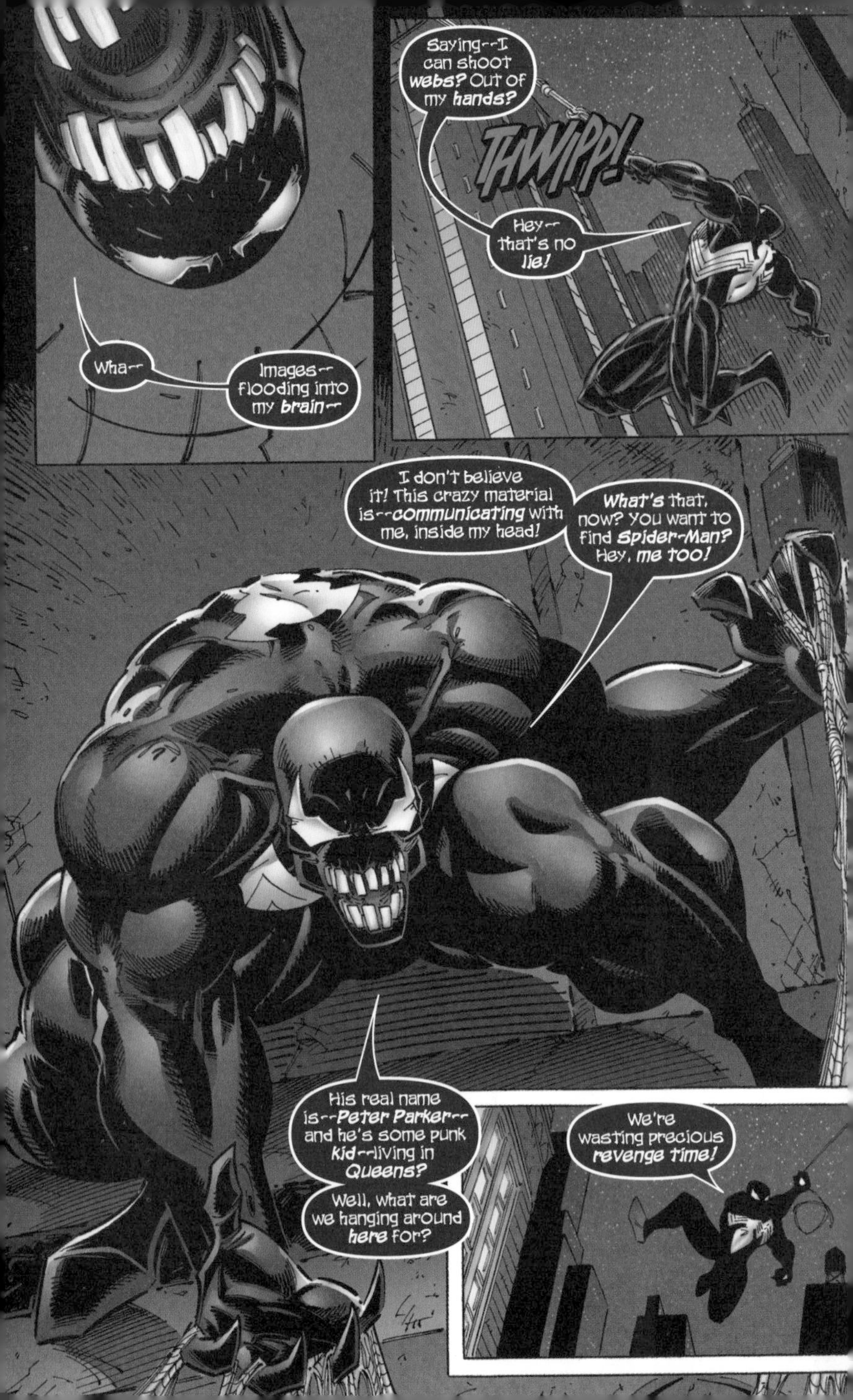
Wha--
Images--flooding into my brain--
Saying--I can shoot webs? Out of my hands?
THWIPP!
Hey--that's no lie!
I don't believe it! This crazy material is--communicating with me, inside my head!
What's that, now? You want to find Spider-Man? Hey, me too!
His real name is--Peter Parker--and he's some punk kid--living in Queens?
Well, what are we hanging around here for?
We're wasting precious revenge time!

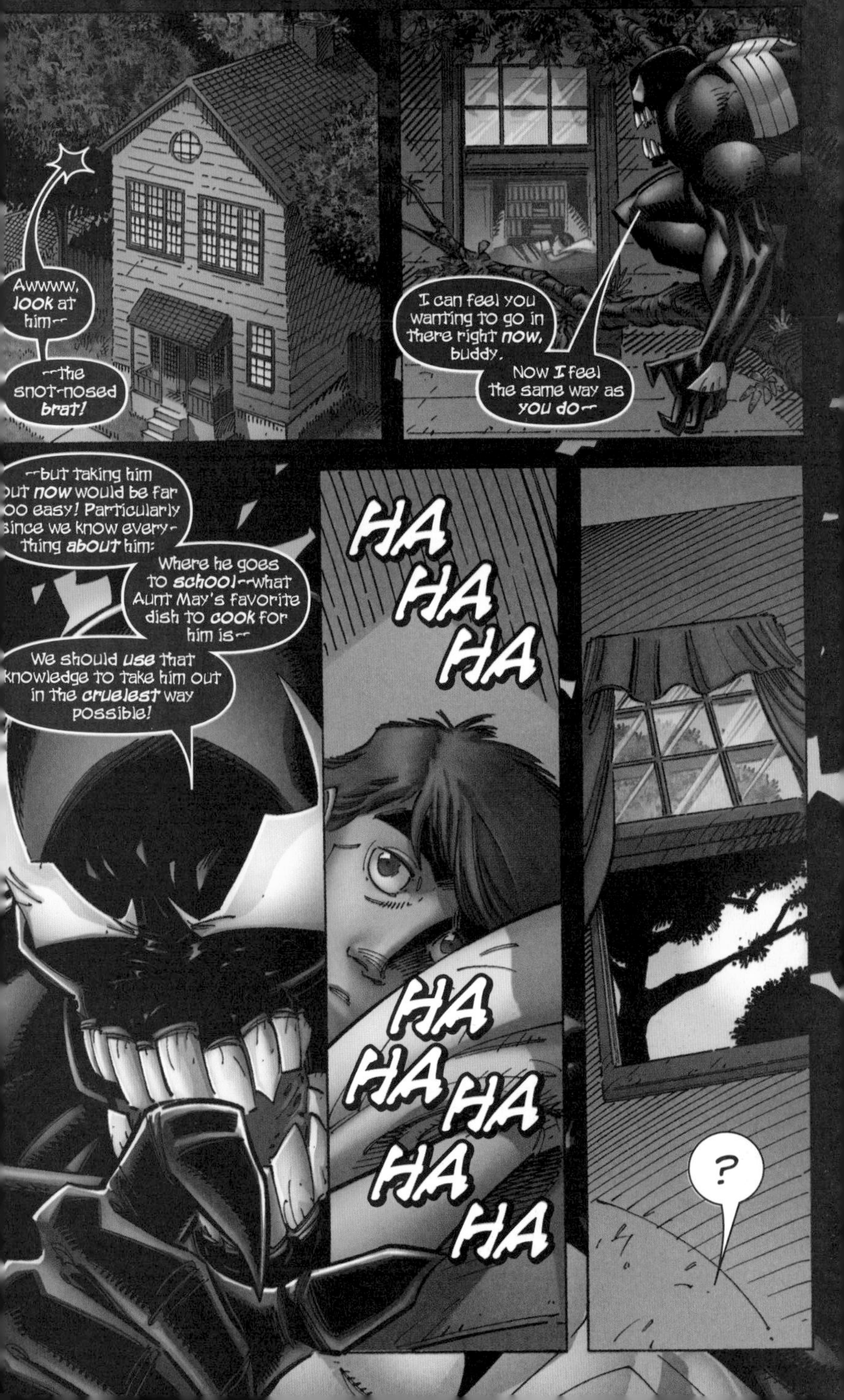
Awwww, look at him--
--the snot-nosed brat!
I can feel you wanting to go in there right now, buddy.
Now I feel the same way as you do--
--but taking him out now would be far too easy! Particularly since we know everything about him:
Where he goes to school--what Aunt May's favorite dish to cook for him is--
We should use that knowledge to take him out in the cruelest way possible!
HA HA HA
HA HA HA HA HA
?

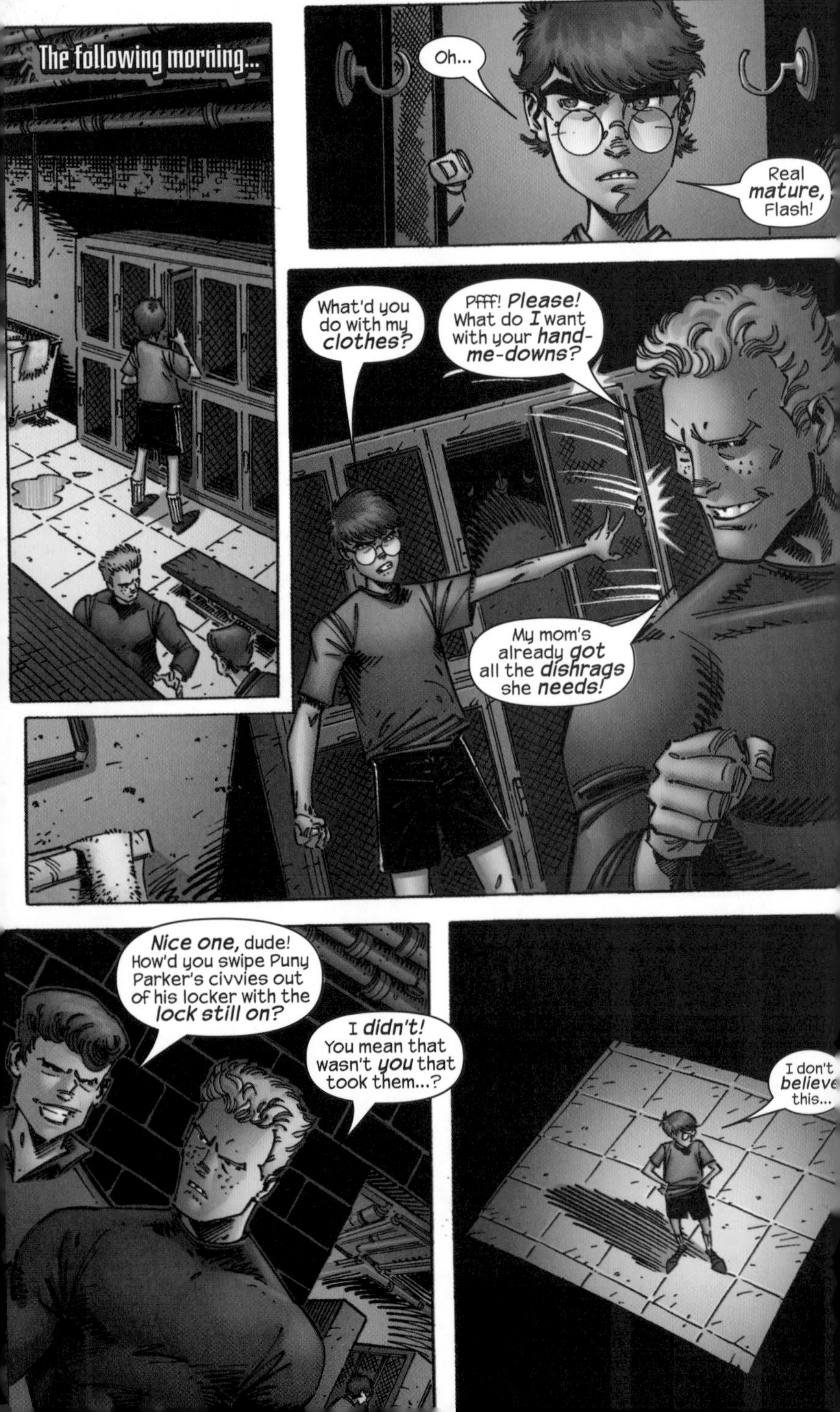

The following morning...
Oh...
Real mature, Flash!
What'd you do with my clothes?
Pfff! Please! What do I want with your hand-me-downs?
My mom's already got all the dishrags she needs!
Nice one, dude! How'd you swipe Puny Parker's civvies out of his locker with the lock still on?
I didn't! You mean that wasn't you that took them...?
I don't believe this...

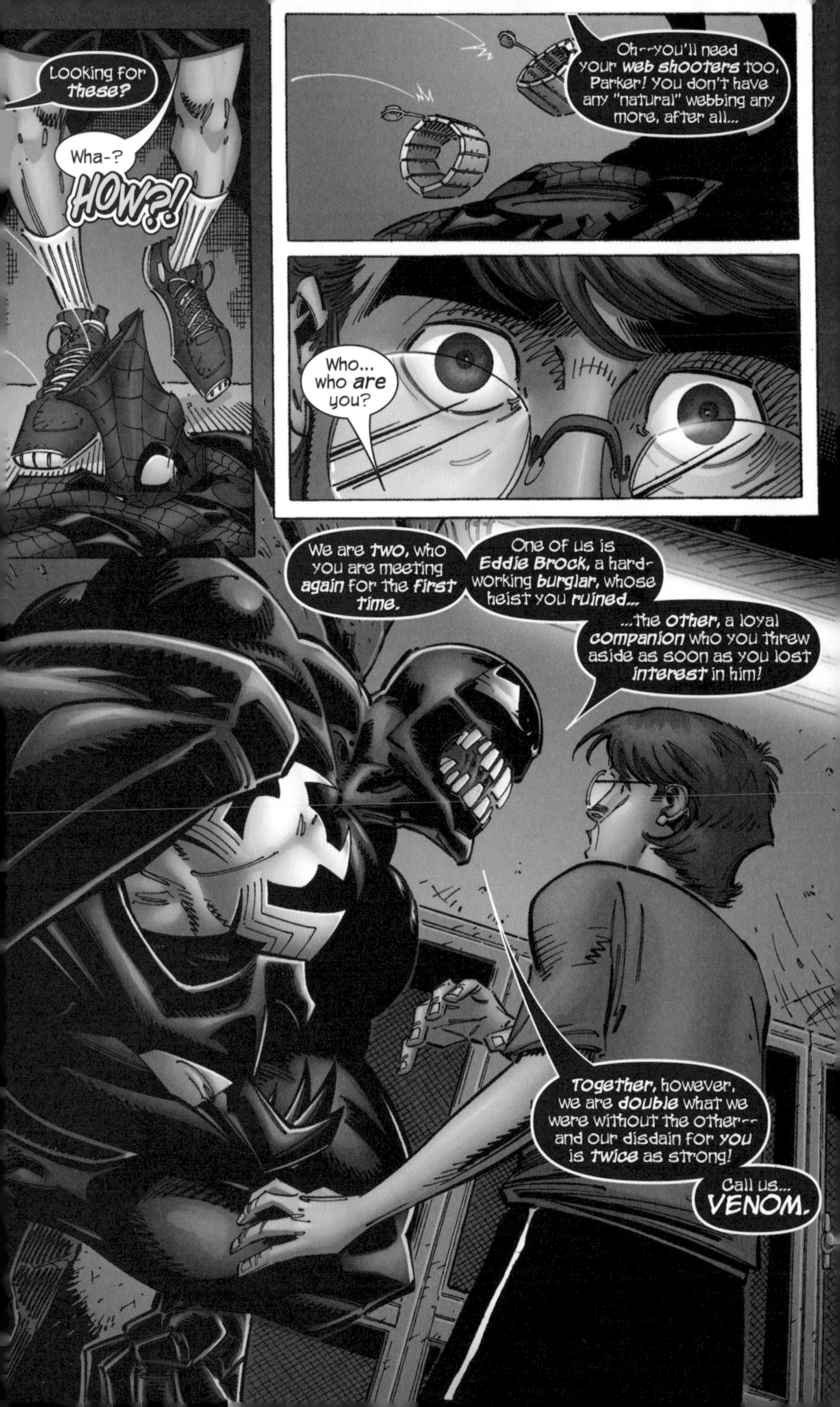
Looking for these?
Wha-?
HOW?!
Oh--you'll need your web shooters too, Parker! You don't have any "natural" webbing any more, after all...
Who... who are you?
We are two, who you are meeting again for the first time.
One of us is Eddie Brock, a hard-working burglar, whose heist you ruined...
...the other, a loyal companion who you threw aside as soon as you lost interest in him!
Together, however, we are double what we were without the other-- and our disdain for you is twice as strong!
Call us... VENOM.

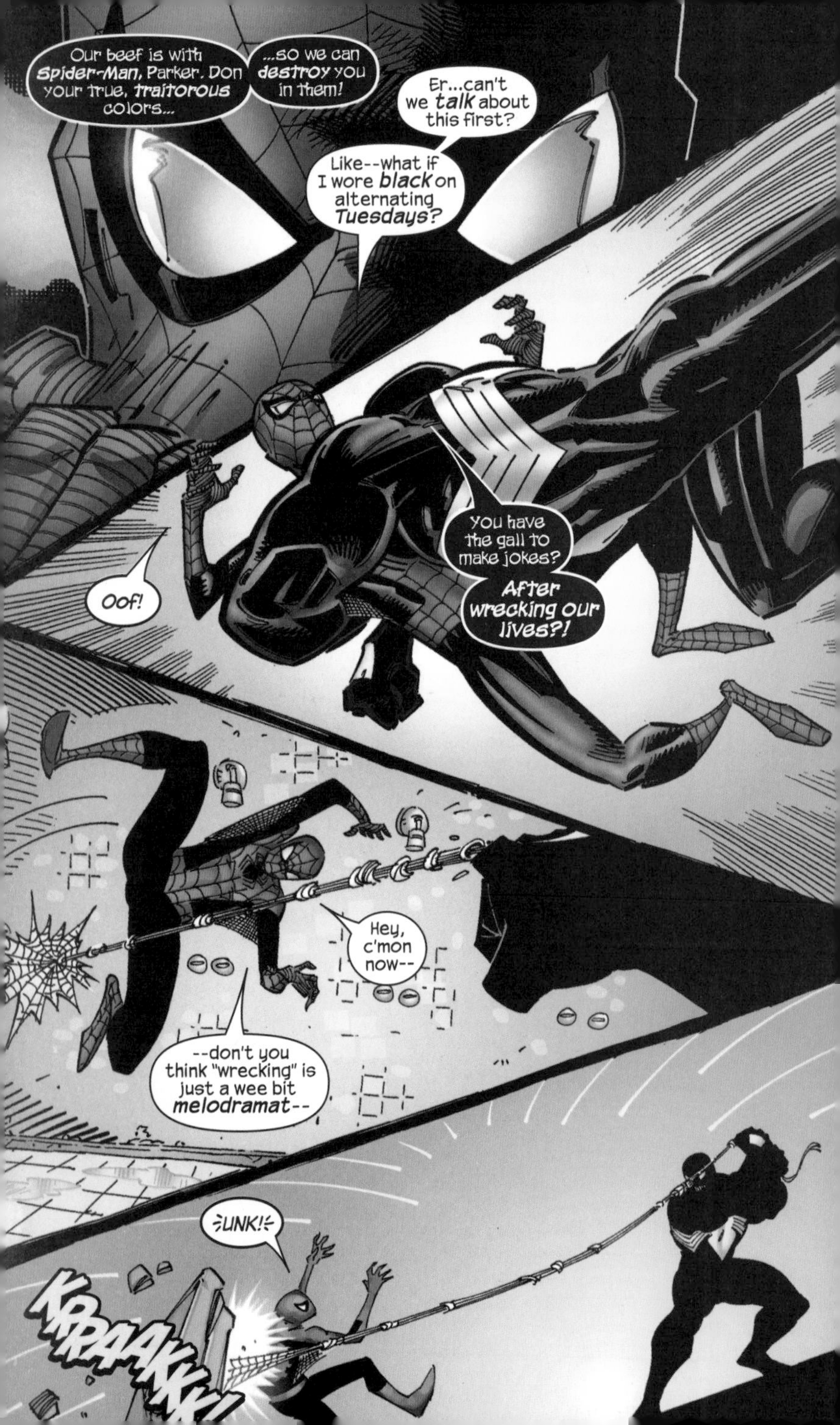
Our beef is with Spider-Man, Parker. Don your true, traitorous colors...
...so we can destroy you in them!
Er...can't we talk about this first?
Like--what if I wore black on alternating Tuesdays?
You have the gall to make jokes?
After wrecking our lives?!
Oof!
Hey, c'mon now--
--don't you think "wrecking" is just a wee bit melodramat--
UNK!
KRRAAKK!

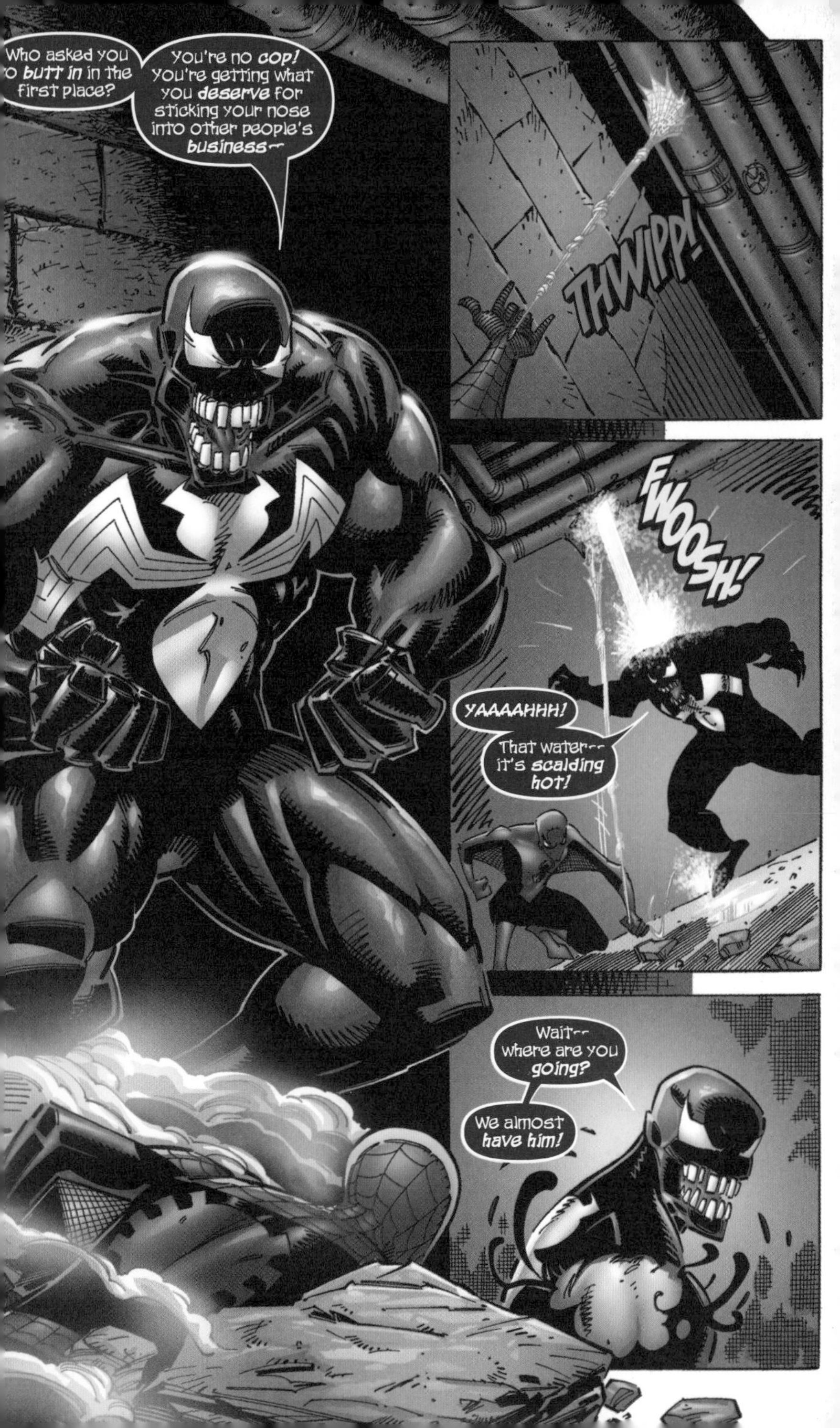
Who asked you to butt in in the first place?
You're no cop! You're getting what you deserve for sticking your nose into other people's business--
THWIPP!
FWOOSH!
YAAAAHHH!
That water-- it's scalding hot!
Wait-- where are you going?
We almost have him!

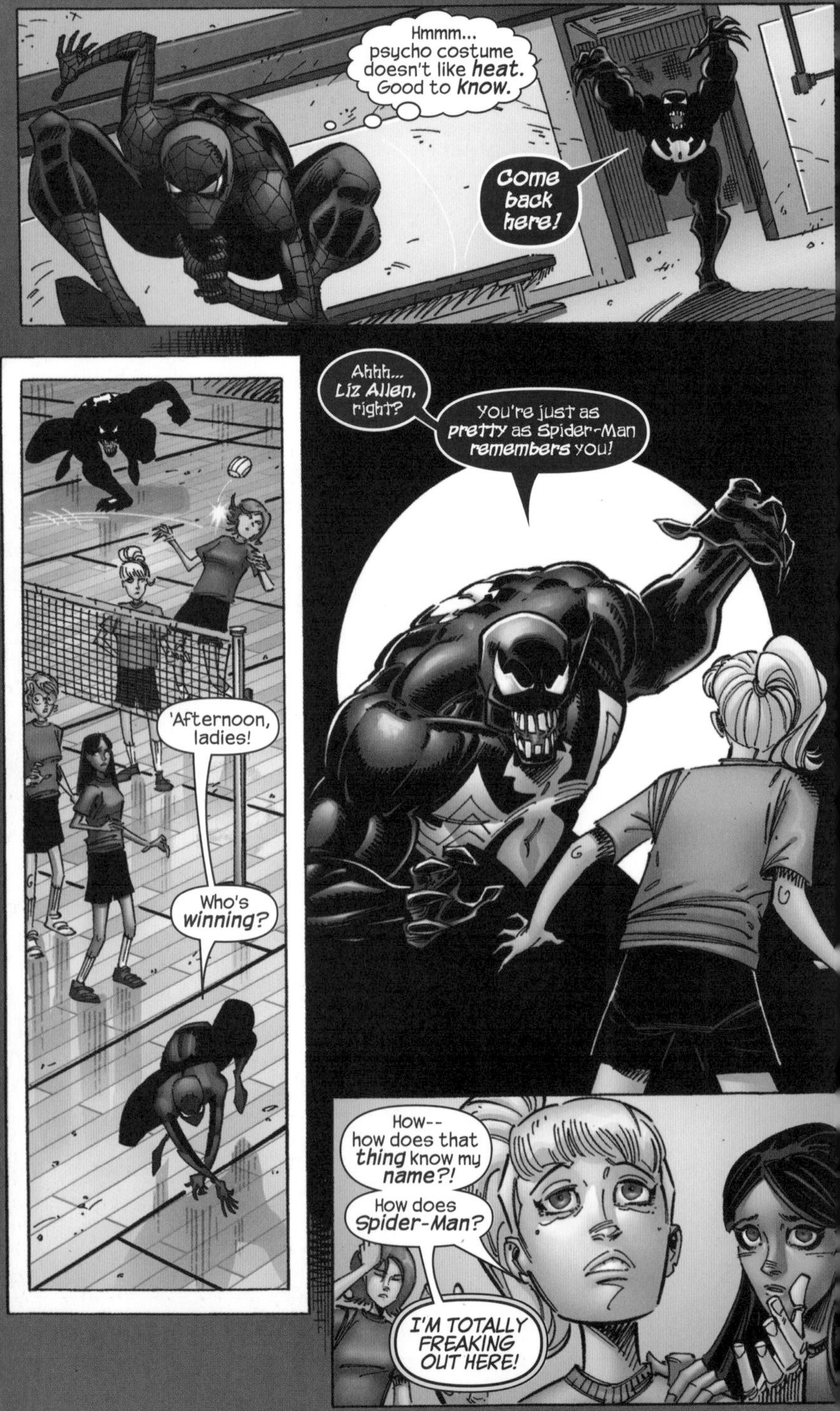

Hmmm... psycho costume doesn't like heat. Good to know.
Come back here!
'Afternoon, ladies!
Who's winning?
Ahhh... Liz Allen, right?
You're just as pretty as Spider-Man remembers you!
How-- how does that thing know my name?!
How does Spider-Man?
I'M TOTALLY FREAKING OUT HERE!

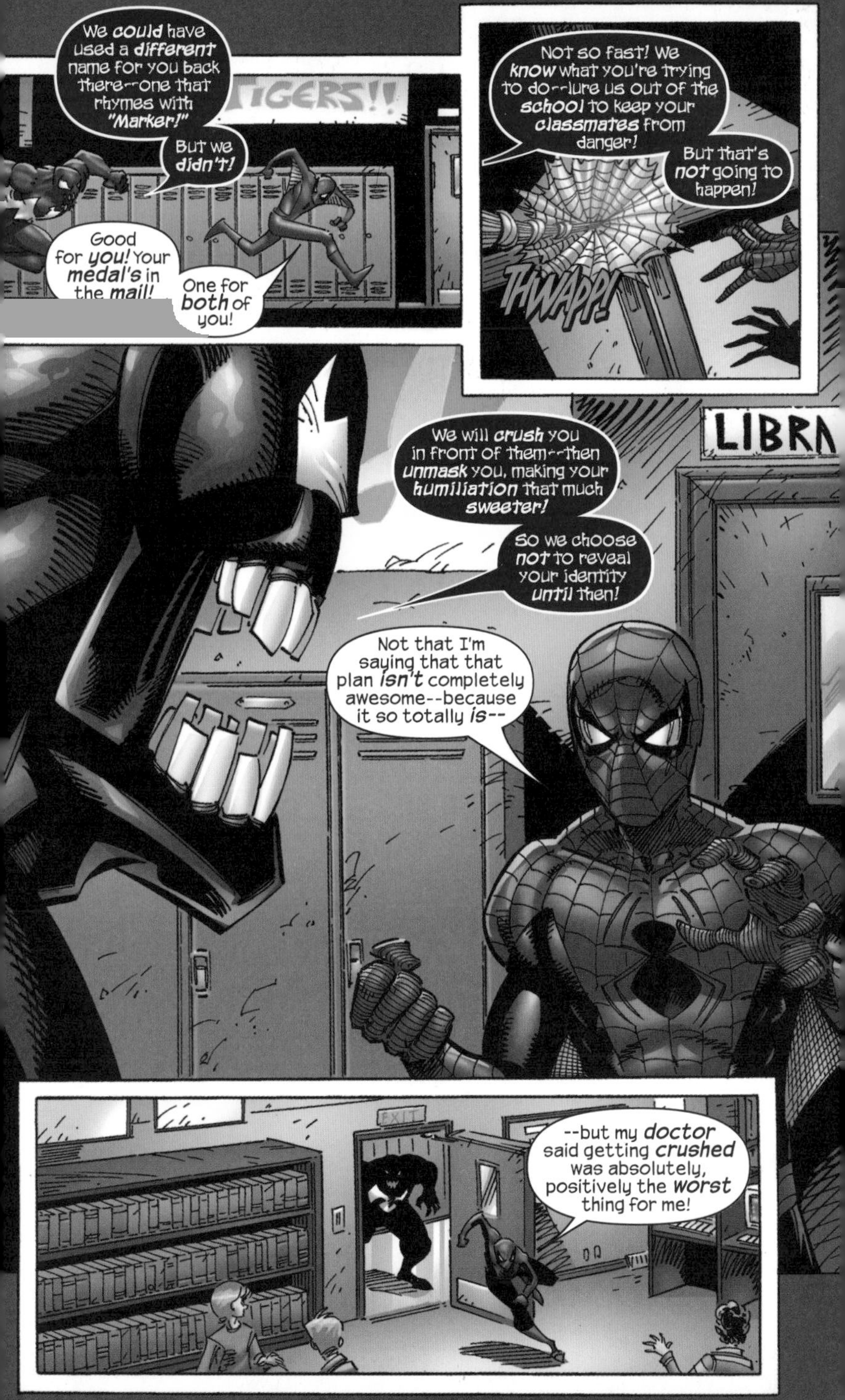

TIGERS!!
We could have used a different name for you back there--one that rhymes with "Marker!"
But we didn't!
Good for you! Your medal's in the mail!
One for both of you!
Not so fast! We know what you're trying to do--lure us out of the school to keep your classmates from danger!
But that's not going to happen!
THWAPP!
LIBRA
We will crush you in front of them--then unmask you, making your humiliation that much sweeter!
So we choose not to reveal your identity until then!
Not that I'm saying that that plan isn't completely awesome--because it so totally is--
EXIT
--but my doctor said getting crushed was absolutely, positively the worst thing for me!

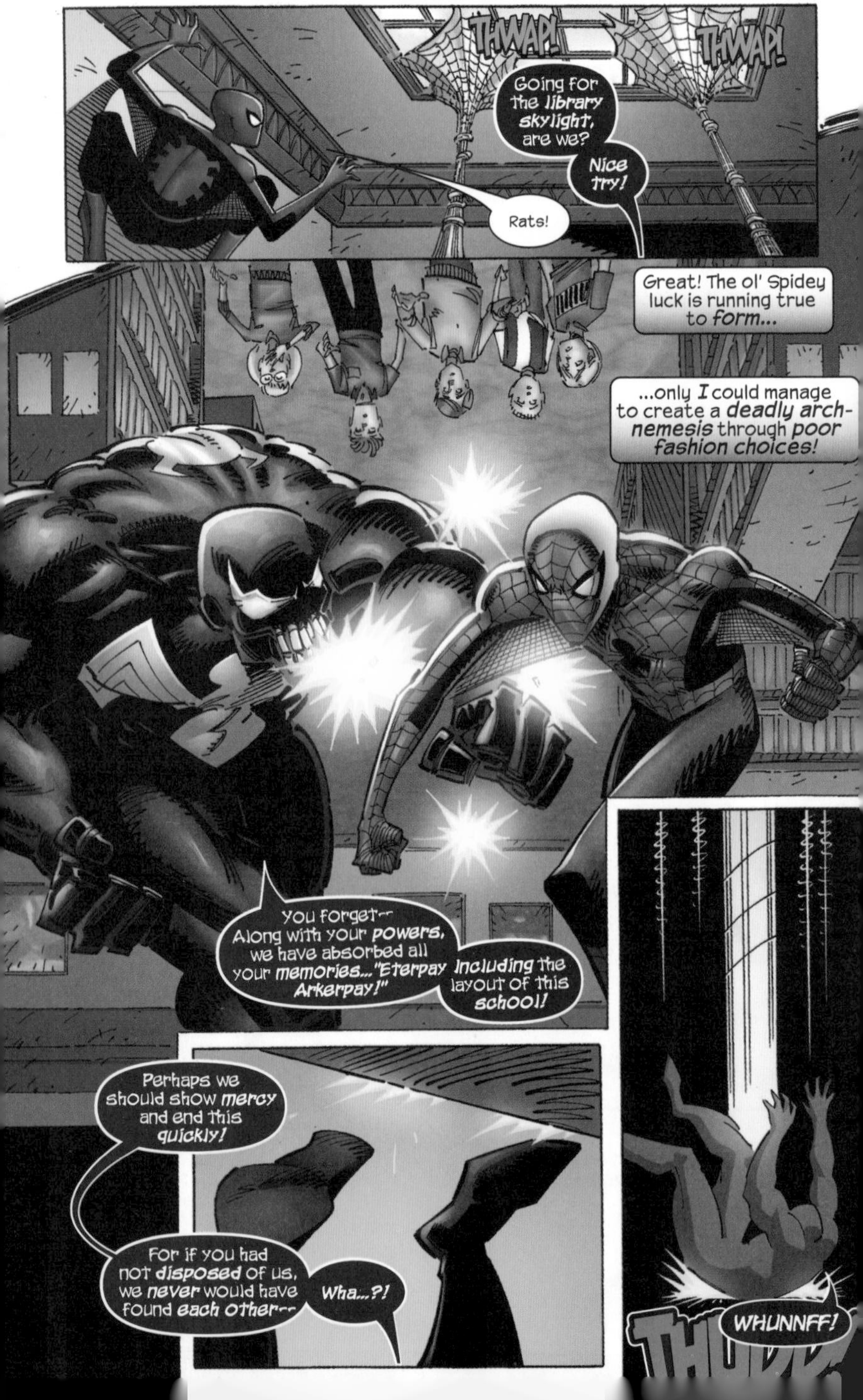
THWAP!
THWAP!
Going for the library skylight, are we?
Nice try!
Rats!
Great! The ol' Spidey luck is running true to form...
...only I could manage to create a deadly arch-nemesis through poor fashion choices!
You forget-- Along with your powers, we have absorbed all your memories... "Eterpay Arkerpay!"
Including the layout of this school!
Perhaps we should show mercy and end this quickly!
For if you had not disposed of us, we never would have found each other--
Wha...?!
WHUNNFF!

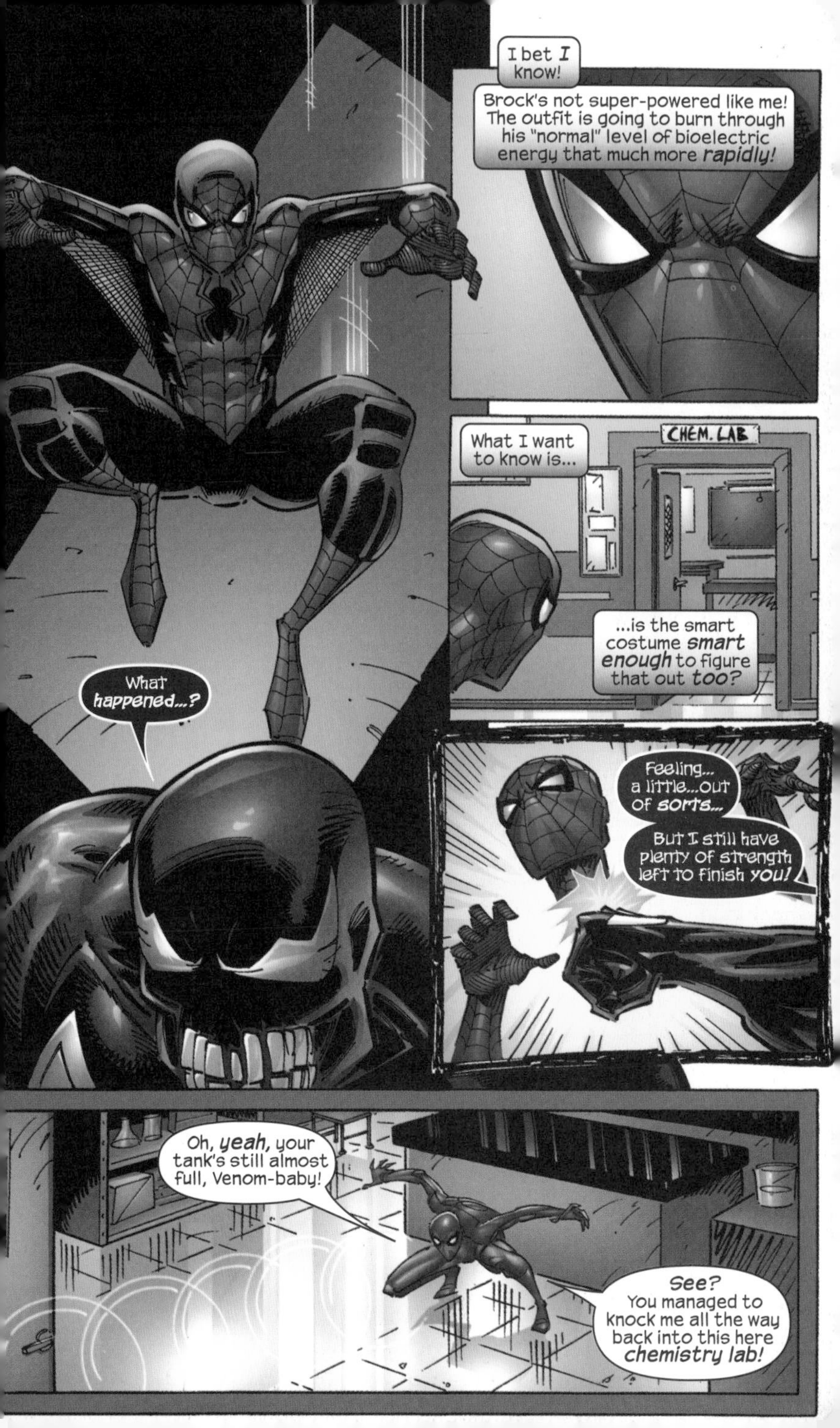
I bet *I* know!
Brock's not super-powered like me! The outfit is going to burn through his "normal" level of bioelectric energy that much more *rapidly!*
What I want to know is...
...is the smart costume *smart enough* to figure that out *too?*
What *happened...?*
Feeling... a little...out of *sorts...*
But I still have plenty of strength left to finish *you!*
Oh, *yeah,* your tank's still almost full, Venom-baby!
CHEM. LAB
See? You managed to knock me all the way back into this here *chemistry lab!*

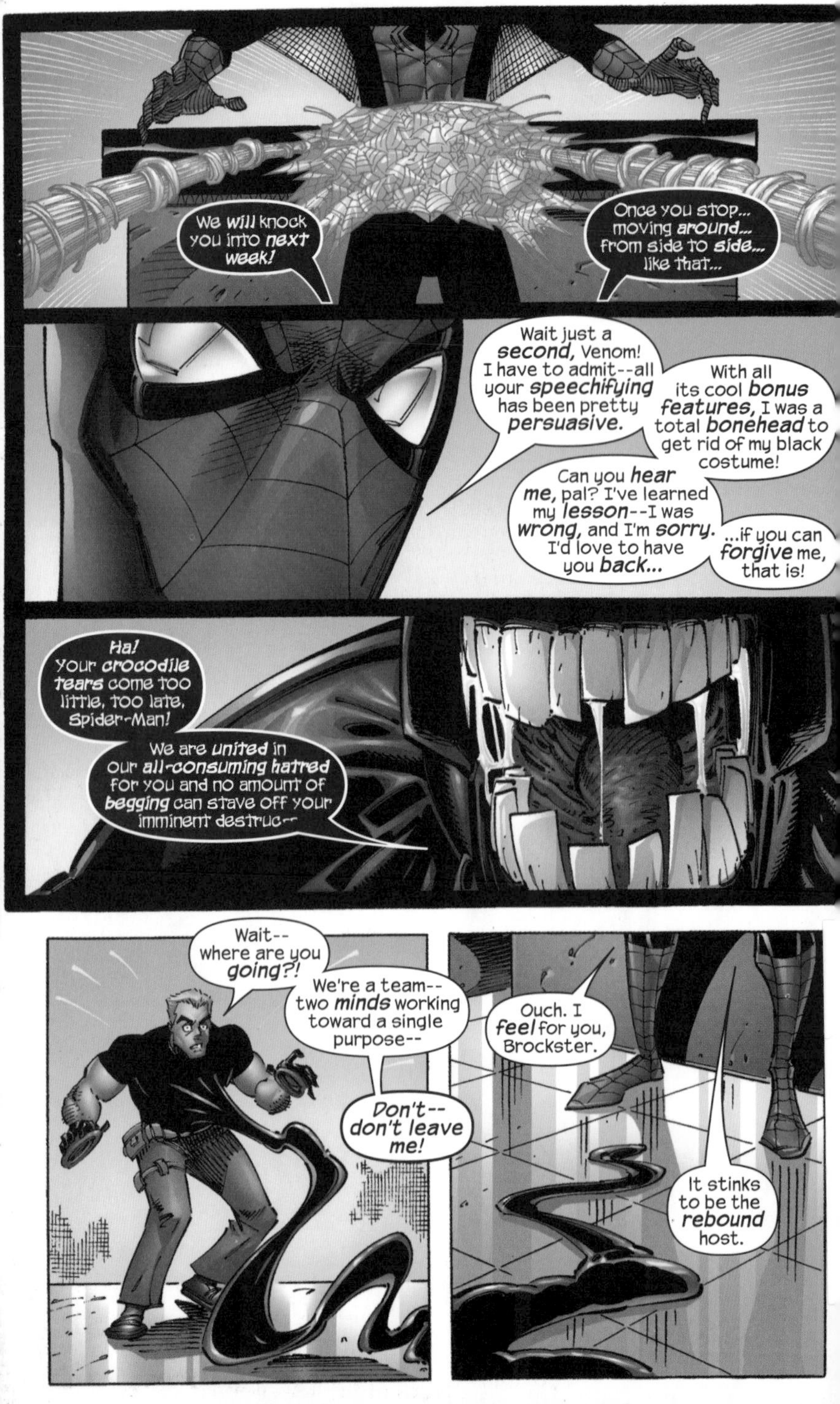

We will knock you into next week!
Once you stop... moving around... from side to side... like that...
Wait just a second, Venom! I have to admit--all your speechifying has been pretty persuasive.
With all its cool bonus features, I was a total bonehead to get rid of my black costume!
Can you hear me, pal? I've learned my lesson--I was wrong, and I'm sorry. I'd love to have you back...
...if you can forgive me, that is!
Ha! Your crocodile tears come too little, too late, Spider-Man!
We are united in our all-consuming hatred for you and no amount of begging can stave off your imminent destruc--
Wait-- where are you going?!
We're a team-- two minds working toward a single purpose--
Don't-- don't leave me!
Ouch. I feel for you, Brockster.
It stinks to be the rebound host.

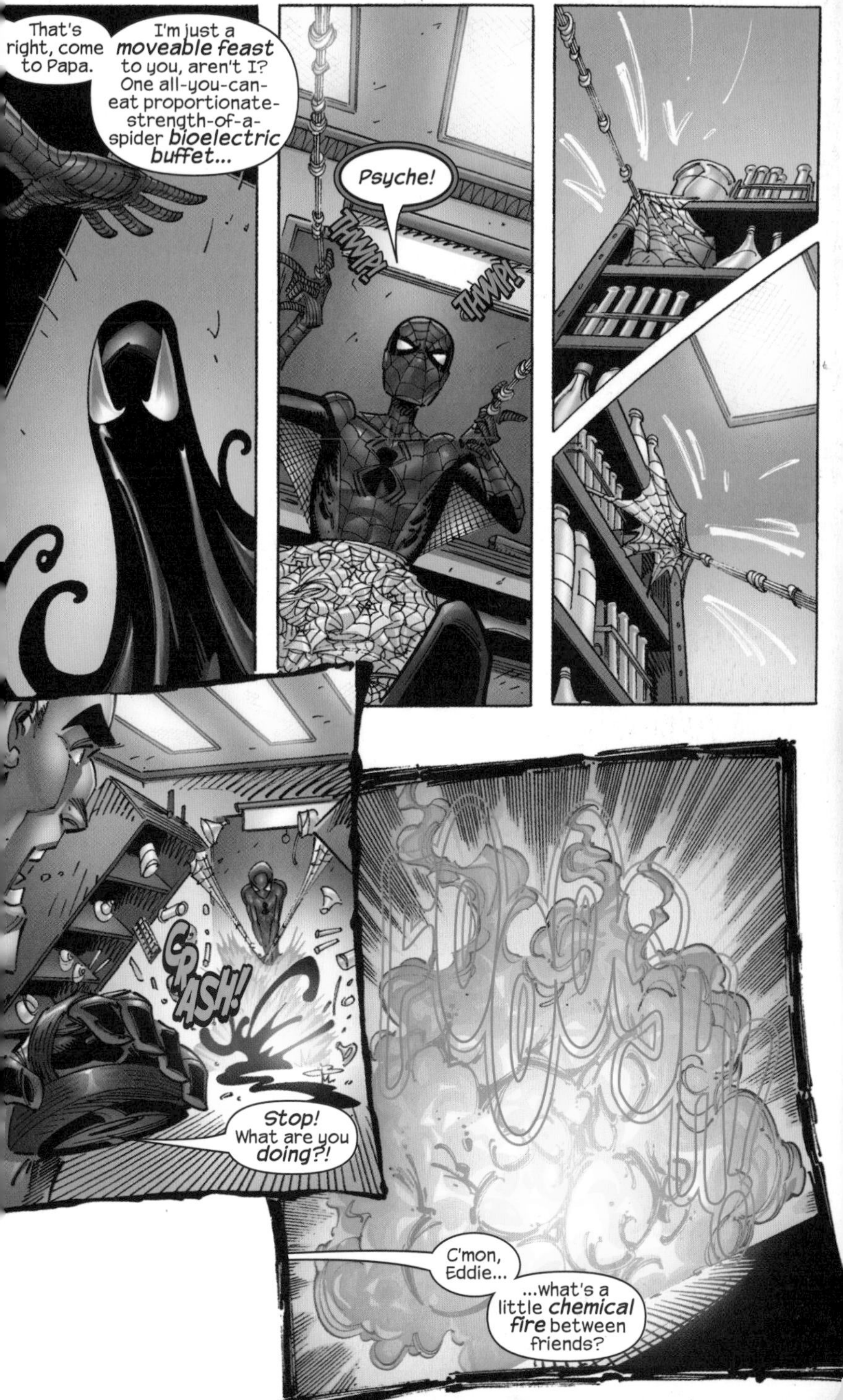
That's right, come to Papa.
I'm just a *moveable feast* to you, aren't I? One all-you-can-eat proportionate-strength-of-a-spider *bioelectric buffet...*
THWIP!
THWIP!
Psyche!
CRASH!
Stop! What are you *doing?!*
C'mon, Eddie...
...what's a little *chemical fire* between friends?

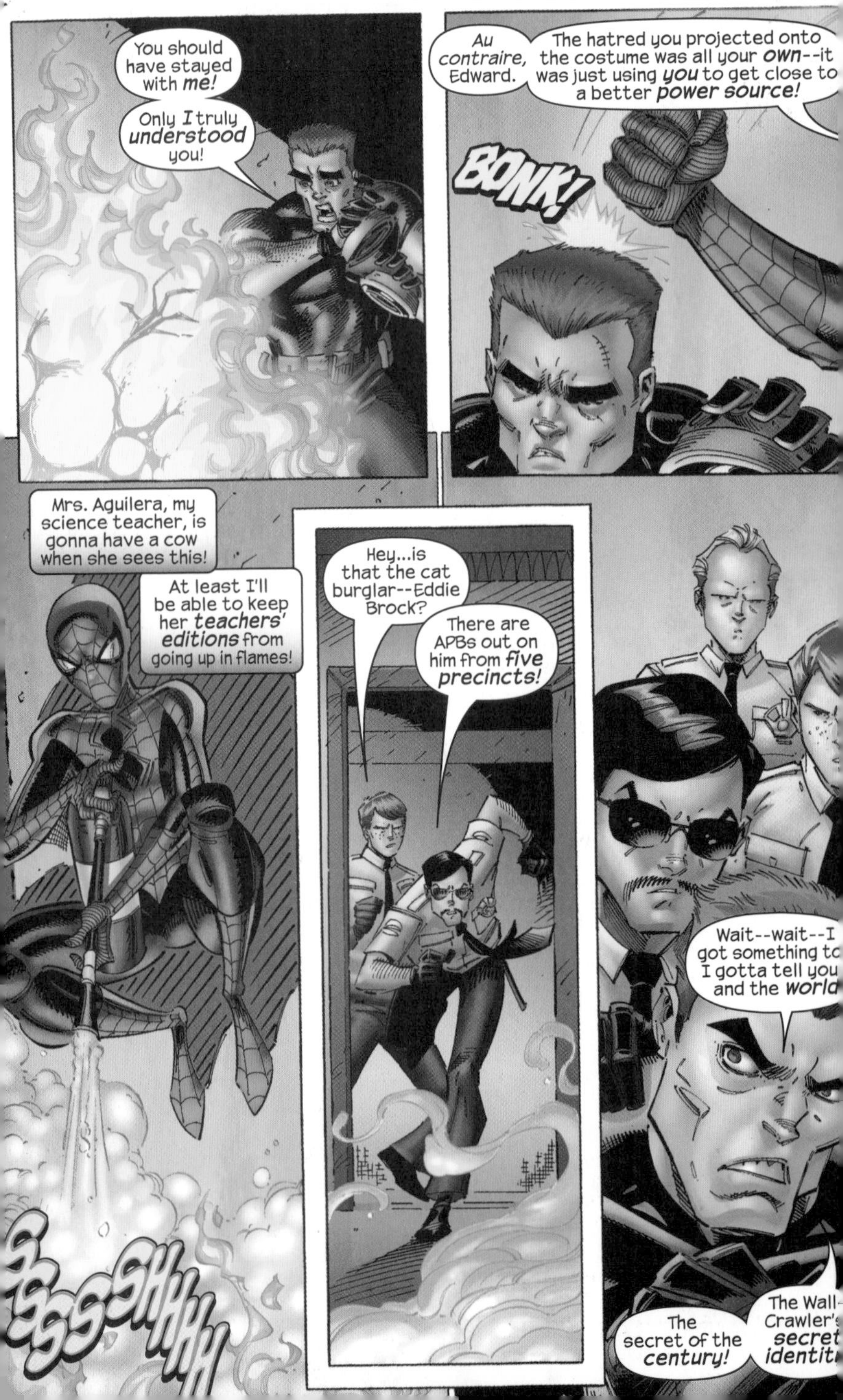
You should have stayed with *me!*
Only *I* truly *understood* you!
Au *contraire,* Edward.
The hatred you projected onto the costume was all your *own*--it was just using *you* to get close to a better *power source!*
BONK!
Mrs. Aguilera, my science teacher, is gonna have a cow when she sees this!
At least I'll be able to keep her *teachers' editions* from going up in flames!
SSSSSHHHHH
Hey...is that the cat burglar--Eddie Brock?
There are APBs out on him from *five precincts!*
Wait--wait--I got something tc I gotta tell you and the *world*
The secret of the *century!*
The Wall-Crawler's *secret identiti*

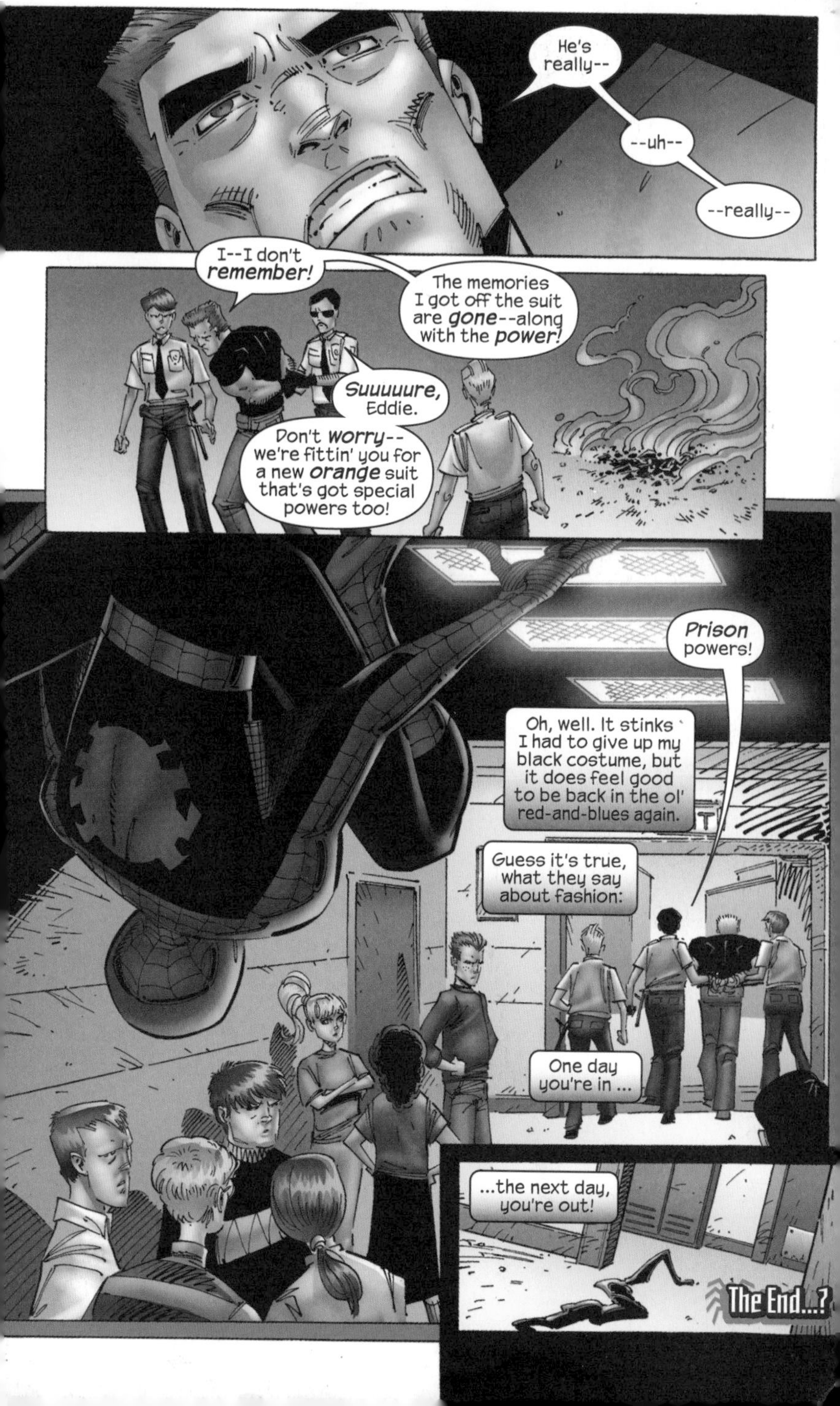
He's really--
--uh--
--really--
I--I don't remember!
The memories I got off the suit are gone--along with the power!
Suuuuure, Eddie.
Don't worry--we're fittin' you for a new orange suit that's got special powers too!
Prison powers!
Oh, well. It stinks I had to give up my black costume, but it does feel good to be back in the ol' red-and-blues again.
Guess it's true, what they say about fashion:
One day you're in ...
...the next day, you're out!
The End...?

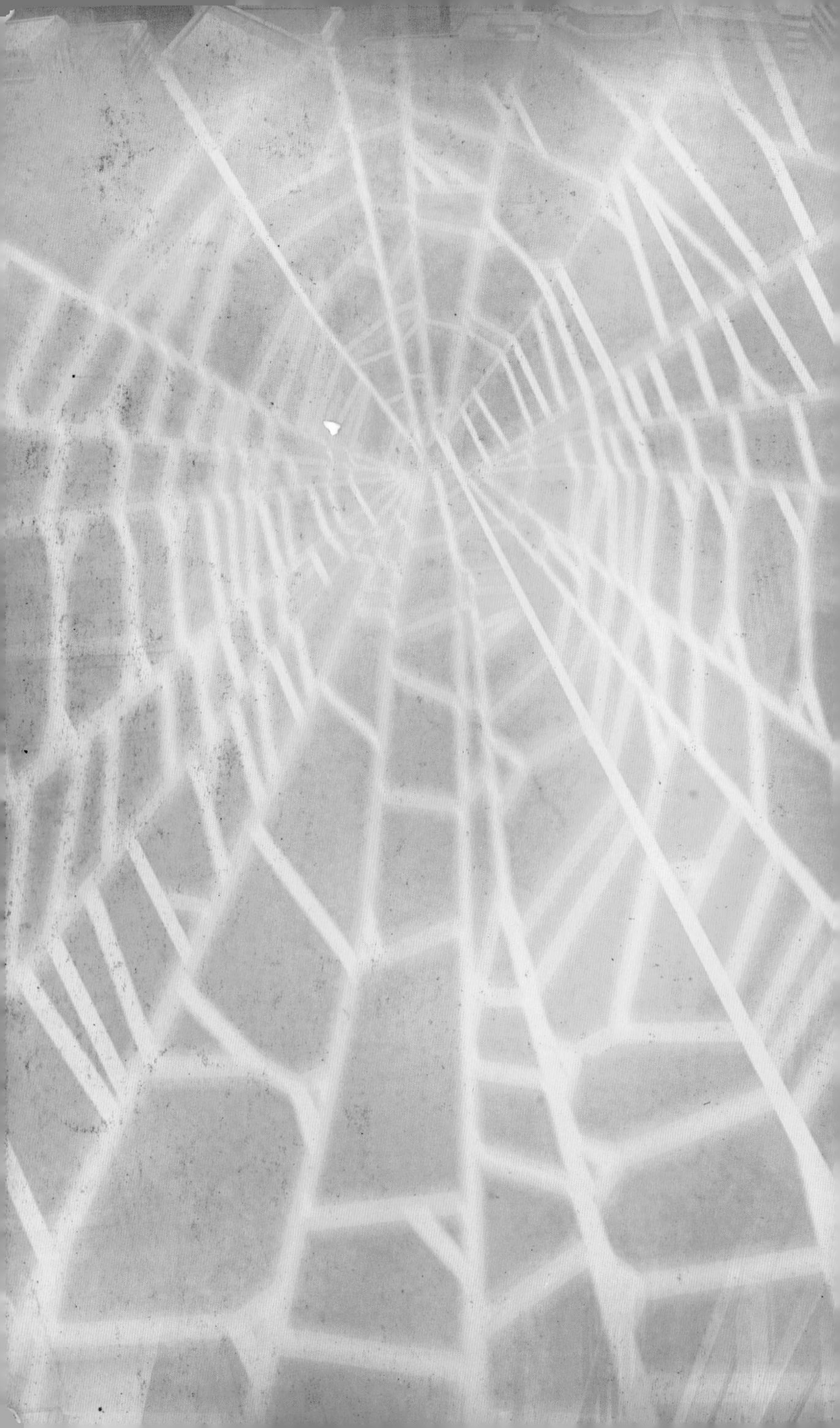